DUB

STEPHANIE HARTE

Boldwood

First published in Great Britain in 2026 by Boldwood Books Ltd.

Cover Design by Colin Thomas

Cover Images: Colin Thomas and Roger Wollstadt / Wikimedia Commons

A CIP catalogue record for this book is available from the British Library.

Paperback ISBN 978-1-80557-741-6

Large Print ISBN 978-1-80557-742-3

Hardback ISBN 978-1-80557-740-9

Trade Paperback ISBN 978-1-80656-475-0

Ebook ISBN 978-1-80557-743-0

Kindle ISBN 978-1-80557-744-7

Audio CD ISBN 978-1-80557-735-5

MP3 CD ISBN 978-1-80557-736-2

Digital audio download ISBN 978-1-80557-737-9

This book is printed on certified sustainable paper. Boldwood Books is dedicated to putting sustainability at the heart of our business. For more information please visit https://www.boldwoodbooks.com/about-us/sustainability/

Boldwood Books Ltd, 23 Bowerdean Street, London, SW6 3TN

www.boldwoodbooks.com

In loving memory of Carmel O'Mahony.
My auntie and constant supporter, who never failed
to encourage my writing.
You are deeply missed and will be remembered forever.
Rest in peace.

PROLOGUE

JOSIE

London, April 1985

People told me that time would heal all wounds. That time would soften things, would ease the pain of losing my husband, Sean. Time had done none of those things. I still ached for him, and a decade had passed. That should have been long enough for the wounds to scab over. Long enough for the nightmares to stop. Long enough for me to become somebody else entirely. And I had, but I remembered every detail like it was yesterday. Some wounds couldn't be healed by time alone. Some scars would never heal.

I'd had to learn how to carry the weight of the tragedy without flinching. The suffering I'd endured over the years would make a bishop weep. I'd had to hide the pain so it wouldn't show on my face, pick up the pieces and start over again without the love of my life. My daughter, Orla, was depending on me, so I couldn't let her down.

I'd been the woman behind the man. Sean had run the business, and I had run the house until the day he was murdered.

When I'd buried my husband in the frozen ground, I'd had to bury the woman I used to be alongside him too. In her place, someone tougher had evolved. I'd changed beyond recognition because I'd had to. My drive to succeed had come from a desire to secure my daughter's future in a world that constantly undermined me.

Rival gangsters, Reggie Bennett and Declan Kelly, had begun circling like vultures the moment Sean had taken his last breath. They'd threatened to take his empire away from me before the earth had even settled on his grave. It wasn't just them doubting my ability, though. Everyone thought I'd cave under the pressure and run back to my hometown of Kerry with Orla. But I had no family left there; my parents were dead, and my siblings were scattered across the globe. None of them were on the doorstep.

I'd had to be brave when I'd faced the future alone. I didn't go back to Ireland as expected. I didn't fold. I didn't crawl under a rock and hide. I stayed where I was. I stood tall. And I fought. I fought with every ounce of strength I had left. In order to succeed, I made a fundamental change. I stopped asking for permission and started giving orders. I took hold of the reins and made sure the business didn't fall apart. My rise to power hadn't been easy. Not all of the decisions I'd made had turned out for the best. But I'd learned from my mistakes. They'd made me stronger and more resilient. I'd survived the worst life could throw at me.

But the men who'd tried to muscle in on Sean's patch still watched from the shadows, thinking distance would keep them safe. They were too scared to show their faces now, even though they'd never admit it. I could smell their fear. If either of them tried to resurface, all hell would break loose. I'd unleash the retribution I'd been holding inside without hesitation or mercy. I wouldn't let them walk away twice.

I didn't smile as easily these days. I didn't trust the same way I used to. I kept a pistol in my bedside cabinet out of fear. When people talked about the O'Connors, they didn't talk about Sean any more. They spoke of me, which didn't go down well with Orla. She was fifteen now and too much like her father for her own good. She had the same fire in her belly as Sean. The same reckless streak. The same refusal to listen to reason or anything I said.

Sean's loss had hit Orla hard. She was hurt, angry and we were at war. I was at my wits' end with her. I'd danced with the devil long enough to know he had his eyes on my child. I was scared of what was coming. Not of the violence on the streets or the men with guns. But of losing my girl and not being able to help her. I had unwavering love for my child. I prayed to God that my devotion to her was enough to save her from the demons that threatened to destroy her.

1

JOSIE

The day I'd been waiting for had finally arrived, but it had been a long time coming. The air felt sharp against my face as I paced along the pavement towards Savills. My brother-in-law, Niall, and I had been caught in traffic, and we were running late, so we hurried inside and took a seat near the back of the auction room.

I cast an eye around the space. There wasn't much of a crowd, just a handful of sharp-dressed men, probably developers, which was good news for us. I didn't care how much it cost. I had to have this building.

'The next property for sale is lot thirteen: The Velvet Ace, Soho. Formerly a casino, it's been closed for ten years and needs extensive refurbishment due to fire damage. The guide price is thirty-five thousand. Who'd like to open the bidding at thirty thousand?' the auctioneer asked.

I said nothing, but raised my hand.

The auctioneer began chanting to encourage someone to bid against me, but no one else was interested in the dilapidated ruin with a bad history.

'Going once, going twice, sold to the lady at the back!'

I hadn't expected to get the property for less than the guide price, but I wasn't complaining. It was going to cost a fortune to restore it.

The gavel dropped, and the sound echoed around the room. I glanced sideways at Niall, who was staring straight ahead. I craned my neck to see what he was looking at when I saw his expression darken. Reggie Bennett, the man responsible for Sean's death, had stepped into the room with a face like thunder. I hadn't seen him for years and his skin was more weathered, his jowls looser. His blond hair had thinned; what was left was a mix of faded yellow with grey streaks creeping through it, but his blue eyes were as sharp as ever, icy cold behind their lids.

I felt heat creep up my neck when his gaze landed on me. Reggie barrelled forward like a charging bull, fury rolling off him in waves. I braced myself as he stormed over to where Niall and I were sitting. He still carried himself like people owed him respect, but the world had stopped giving it to men like him. Men who had nothing. There was an arrogance about him, which he wore like a badge of honour, and a stiffness in the way he moved. He was showing his age.

'I should have known you wouldn't be able to resist sniffing around the bones of my place. You're fucking vultures!' Reggie's cockney voice boomed out.

Heads turned in our direction. The men in suits were far more interested in the scene he was making than they'd been in his precious casino, which was hardly surprising as it was a total wreck despite its prime location. The air was thick with anticipation, but I wasn't going to have a public showdown with Reggie no matter how much the captive audience wanted me to.

'I've not come here to argue. I came to buy a property and now The Velvet Ace belongs to me,' I replied, getting up from my seat. I smoothed down the pencil skirt of my charcoal grey suit while a small, satisfied smile played on my lips.

Niall followed my lead as Bennett glared at us. I was calm, composed. Reggie was livid, boiling mad. He almost had steam coming out of his nostrils and ears, but he didn't rattle me.

'You've got a brass neck, I'll give you that,' Reggie replied, shoving a chubby finger in my face.

I didn't flinch. I'd had years of practice dealing with bullies like him. I'd learned to carry myself with a confidence that made men twice my size step aside.

'You think this is funny? You smug little bitch. I've got a good mind to wipe that smirk off your face,' Reggie threatened, curling his sausage fingers into a ball at his side.

'That's no way to speak to a lady. I suggest you apologise to Mrs O'Connor right now,' Niall said as he loomed over Reggie.

'It's OK, Niall, I'll handle this,' I said to my brother-in-law before I took a step closer to Reggie. 'I can see you're upset, but if you ever speak to me like that again, it'll be the last thing you do.' My face was inches from his. He knew I didn't make idle threats. As my words registered, he shifted his weight; his bravery was deserting him.

'Of course, I'm upset. The Velvet Ace is mine. Always has been. Always will be. There's no way I'll sell it to Irish scum,' Reggie fumed. His breath was sour, his voice low.

I let his insult go over my head.

'You're not in a position to refuse my offer. It's not as though you had any other takers.' I glanced over at the men.

Reggie looked down his nose at me before he fixed his eyes on the small group who were engrossed in our conversation. 'How come none of you bid against her?'

One of them laughed. 'Are you serious? I wouldn't give you

ten grand for that piece of shit. No offence, love,' he said, looking at me.

'I'd sell it to you for five rather than let her get her grubby mitts on it. If her husband hadn't torched the place, none of this would have happened.' Reggie flashed me a look that could kill before turning away again. 'What do you say? Five grand? Have we got a deal?' Desperation coated his words.

'The deal's with me,' I interrupted before the man had a chance to reply. 'It's too late to back out now. The sale is legally binding. You're broke, and the bank wants its money back.'

'I swear to Christ, if you open my casino with your name above the door, I'll...'

'You'll what?' I asked without raising my voice.

He stared at me, breathing hard. Something dangerous flickered in his eyes. He wasn't just angry, he was humiliated. He was a man with nothing left to lose so he was still a threat to me, but I was more ruthless than he was giving me credit for. Try crossing me again, I thought. I was looking for a reason to stop holding back.

'You're going to regret this. You think you've won. But I know your weaknesses, Josie. And mark my words, I'll never let your venture get off the ground.'

'Really?'

I walked past him, calm and deliberate, as my stiletto heels echoed on the polished floor. He'd been beaten down, but he still had fight left in him. He wasn't finished. Not yet. He was a man I once feared beyond measure. Now the tables had turned, and I was the one in the power seat. He'd do well to remember that.

2

REGGIE

I'd skulked back to the place I now called home to lick my wounds after Josie O'Connor's latest victory, popping into the corner shop on the way to buy an overpriced four-pack of tramp juice. Brandy used to be my tipple of choice, but I couldn't afford that now, so I had to settle for Special Brew instead. It tasted vile, but it did the job.

I turned on the TV before I flopped down on the lumpy armchair and opened a can. The bedsit was small and squalid and had damp creeping through the peeling wallpaper. The carpet was threadbare and stained. It was a far cry from the luxurious penthouse above The Velvet Ace, but beggars couldn't be choosers, and it was better than dossing down in Brompton Road any day.

After my livelihood and all my hard-earned cash had gone up in smoke, I'd spent the first year sleeping rough on a mattress scavenged from a skip, in the old station that lay beneath Piccadilly like a forgotten scar. I was in dire straits. I had nothing. My men had deserted me when I couldn't pay their wages. It was hell on earth. Filth and the ever-present hum of London overhead plagued me. It was like being buried alive in a tomb of regrets.

During the Blitz, abandoned Tube stations had served as air raid shelters, protecting thousands of civilians. That was what gave me the idea in the first place. Churchill himself had a bunker at Down Street station. If it was good enough for the wartime leader, it was good enough for me, I thought. But unlike Winston, I didn't have access to a bathroom, caviar and vintage champagne. I only had rats and mildew for company.

Life in the tunnels was depressing. The walls were streaked with old graffiti, and water dripped steadily from rusted pipes. It was enough to do your nut in. Things got so tough, I briefly considered turfing my tenant, Mary O'Hara, and her kids out of my flat. Truth be told, the only reason I didn't evict them was that I needed the rent money to keep food in my belly until I got back on my feet.

Three sharp raps on the door drew my attention away from the horse racing results scrolling past on the TV. I recognised the knock, so I unlocked the door without hesitation. Freddie entered first, a wall of muscle with a busted knuckle wrapped in tape. Pistol Pete followed a beat behind, wired and twitching as always. His eyes darted around the bedsit with barely disguised disgust. Cheeky fucker. Who did he think he was?

'It smells of shit in here, Reg.' He wrinkled his nose and then did a double take when his gaze landed on a battered cage in the corner of the room. Inside it, a black rooster was preening its glossy feathers.

'What the fuck is that?' Pete asked, peering at the bird with wide eyes.

'What you see before you is a prize-winner,' I replied with pride, puffing out my chest.

'Where did it come from?' Freddie asked.

'Never you mind!'

* * *

The dimly lit basement beneath an old East London pub smelled of spilt beer and damp brickwork. I walked towards the centre of the cellar, where the pit had been marked out with chicken wire. Freddie and Pete trailed along behind me. There was a decent turnout for a Monday night. Men circled the enclosure. They were jostling to get a closer look at the champion I'd arrived with. Do-gooders viewed cockfighting as a cruel and barbaric practice, but that didn't stop it from happening. When something was forbidden, it just added to the thrill if you asked me!

'Fred, you're going to have to do the honours. I need to run a book,' I said with a wide grin on my face as I lowered the cage to the ground. I was eager to relieve the punters of their hard-earned cash.

'Why me?' Freddie quizzed.

'Because I said so,' I replied. The smile slid from my face and was replaced with a look of fury.

'But I don't know the first thing about handling birds, Reg.'

'Well, it's time you learned!'

I'd been assured my rooster was undefeated. We hadn't even started the fight, and I could already feel the winnings burning a hole in my pocket. Regaining my throne was taking longer than expected, but finally, I was on the way up.

I stood just beyond the ring, coat collar up, a fat cigar wedged between my fingers as Pistol Pete did the rounds, prowling the edge of the crowd, collecting money in a steel cash box. The bets weren't much, fives and tens, the odd twenty thrown in for good measure, but they were cash that I didn't have, so I wasn't about to complain.

'Five on the black one! Break that golden bastard's neck!' a man at the back called out, waving his note in the air to get Pete's attention.

The crowd jeered in agreement, and the energy in the basement swelled. It was time to start the fight, so I nodded at the handlers. Freddie hesitated, but followed the other man's lead. He opened the cage door and stepped away from the cockerel.

The pale gold bird sized up its opponent. Its eyes were wild with fury. A second later, the roosters flew at each other in a flurry of feathers. The crowd roared. Blood sprayed on to the ground as the golden rooster staggered. It had been sliced across the wing by the tiny, curved blade bound to my bird's claws. My champ drove in again, talons flashing. Savage. Fast. Brutal. It performed just as expected. I puffed on my cigar and watched the money pour in, imagining how I was going to spend it.

Just then a lanky, underfed teenager, still growing into his frame, with a dark brown mullet and a navy Fila tracksuit, slipped down the stairs and breezed across the room like he was somebody important. Heads turned momentarily before they lost interest in the nobody. The fight was too good to miss. He stopped in front of me and handed me an envelope with a sneer on his face.

'This is from Lewis Slater. Put the lot on the favourite. He wants to know if you're interested in buying some cocaine.' The lad spoke in a London accent.

I'd never seen the boy before – he was all elbows and sharp shoulders. The new kid on the block, no doubt.

I opened the envelope, mulling over what he'd just said. A thin wad of notes was inside. Not enough to get a hard-on over. But enough to say I wasn't invisible to other people any more.

'Lewis Slater, you say. Never heard of him,' I replied.

The teen snorted, put out by his boss's lack of recognition.

'Well, you should have. He's running Camden, but his patch is getting bigger by the day,' he bragged.

'Tell him from me, if he wants to do business with me, he'll need to come and see me himself. I only deal with the organ grinder, not the monkey.'

A flash of anger spread over the youth's features, so I couldn't resist taking a drag of my cigar and blowing the smoke into his face. My lips stretched into a smile as he walked away without responding, coughing and spluttering like he had a dose of TB.

I tore my attention away from him when I heard the crowd shouting and swearing, and a rooster squawking. While I'd been distracted by Jack the Lad, disaster had struck, and the golden bird must have got the upper hand. There was blood all over the floor, and the black cockerel was staggering around the pit, one wing drooping, like it had been on a bender and drunk ten pints, before it keeled over and lay motionless. Its glossy feathers were matted with blood. Its eyes, once wild and sharp, looked dull. Its third eyelid was drawn across like it had closed the curtains. I couldn't believe what I was seeing.

I stepped into the chicken wire enclosure, paced over to it with my nostrils flaring and gave it a couple of prods with my foot. It responded with a low moan. All the fight had been drained out of it.

'Fucking useless bastard!' I roared, then spat on the bird, lying in its own filth. 'You were meant to be a champ – bloodline from the Midlands. Cost me two hundred quid. And for what? A couple of rounds and you're gasping like a pensioner with a collapsed lung.' I glared at the rooster as though I was expecting it to answer. The dying bird let out a soft, rasping croak. 'Is that all you've got to say for yourself? I should've wrung your neck the minute I set eyes on you. I should never have let you through the fucking door!' I stared at it with my eyes narrowed, judging it as though it had personally betrayed me. The bird didn't move.

'What the fuck's going on? Have you completely lost the plot, Bennett? Stop talking to the fucking cockerel and pay us what we're owed,' yelled a huge thug with a face like a baboon's arse.

I glanced over my shoulder and saw Freddie and Pete trying to hold back the baying mob. The stench of beer and bird shit hung in the air around us, which crackled with tension. On the far side of the basement, two punters were at each other's throats, shoving and shouting.

'That was a fix! Your bird took a dive! Give me my money back, you thieving old bastard!' a man with rotten teeth yelled as he tried to break free from Freddie's iron grip.

The mouth on legs had just said what was on everyone's mind. I'd used that tactic before, and now my dishonesty had come back to bite me. Fixing fights was one of my favourite pastimes, but hand on heart, I hadn't rigged this one. I didn't think I needed to. The black demon was meant to be a sure bet.

I stood in the centre of the ring with my jaw clenched, as chaos erupted around me. When was I going to get a break? Why did everything I touched go tits up? Humiliation clung to me like a second skin.

I glanced down at the supposed champion. It lay twitching with one wing crushed, and its neck bent at an unnatural angle, rasping its final breaths. The golden bird had torn through it like paper. Punters were shouting louder now. The whole room was a ticking time bomb. I could feel everyone turning on me. Hatred radiated towards me in Tsunami-sized waves. I had to do something before all hell broke loose.

'Oi!' I barked, my voice cutting through the noise. 'You think I rigged it? You think I wanted to lose two grand on a crippled chicken not fit for the pot?' Boos and catcalls rang out around me, making my head throb, so I reached down and grabbed the half-dead bird by the legs. 'Look at the fucking state of it!' I roared, holding it aloft by its spurred feet. 'Do you seriously think I threw this fight? Why would I do that? This bird has cost me more than most of you make in a year!'

The cockerel attempted to feebly flap one wing as blood dribbled from its beak. The crowd suddenly hushed as uncertainty spread through the air. They eyed me with suspicion, unsure what I was going to do next. But there was only one thing I could do. I snapped its neck with a single brutal twist. Then tossed the limp body on to the sawdust. Truth be told, I'd put it out of its misery, but that wasn't why I'd killed it. I'd snuffed out the champion to prove a point, gain some respect and regain control from the punters.

The room gasped. Silence followed. People seemed shocked by the violent action, but they weren't at a nipper's tea party. They were spectators in the illegal world of underground cockfighting.

'There'll be no refunds – only payouts for the bets on the golden bird. Now stop behaving like savages and form an orderly queue. But if any of you come at me, accusing me of fixing fights again, you'll end up like my feathered friend here,' I said, giving the mangy rooster a boot for good measure. Then I stepped out of the pit with my chin up, hoping I had enough in the tin to pay what was due.

3

DECLAN

Dublin, April 1985

I'd been waiting for Fergal in an alleyway off Parnell Street, with my collar turned up against the cold and rain, watching people going about their business. The wind whipped up discarded litter as the crowd rushed to escape the bad weather.

The city hadn't changed much in the last ten years. There were a few different gangs on the scene, new faces, but the same rules applied. I didn't regret my decision to come home to recuperate one bit after Josie outmanoeuvred me. The O'Connors' business had been there for the taking, so we'd expected a landslide victory when we'd ambushed them at Down Street station, but things hadn't ended well for the Kellys. Josie had killed my brother, Aidan, and then her men had beaten me to within an inch of my life. Once Josie forced me out, I realised I could run my whiskey smuggling operation just as efficiently from the Irish side, so I wasn't tempted to go back to London. It held too many bad memories. Too many ghosts.

Where the fuck was Fergal? He was late. Again. I'd be frozen stiff by the time he arrived. I lit a cigarette, striking a match that hissed in the drizzle, to pass the time. I turned to face the mouth of the alley when I heard footsteps echoing through the puddles, sharp and quick. Fergal's shoulders were hunched, and his chin was tucked into the collar of his denim jacket.

'We're going to be late. What kept you?' I asked flatly.

'I'm sorry, I got held up. I was just leaving the house when Cormac rang to say there's been a change of plan...'

My eyes narrowed as my suspicion spiked. I didn't like the sound of this. 'How come?'

'He didn't say, but we're not meeting in O'Connell Street now, he's going to pick us up by the Garden of Remembrance in Parnell Square at three o'clock,' Fergal replied.

'Do you think it's a set-up?'

'I doubt it. More likely, Cormac's just being cautious. We don't have history to fall back on. We hardly know each other. He probably wants to make sure we're not going to do the dirty on him,' Fergal replied.

I couldn't argue with the voice of reason, but that didn't mean I was happy about the situation. Enemies were easy to come by. I glanced down at my watch. It was 2.55 p.m.

'We'd better make tracks then,' I replied, although I still felt uneasy.

Five minutes later, we arrived at the designated pick-up point. Fergal stood beside me, chewing his lip, hands buried in the pockets of his battered jacket. We waited in silence. Tension was almost crackling between us as time ticked by. I checked my watch again. It was 3.15 p.m. And there was no sign of Cormac.

'He's late,' Fergal muttered before I had a chance to speak.

'Either that, or he's not coming,' I replied.

The sky over Parnell Square was the colour of dirty dishwater. The rain had stopped for now, but the clouds were darkening, threatening another downpour. I had no intention of getting soaked to the skin, so Cormac better get a move on, or he wouldn't see me for dust. I wasn't going to wait much longer.

Fergal and I stood stony-faced, watching the slow crawl of cars as they inched their way through the city. My temper was simmering. It wouldn't be long before it came to a boil. I checked my watch again. My jaw was tight. Cormac was twenty-five minutes late. My eyes swept the street. I felt exposed.

'He's taking the piss,' I said through gritted teeth. 'Amateurs keep people waiting. Professionals don't.'

Fergal gave a shrug, but he looked uneasy too.

'Maybe he's caught in traffic.'

'Or maybe he's playing games,' I grunted.

A battered Ford Fiesta with sun-bleached red paint lurched around the corner and pulled up beside us without indicating. The car was barely roadworthy. The wheel arches were rusted, and the passenger wing mirror was taped into position. The driver leaned over and rolled down the window, which squealed in protest as the engine idled noisily.

'Get in,' the man said in an accent that wasn't local.

No introduction. No apology. No explanation.

'Cormac Walsh?' I asked to highlight his ignorance.

The man with dark, slicked-back hair nodded. He was young, barely thirty. He had a crooked nose and a gaunt face, with hollow cheekbones. His expression was unreadable. He didn't smile. Didn't offer a handshake. He hadn't made a great first impression and had set the tone for an uneasy partnership.

Fergal and I exchanged a look, but climbed in without a word. My lip curled slightly as I opened the back door and slid in. Fergal followed. The interior reeked of cigarettes and damp wool, and something else: charcoal, sulphur, maybe spent ammunition, I couldn't be sure.

Cormac pulled away without looking at us, weaving through the traffic, heading towards the quays with one hand on the wheel, the other resting on the gearstick like he was out for a Sunday drive. I studied him in the rear-view mirror, taking in his lean jaw, his clenched mouth, the tension behind the stillness. Military, maybe. Or paramilitary. I couldn't tell yet. But one thing was clear – Cormac didn't care who I was. And that fucked me right off.

'How come you're late?' I asked with deliberate hostility.

Cormac didn't reply.

'Why the change of plan? Too public for a meet like this, was it?'

Still no response. It was like getting blood from a stone.

'It would've been nice to know you were running behind schedule before I froze my bollocks off.' I couldn't disguise the anger creeping into my voice.

'For the record, I don't waste time explaining myself, so do us both a favour and let the matter drop,' Cormac replied, flashing me a look in the mirror before his gaze returned to the road.

Fergal shifted uncomfortably in the seat next to me as he watched the Liffey drift by. I didn't like this set-up. There were too many variables. Too little respect. I was used to calling the shots. I'd keep quiet for now because the deal was too valuable to blow on bruised pride, but I'd already decided, if this cocky young bastard stepped out of line, even once, I wouldn't give him the chance to do it twice.

Cormac turned off the main road and cut through a series of narrow lanes lined by poorly maintained redbrick terraced properties with crumbling paintwork and overgrown front gardens the size of postage stamps. Then he drove past a run-down social housing estate where washing lines were strung between windows like bunting.

He pulled up outside an old scrapyard behind a boarded-up shopfront in the Liberties district and killed the engine. 'We're here,' he said as he got out of the Ford Fiesta.

Fergal and I followed. Our shoes crunched on the broken glass and debris littering the floor. The smell of oil and rust clung to the air as we waited for Cormac to unlock the Portakabin, which stood beside a stripped-down van. He glanced over his shoulder, scanning every direction. It was the first time he'd looked uncomfortable. Up until now, he'd been brimming over with confidence. I was surprised he'd come to the meet alone. Surely bringing backup would have been the sensible thing to do.

'What's wrong? Do you think we're being watched?' I asked.

He was doing nothing to put my mind at ease. I was beginning to wish I'd stuck to whiskey smuggling now and hadn't been tempted to venture down this path.

'If you've brought anything you shouldn't have with you, don't bother coming in,' Cormac replied before he pushed open the door.

My jaw tightened, but I said nothing. The air inside the lock-up was cold and metallic. Uninviting like Cormac himself. He picked up a crowbar and set to work freeing the lids from the wooden crates lining the far wall. He moved around the room, silent and hard-eyed. When he pulled out the straw, I saw the handguns, rifles and silencers, and my breath caught in my throat.

'You've been smuggling whiskey for a good while, have you?' Cormac asked, pausing by the last crate in the line with the crowbar still gripped in his hand.

I nodded. 'Twenty-odd years.'

'Easy money. Safe. Civilised. What makes you want to get involved with gunrunning?'

I was terrified of running into Josie again after my last encounter with her. This move would put some distance between our businesses, and we'd no longer be in competition. Greater rewards came with greater risks, didn't they? I stood to make a small fortune if everything went to plan. Wealth equalled power. And once I was back in the driving seat, I'd take my revenge on Josie for what she'd done to me, but I didn't want Cormac to know my reasons. I shrugged. 'An opportunity's come my way and it's time for a change.' I'd been approached by a bloke who needed to buy weapons for a Camden drug cartel.

'It's not as easy as it looks. You have to be able to stay calm under pressure,' Cormac replied while sussing out whether I was up to the job.

Although I was preparing to smuggle guns into the UK, unlike Cormac, I didn't have political motives.

'I wasn't aware I'd have to undergo a psychiatric evaluation before we could discuss terms.'

My words were laced with sarcasm. This jumped-up little prick was barely old enough to shave, but without him, I couldn't get access to the weapons. He was the contact on the Irish side of the arms operation. He served as the fixer and broker between the Republican elements in the North and shadowy suppliers across Europe.

'I need to be sure you've got the right type of character – not everyone's cut out for it – but if you've got a problem with that, you know where the door is.' Cormac narrowed his eyes and glared at me.

'That's fair enough. There's no problem. I get where you're coming from.' The words almost got stuck in my throat. Cormac was going to make me work hard before he brought me in on the deal. 'I can assure you, whiskey smuggling isn't a walk in the park either. We've had some hair-raising moments over the years, but we've lived to tell the tale. Haven't we, Fergal?'

'Isn't that the truth,' he replied.

'How do you intend to run the guns?' Cormac asked.

'Through our whiskey routes,' I replied. The men I used knew the contents of the crates they were transporting were illegal, but they didn't give a shit what was inside, as long as they were well paid.

'Fine. But if you bring heat on me, I'll make sure you live to regret it. I got out of the game for good reason. I no longer carry weapons myself. I just facilitate their movement,' Cormac said, as though he was a seasoned veteran.

'How come?' I asked. He'd piqued my curiosity. He didn't seem old enough to have amassed a wealth of experience.

'When you live in the shadow of the Falls Road, they start you off young. I've done my time. Paid my dues to my brothers in arms...'

I wondered what he'd meant by that, but before I had a chance to delve any further, he put a stop to the conversation.

'Enough of the questions. Do you want the weapons or not?' Cormac asked, flashing me a look that could kill.

He was a closed book. He wasn't giving much away. 'Of course I do,' I replied without hesitation.

'This is what you asked to see,' Cormac said, lighting a cigarette as he gestured to the haul.

I wasn't sure it was a good idea to smoke around all this ammunition, but I decided to keep that to myself in case he pulled out of the deal. I stepped forward and inspected one of the crates.

'It's Eastern Bloc stock. Clean enough, but the price has gone up...' Cormac exhaled smoke slowly as he let the news sink in.

Fergal and I had had multiple telephone conversations with

him to get to this point, but this was the first time I was hearing about the increase. 'How come you never mentioned this before?'

'I just did,' Cormac replied. His tone was flat.

I stiffened. I knew what he was playing at. Raise the price at the last minute, squeeze the last drop out of me, test how far I'd bend before snapping. I was pretty sure my customer would be fucked off to hear this, but Cormac had me over a barrel. It wasn't as though I could use another source.

'How much are we talking?' I narrowed my eyes and fixed them on him.

'Handguns and shotguns will be an extra hundred each. AK-47s, AR-15s, Uzis and submachine guns will be an extra two hundred each,' Cormac replied, meeting my gaze. He stared at me unblinking.

'Jesus, that's a bit steep, isn't it? I'm not sure my contact will go for that,' I said, hoping to beat him down.

'Take it or leave it.' Cormac tore his eyes away from mine and started putting the lids back on the boxes.

The man might be young, but he had balls of steel, I'd give him that. I reached into my coat, pulled out an envelope, and tossed it on to the nearest crate. Cormac picked it up and started counting the contents. 'I'll leave that as a deposit. There's three grand in there. I want ten handguns, ten shotguns, five AK-47s and five Uzis. Fourteen and a half grand in total, I make it. How about I give you another ten grand on delivery and we call it quits?'

'Go fuck yourself. The price is fixed. Non-negotiable,' Cormac replied and then went back to leafing through the wad of cash.

'You drive a hard bargain. God loves a trier.' I smiled tightly.

Cormac put the money back in the envelope, and then he flashed me a black look. 'He might, but I think you're a wanker.

There'll be no delivery. You need to collect the weapons from me. When can you get hold of the rest of the cash?'

'In a day or two.'

'Phone me when you've got it and I'll arrange a meet.' Cormac walked over to the door and flung it open. 'I've got an important call to make, so...' He gestured with his thumb for us to vacate his premises.

I was taken aback to be turfed out on to the street. I'd thought the least he could do was drop us back to Parnell Square, but then again, Cormac had already told me he thought I was a wanker, so he wasn't going to worry if his lack of manners offended me. He'd been disrespectful from the moment we'd met. Something told me I was going to have to get used to his behaviour. I needed him more than he needed me.

4

ORLA

London, April 1985

'Hurry up, Orla, or you'll be late for school!'

Mum's voice came slicing through the bedroom wall like a scalpel. I rolled my eyes so hard I could see the back of my skull. I'd been standing in front of the mirror, putting the finishing touches to my uniform. These things couldn't be rushed. I gave myself a final once-over to check everything was as it should be. My tie was loosened. The waistband of my skirt was rolled over several times so it barely skimmed my buttocks. I'd plastered on the Leichner Theatrical Clown White paint I'd bought from Camden Market that I'd mixed with my foundation. I was so pale I could never find anything light enough to match my skin tone, and I'd circled my eyes with heavy black eyeliner. Then I'd back-combed my auburn curls as big as I could get them and sprayed them in place with a gallon of hairspray so they'd stay put.

'Orla, did you hear me calling you?' Mum asked as she burst into my room without knocking. She took one look at me and her mouth flattened into a thin line, so I glared at her in the mirror before slowly turning around to face her. 'I thought I told you last night not to do that to your skirt!' Mum walked over to where I was standing. Her face was getting redder by the minute. She looked like she was about to explode, which brought a smile to my face.

'What's wrong with it?' I asked, feigning innocence. 'This is how everyone dresses.' I threw my hands up as I glanced down at the navy pleats.

'You look a right mess,' Mum said, pulling at my skirt, trying to yank it down.

I slapped her hand away. As she stepped back, something flickered across her face: anger, hurt, maybe both. 'Don't touch me!' I barked. My heart was racing. I didn't want to look like a Catholic schoolgirl. I was trying to imitate my idol, Siouxsie Sioux.

'Lord have mercy, wait until Sister Basil and Mother Superior see you,' Mum muttered, crossing herself before gearing up to give me a lecture, which had been a morning ritual for as long as I could remember. 'You're going to end up in detention again for not respecting your uniform and for having that muck plastered all over your face. You look like you're heading to a nightclub, not the Sacred Heart Catholic School for Girls!'

'I get a detention no matter what I wear, so why should I care?' I snapped.

'Because otherwise you're going to find yourself expelled!' Mum put her hands on her hips and fixed me with her sternest look.

'Good! I hate that place. It's not a school, it's a prison! The nuns are evil. Absolute sadists,' I yelled. Then I pushed past her as she stood in the middle of the room with her mouth opening and closing and a horrified expression pasted on her face. I stomped down the stairs, grabbed my bag and blazer from the coat rack in the hall, then I flung open the front door.

'Orla, wait, what about your breakfast? You can't go to school on an empty stomach,' Mum called from the top of the stairs.

I slammed the door behind me without bothering to answer. I didn't have any intention of going to school today, so I didn't need a bowl of porridge sloshing around in my stomach. I hoofed it to the corner shop, bought myself a packet of ten Silk Cut and a can of Coke, then headed to the park to meet Majella. My best friend was already waiting for me on the bench closest to the entrance.

'Hi,' I called as I got closer. She'd been looking for something in her bag, but looked up at the sound of my voice.

'What kept you?' she asked as she dangled a small bottle of vodka in front of me.

'Mum was kicking off as usual. Where did you get that?' I felt my blue eyes widen.

'It was stuffed down the side of the sofa. Finders keepers,' Majella laughed before twisting the cap off with her teeth. 'It's the breakfast of champions.' She held the bottle up before taking a swig. Then she wiped her mouth and passed it to me.

I hesitated, but followed suit. The neat alcohol burned a trail down my throat, making me cough. 'Oh my God, that's vile,' I said, opening the can of Coke I'd just bought and glugging half of it to take the taste away.

'I wish you'd told me you'd got a mixer before we downed it from the bottle.' Majella laughed, then took the can from my hand and poured a hefty measure of the firewater into it. 'One day, you'll thank me for corrupting you,' she said.

We sat on the bench, passing the drink backwards and forwards for a while. When I glanced down at my watch, I realised it was just before nine. 'We'd better go and do the deed,' I said. We trudged over to the telephone box and I dialled the school's number. 'I'm Majella Lynch's mum. I'm just phoning to let you know she won't be in today. She's got a very bad cold,' I said to the secretary while trying to disguise my voice.

'How did it go?' Majella asked when I stepped outside.

'She said she hopes you feel better soon.' I smiled.

'I feel better already,' Majella replied.

'Will you phone in for me? Say I've got a stomach bug. We don't want them getting suspicious.'

* * *

The market was only just starting to wake up when we arrived at Camden. Traders were unlocking battered shutters and dragging out crates of old records and second-hand coats as we walked past. We perched on a metal railing above the canal, sharing a cigarette. My gaze dropped to the water below as a slow-moving, red-and-yellow barge drifted past. The smell of frying bacon wafted up, making my stomach rumble.

'This beats going to school any day,' I said. 'But it's the third time we've bunked off in the last two weeks. Do you think we'll get away with it?'

'I don't give a fuck, and neither will my mum. She gave up nagging me months ago. Said she'd got enough on her plate holding down three crappy part-time jobs without trying to keep me in line,' Majella replied, as smoke drifted down her nostrils.

'Lucky you. My mum will murder me if she finds out.'

Mum liked to control everything – including me. She used to be warm and caring. Now she was cold and detached. She left me to my own devices for hours on end while she kept the men in line and she wondered why I rebelled at every opportunity. She was so obsessed with running the business, the only way I got any attention was when I acted up.

Majella hopped off the railing and tugged at my sleeve. 'Come on. Don't be down. We might as well make the most of our day off. Let's see if that record shop has any new singles in,' she suggested, her big dark brown eyes glittering under her heavy fringe.

I jumped down and pushed all thoughts of my mum from my head as we disappeared into the labyrinth of stalls and alleyways that had become a haven to us in recent weeks. We loved it here. We could blend into the diverse crowd with no questions asked. Amen to that!

5

JOSIE

London, May 1985

A week after the auction, Niall stood beside me on the pavement. The Velvet Ace was a shadow of its former self. The building was a mess, with boarded-up windows, flaking paint and a crooked sign that creaked in the wind. Soot still clung to the bricks even now, years after the fire.

'Are you sure you know what you're doing?' Niall asked.

I didn't want to tell him I was apprehensive. He'd probably already guessed as much. It had taken me seven sleepless nights to pluck up the courage to come here. I stepped closer to the padlocked door without replying. The bunch of keys was burning a hole in my hand. Niall hovered behind me with his hands jammed deep into the pockets of his wax jacket. A deep frown rested on his face. He looked troubled.

'This is ghoulish, Josie,' he said, his voice low. 'I don't understand why you wanted to buy the place where Sean died. Where Reggie took him from us. We'll be surrounded by bad memories;

worse, ghosts. Are you sure you can stomach this? Won't it be too painful for you?'

I didn't dare turn around. I didn't want him to see the tears that had welled up in my eyes. I sniffed them back and let my gaze roam over the sign. The letters had faded from the fire and years of neglect. Once I'd composed myself, I faced him.

'I'm well aware that this is where my husband took his last breath, and I don't expect you to understand, but I can still sense his presence here, so it makes me feel close to him.'

My voice wasn't trembling; it was as sharp as a broken bottle. Niall shifted and glanced up and down the empty street. I'd thought I'd be able to count on him for support, but he seemed spooked by the whole idea, which was strange as he'd never mentioned anything to me when I'd told him I intended to buy the place when it went up for auction.

'I think there's more to it than that. You want to punish Reggie, too, don't you? By taking the thing he loved the most and making it yours. That's it, isn't it?' Niall pressed.

I let out a slow, deliberate breath as I craned my neck to look into his face.

'Of course I want to punish Reggie. He thought he could destroy my life. He shattered my world. My heart. And he walked away grinning. Revenge has been a long time coming.' The words tasted bitter in my mouth.

'There are other ways to get back at Bennett. Not that he's got anything left to lose. He's on the scrapheap, has been for years. I really think you should reconsider. You've bitten off more than you can chew,' Niall replied.

I felt my anger spike, although I managed to contain it. I'd kept the business afloat for years. I knew what I was doing. 'That's your opinion, and you're entitled to it. But I'm determined to rebuild the place with or without you. I want to branch out and make Sean proud. I'm doing this in honour of him. Are you coming to have a look around Mulligans or not?' I asked. My name was on the deeds. My name would be above the door.

'Mulligans? You're using your maiden name? Why aren't you calling it O'Connors if it's a tribute to Sean?' Niall asked with a puzzled look on his face.

He had no right to question my decision, as it was clear he had no interest in the restoration. He wouldn't understand that I wanted to reclaim my own identity. It was a quiet rebellion to the people who thought that I only existed in relation to my late husband. I was somebody before I became an O'Connor. I was strong, resourceful, independent and capable in my own right.

I pushed the key into the lock and, with a decisive twist, released the rusted padlock. It opened with a reluctant clunk. The main door was stiff. The wood had swollen from exposure to the elements and lack of use, so I put my shoulder against it and gave it a barge. Then I took a deep breath to calm my racing heartbeat and stepped inside.

The air still smelled of smoke. Bits of charred wallpaper had curled away from the damp walls. The scorched timber beams stuck out like a ribcage picked clean by vultures. Shards of broken glass littered the floor. I stood in the middle of the gutted room, staring up at where the chandeliers used to hang. It was shocking to see the result of Sean's handiwork. He'd achieved what he'd set out to do. He'd destroyed Reggie's empire. I wondered what he'd think about my plans for the place.

I glanced over my shoulder and saw Niall watching me. His thick, dark eyebrows had knitted together as he observed my movements. He seemed uninterested in inspecting the building's condition. I was commanding his complete attention.

'You never answered my question, Josie. Why are you calling

the place Mulligans?' He spoke slowly as though I might not understand.

'Why not? It's my name.' I didn't look at Niall when I replied. I pressed my fingers onto a scorched beam and let my thumb trace a splinter.

'It *was* your name. You're an O'Connor now.'

I spun around and stared at him. 'I know that, but it's my way of keeping my lineage alive. I'm proud of my roots.' My voice came out sharper than I'd expected. Niall shifted his weight and looked uneasy.

'I understand that, but the O'Connor name carries weight. People know it. They'd line up at the door, lured by that alone.'

Niall's insistence was getting on my nerves. This wasn't a joint venture, so he had no right to be so opinionated.

'You know I loved Sean with all my heart, God help me. But I don't want this place to be just a shrine to a man who's no longer with us...' I let my sentence trail off in the hope that Niall would let the matter drop. He opened his mouth to say something, so I pressed on. 'I was a Mulligan before I was Sean's wife. Before I was Sean's widow. Before the smuggling, the guns, the violence and the bloodshed. Before I was thrust into this situation.'

I couldn't change what had happened, but I needed to forge my own path. My married name was tied to Sean and the world he'd built. I was ready to step out of his shadow; write my own story and show everyone I was here to stay. This was the start of something new. And I wasn't about to let my well-meaning brother-in-law ruin it for me.

Niall's shoulders sagged. He looked defeated. Silence settled heavily between us. 'I can see your mind's made up. Mulligans it is, then.' He let out a slow, grudging breath, and a small, sad smile tugged at the edge of his mouth. 'Do you really think you'll be able to find peace in the place where Sean was murdered?'

My breath caught in my throat and tears threatened to spill. But I wouldn't let myself fall to pieces. Niall should have known better than that. I'd toughened up in the last ten years. His words were designed to hurt me, to make me reconsider. I wasn't trying to force him to be part of something that made him feel uncomfortable. We'd have to agree to disagree. I wouldn't be bullied into changing my plans.

I slowly shook my head as I stared into Niall's dark brown eyes. 'I'll never be at peace. You should know that. I'm not asking for your blessing, but please don't try to stand in my way.'

Niall had made no secret of the fact that he thought I was mad for buying the place. Maybe I was. I couldn't explain it, but when I imagined the new bar, I didn't see the fire-blackened beams or the charred remains. I saw Sean's strong shoulders moving behind the counter, that big, easy grin of his splitting his face. The smell of pulled pints and cigarette smoke, the sound of music drifting from the jukebox.

My husband was gone, but here, in this wreckage, I felt closer to him than anywhere else. I could almost hear his laughter bouncing off the crumbling walls and feel the warmth of his hand on mine. I couldn't bear to tear the building down or to let someone else own it. I owed it to Sean to keep the walls standing. I owed it to Orla to keep his memory alive. Niall had no right to make me feel like this. I brushed off his unkind words. I was way past caring what anyone else thought about me.

6

ORLA

Camden was alive with the sound of music blaring from pub jukeboxes. Neon signs flickered above shops, and graffiti covered entire walls. Majella and I were wired from the pills we'd taken an hour ago. We were laughing loudly as we stumbled out of The World's End with a cider bottle tucked into the crook of our elbows.

I lit a cigarette with shaky fingers and then offered one to Majella. Exhaling smoke into the damp air, I felt invincible. Untouchable. Deep down, I knew I wasn't either of those things. The shit was really going to hit the fan when I went home, but I pushed that thought from my head. I didn't want to ruin the moment.

Majella and I leaned against a rusted railing outside the tube station, taking in the buzz of Camden after dark, and that was when I spotted him. He was leaning on the same railing as us, ten feet away, smoking a roll-up. He looked like a bad boy, which made him doubly attractive.

'He's fit,' Majella whispered, nudging me.

I'd been thinking the same thing. He had a dark brown

mullet, short and neat at the front and sides and longer at the back, with a slight natural wave. His face was sharp, all cheekbones and jawline. He was wearing a burgundy Fila tracksuit, zipped halfway up with a gold chain around his neck. He was tall, taller than me, by the looks of it, which was an added bonus. He looked over at us, and I felt my cheeks flush. As his eyes swept over me, my stomach flipped, and a jolt shot through me.

'What are you staring at?' I called to try to hide my embarrassment.

He didn't answer straight away, but he continued to watch me. 'I could ask you the same thing,' he finally replied in a cockney accent. 'That cider's made you mouthy!'

'Don't blame the cider! Orla's always like this!' Majella laughed.

Heat rushed up the back of my neck, so I took a swig and hoped the ground would swallow me whole. I gave my best friend a dig in the ribs while throwing her a black look.

'So you're Orla. I'm Shay,' he said.

'I'm Majella,' my best friend piped up from behind me.

Shay ignored her. His eyes were locked on mine as though the rest of the world had vanished. He took a final drag of his cigarette and then threw the butt into the gutter. My heart started pounding when he pushed off the railing and sauntered over to where we were standing. 'You from around here?'

'Kilburn,' I replied. 'Why are you asking? Were you planning to follow me home?'

That got a smile from him. 'You wish.'

Up close, I could see he had icy blue eyes, which were striking against his dark lashes. He had a thin scar at the corner of his mouth and a tiny chip at the edge of his front tooth. I liked the imperfections. They made him look cool. Reckless.

'So what brings you to Camden? Are you lost?' Shay asked.

'Do we look lost?' I snorted.

'Nah. You look like trouble.' Shay grinned.

Majella giggled from behind my shoulder.

'Is that so?' I smirked and then flicked my cigarette ash at his feet.

'I know this place better than anyone. Do you wanna see the real Camden? The bits they don't show the tourists?'

My pulse was hammering so hard I felt dizzy. I glanced sideways at Majella. It was clear by the way she was eagerly nodding her head that she was sold on the idea. Decision made. 'Lead the way, then,' I said, doing my best to play it cool while trying to suppress the smile threatening to stretch from ear to ear.

Shay smiled over at us before he turned and started weaving through the crowd, without looking back to see if we were following, which, of course, we were. We scurried after him, grinning at each other, drawn by a pull we didn't try to fight. We eagerly disappeared into the dark recesses of Camden. I knew there would be hell to pay, but the promise of a good night was impossible to resist.

Shay paused outside a scruffy terraced property and waited for us to catch up. The front door was ajar, so he didn't bother knocking, he just stepped inside. The party was in full swing. The music was louder than our laughter. The room started spinning from the booze running through my veins. I could feel it in my chest, a heat that wasn't just from the alcohol; it was from Shay's presence beside me. He was close enough that my skin tingled when he accidentally brushed it.

Before long, Majella began slow dancing with a guy we'd been introduced to at the house party. His hands were on her arse, his tongue down her throat. I desperately wanted to get off with Shay, but he seemed a bit standoffish. Maybe he was nervous, too. Things had been a bit awkward between us since we'd arrived, which made me think Shay liked Jella, not me. He hadn't said anything to me in a while, and I was wondering if I should go when he suddenly leaned into me. I turned around and smiled at him.

Shay took my hand and led me out of the room and into one of the empty bedrooms. I knew what was going to happen before he started undressing me. It was as though everyone else in the house didn't exist. It was just him and me. His hands were trembling as they hovered over my body. Mine were, too.

The strangest feeling had come over me. I yearned for something I knew existed, but didn't fully understand. It was awkward. Fumbling. And just like that, it was over. There hadn't been any fireworks or fanfare when I'd lost my virginity. My heart was thudding as Shay rolled off me and propped himself up on his side. He stared at me, but both of us were too drunk, too inexperienced and too stunned to have a meaningful conversation. I wanted to get away before I died of embarrassment, so I threw my clothes back on and hurried out of the room.

* * *

My key jabbed the lock like it was a moving target, but I eventually managed to open the front door and stumble inside. I tried to close the door softly, but I shoved it harder than I'd intended, and it slammed shut behind me with a bang loud enough to wake the dead, let alone my mother. A heartbeat later, the hallway light snapped on.

Fuck! Fuck! Fuck!

My head felt like it was about to explode. Mum was standing in front of me in her dressing gown. Her arms were folded so tightly that it looked like she was trying to hold herself together. Her olive-green eyes cut through me, sharp and cold as a blade.

Niall hovered behind her. His jaw was tight as his eyes flicked over me. I knew I was in the shit even before they said a word. I tried to straighten up, put on a brave face, and deal with the consequences, but the floor seemed to tip sideways under me. I staggered a couple of steps before I could steady myself. I held on to the wall as I did my best to focus on the blurred figures.

'Orla, where have you been?' Mum's voice was low, like the rumble of thunder before a storm.

'Out,' I slurred. Then I forced myself to point my chin towards the ceiling in a show of defiance, even though my stomach was churning like the spin cycle of a washing machine.

'Out where?' Niall snapped. His Dublin accent was sharper than usual, as though he couldn't keep the worry out of his anger.

I shrugged. 'What's it to you?'

'Don't you dare speak to your uncle like that! We've been worried sick about you. Do you know what time it is?' Mum unleashed a barrage of questions as I swayed in front of her. 'Look at the state of you.' She paused, gesturing to the mirror on the wall next to me.

I squinted into it, and I had to agree I wasn't looking my best. My hair was like a bird's nest, and my black eyeliner was smudged halfway down my face. I started grinning at my reflection, which didn't go down well and provoked another extreme reaction.

'You come crashing in after midnight on a school night, and you think it's funny? It's not. You're fifteen years old, Orla! I'm not putting up with this behaviour.' Mum stepped forward like a fire-breathing dragon, and for a second, I thought she was going to slap me. Instead, she just stared at me, her eyes burning into mine. She almost had smoke coming out of her ears. I couldn't remember ever seeing her so mad. 'You smell like an ashtray, and you're drunk out of your mind. Anything could have happened to you. I've been beside myself with worry, so has Niall. You're lucky I didn't call the police. I thought about it,' Mum spat. Her face was pale and tight with rage.

My conscience told me that now would be a good time to apologise, but my stubbornness wouldn't allow it. Not that I'd have been able to string the words together even if I'd wanted to. I was pissed out of my head, so they'd jumble together and tangle on my tongue.

'Go on then, say something smart,' Mum dared, glaring at me with her hands on her tiny hips.

My head throbbed so badly I thought it might split open in the hall. I didn't want to have a showdown. All I wanted was to go to bed. While she waited for me to reply, her jaw worked overtime like she was grinding her teeth to dust. The idea of that brought a smile to my face.

'Orla, I'm warning you, this is no laughing matter,' Mum said, wagging a disapproving finger at me.

I opened my mouth, but before I could say anything, my stomach lurched. A second later, my mouth flooded with vomit, hot and sour, and I was sick everywhere.

'Oh, Jesus!' I heard Niall mutter as it hit the floor and splashed up the wall.

I could tell there was more to come, but I was glued to the spot. I couldn't get my feet to cooperate with my brain. I doubled over, my hands gripping my knees as I retched again, once, twice, then it all came up. Vodka, cider and something greasy I barely remembered eating splattered all down the front of me. I was powerless to stop it. Mum let out a horrified, strangled sound. The smell was disgusting. I knew it would penetrate deep into the wood and cling to the grain for days on end, filling our lungs every time we breathed.

I straightened my posture and wiped my mouth with the back

of my hand. My vision was swimming. My hair clung to the side of my face. It stank of smoke and now vomit. I pushed it over my shoulders so I wouldn't have to smell it.

'She's going to destroy herself, Niall. She's going to end up in the gutter if she carries on like this.' Mum spoke as though I wasn't in the room. Her voice was trembling, cracking with emotion, which sent guilt flooding through me.

Niall's large feet tiptoed around the piles of puke, and he grabbed hold of my arm to steady me. 'Come on, love. Let's get you upstairs to bed.' His voice was soft and sympathetic, which was more than I deserved.

Mum didn't say a word or move a muscle. Her eyes were wide with shock, and she looked like she'd just seen a ghost. I knew I was hurting her, and part of me hated myself for that, but I was angry because I felt abandoned even though I'd never admit that out loud.

I let Niall guide me as my legs were barely working. I felt Mum's gaze burning into the back of my skull all the way up the stairs. She was emitting a mix of fury, disapproval, and something worse, something that felt like heartbreak.

When we reached my room, I collapsed on to the bed without even kicking off my shoes. My stomach was twisting and turning like it hadn't finished punishing me. It wanted to make me pay for drinking, smoking and taking drugs. An imaginary puppet master was pulling the strings, sending waves of nausea crashing through me one after the other.

'Get some sleep. It's late,' Niall said from the doorway, and then he disappeared out of sight.

There was nothing I'd have liked better, but at that precise moment in time, I felt too sick to drop off, so I curled into a ball. My head was pounding as tears started running down my face. My life was a mess. Was Mum right? Would I end up in the gutter? If I did, I'd only have myself to blame. I hated being at war with her, but we were stuck in a rut, and I didn't know how to get out of it. Things were getting worse by the day. Mum was impossible to talk to. I felt judged and misunderstood. She was consumed by work and had no time for me any more. She'd stretched herself too thin at my expense. I'd already lost one parent to the business, and now I was losing the other.

When I woke the next morning, the haze of alcohol had gone, which left me with a feeling of dread. My stomach sank in a way that had nothing to do with hangovers. I'd done a stupid thing. And now everything had changed. I couldn't shrug it off or laugh it away. I barely knew Shay, and yet I'd let him take my virginity. What was wrong with me? Now he'd think I was a slag and wouldn't want anything more to do with me. I had nobody else to blame. I'd brought this on myself.

7

DECLAN

Dublin, May 1985

Gavin Davis had been a small-time enforcer when I'd first arrived in London. He was a man who specialised in sorting problems. Bad debtors, loose-lipped doormen, and cowardly individuals who needed a rocket put up their arses were his bread and butter.

Gavin and I had nothing in common, but we shared a mutual respect having done a few jobs, shaking down bookmakers and corner-shop owners where backup was required. I'd been a teenager then, but I'd grown up in a rough neighbourhood in Dublin and learned early on that power belonged to those who were willing to take it. My father had been an enforcer for a local gang, so I'd known what was required of me.

I was leaning against the battered metal desk, watching Fergal pacing nearby. He was chain-smoking, and his eyes flicked to the entrance of the draughty warehouse every few seconds. He was becoming more agitated by the minute.

'What's keeping him?' Fergal asked, chewing the nails on his left hand in between puffing on his Major.

'How should I know?'

I'd arranged to meet Gavin in my lock-up, which was one of the many redundant buildings in the vast North Wall area of Dublin Port. The smell of salt, diesel and damp concrete hung in the air, and stacks of crates marked 'Agricultural Equipment' lined the wall on the right. They concealed the finest whiskey Cork, the Rebel County, had to offer. If things went to plan, this could well be the last shipment of single malt I smuggled.

I was beginning to think Gavin wasn't coming when I heard several sets of heavy footsteps echoing outside, and a moment later, he appeared in the doorway, framed by two big lads in bomber jackets. He eyed the cavernous space with a suspicious glance, then he stepped inside.

Gavin hadn't changed much since I'd last seen him. He was in his mid-forties, a big-framed Englishman with a thick neck that always seemed too wide for his shirt collars. His nose had been smashed and reset countless times, and he had deep lines around his mouth from years of shouting orders and laughing at his own jokes. His hair was dark, but it was starting to go grey at the sides. It was still in the same style as before, cropped close to the scalp in a no-nonsense cut.

'For fuck's sake, Declan. This place is miles away from the passenger terminal,' Gavin said in his thick East End accent.

'Miles away? It took me fifteen minutes the last time I walked it. I was wondering what was keeping you. I'd thought maybe you'd decided to swim over from Holyhead instead of getting the ferry,' I fired back.

'Don't be such a smart arse. Fuck me, it's freezing in here. Couldn't you have found somewhere with a heater? I didn't grow up in a bog like you lot.' Gavin rubbed his hands together.

I'd picked the warehouse because it was a stone's throw from where the boat came in. I thought I'd made life easy for Gavin, but he was in a foul mood, and I wasn't going to take the bait. I didn't move from my position. I watched him approach, staying calm and composed. 'It's good to see you made it across the water in one piece. How was the crossing?' Gavin wasn't going to like what I had to say, so I didn't want to start off on the wrong foot. His two companions were both watching me like guard dogs waiting for their master's signal.

'It was fucking awful. That boat's a rusty old tub. I'm surprised it's seaworthy. There was nowhere to sit – the carpets stank of puke and stale beer. And don't get me started on the state of the crappers. Never again. This is the first and last time I'm coming to this shithole. Next time you want to speak to me, we'll do it on my turf.' Gavin eyed the crates, then turned his attention to me. 'Are those the toys?'

They weren't, but he didn't need to know that. I didn't dare look at Fergal in case he gave the game away. I'd never seen him acting so uneasy before. He'd been in the whiskey smuggling game as long as I had, but the change of cargo had him rattled. 'They are, but they're not yours. They're for another customer. I can't move your order until I get the rest of my money.'

Gavin clicked his tongue and stepped closer, leaning in so close that I could smell the stale cigarettes on his breath. 'The cops raided one of my client's warehouses in Bethnal Green last week. He had a lot of gear seized and cash flow is tight,' Gavin said, dropping his voice low.

I clenched my jaw. 'How tight are we talking?'

Gavin smirked, and his gold tooth glinted in the warehouse light. 'The buyer can't afford to give you more than ten grand. And don't start crying about it. I'm not in the mood.'

Fergal stepped forward, so I shot him a look to stand down. The meatheads Gavin had brought with him were primed and ready for action, but we hadn't come here to fight. We were meant to be closing the deal. 'I'm not sure I heard you right. Did you say ten grand?'

Gavin nodded and let out a short, barking chuckle, highly amused by the situation. But this was no laughing matter.

'You're taking the fucking piss. Your client owes me forty-five grand. It was half up front. Half on delivery. Remember?'

I glared at Gavin, barely able to contain my fury.

'Ten grand it is. It's non-negotiable. Take it or leave it,' he grunted and waved a dismissive hand at me.

'That's not the figure we agreed on,' I replied, staying calm but cold. 'I put this order together at great risk and expense to myself. Your client's not the only man in London looking for stock, as you know.' I was bluffing. I needed his money to be able to secure the order with Cormac and I didn't know anyone else I could sell the weapons to if the deal fell through.

Things were turning to shit before my very eyes. Cormac had fleeced me on the purchase price, and now Gavin was trying to ride me, too. I'd be lucky to break even at this rate. I had years of experience behind me, but whiskey smuggling and gunrunning were poles apart. It was a mug's game.

'My contact in London wants these crates yesterday. He can't afford to wait while you throw a tantrum.' Gavin straightened his posture and then adjusted the rows of gold rings he wore on both hands, like a poorly disguised set of knuckle dusters.

'Who's throwing a tantrum?' I prided myself on never raising my voice, even when under immense pressure. 'I can arrange the shipment quickly, but nothing's leaving this warehouse unless I get what I'm owed.'

Silence fell between us. Gavin's men shifted behind him, ready for trouble. 'Sell them to the Paddies in Kilburn if you want. But if you go back on the agreement, you're done. My client will make sure of that,' he sneered.

My heart was pounding. I'd bitten off more than I could chew, but I couldn't afford to lose face. I took a deep breath, then stepped forward so that I was inches from Gavin. 'I'm not an unreasonable man. I'm prepared to take pity on your client's predicament on this occasion and accept the ten grand. But don't mistake my generosity for weakness. You push me again, I'll make sure you never come back on Irish soil. You hear me?'

Gavin grinned, but his smile wavered for just a moment. He held my stare, and then he clapped me on the shoulder. The sound echoed in the cold warehouse. 'I'll leave you to make the arrangements. The cargo needs to ship ASAP,' he said, pulling out a wad of notes from the inside of his jacket and handing it to me. He turned and barked orders to his men before they disappeared out the door.

Once they were out of earshot, Fergal paced across the room. 'You let that bastard rob us!' he fumed.

'What was I supposed to do? Would you prefer a price on our heads?'

Fergal glared at me, but didn't reply.

'It's better to take the cut now than be left with stock we can't shift and a mob of gangsters baying for our blood. Next time, we'll set the price higher and demand the money up front. If he tries to shaft us again, he won't leave Dublin alive.'

'I'm holding you to that,' Fergal replied.

'Gavin might think he's got one over on us, but we still stand to make a huge profit. Far more than we'll get for shifting this lot.' I gestured to the crates of whiskey lined up along the wall.

Gavin hadn't had the last laugh. I was already planning my next move. One that would remind the Camden crew exactly who they were dealing with. But I'd have to hold the thought. I had whiskey to ship, and the tide waited for no man.

8

JOSIE

London, May 1985

I trudged up the steps of the council offices in Westminster, dreading the meeting I'd been summoned to. The refurbishment had taken over my life. All I seemed to do was work these days. I was barely able to contain my temper when I was called, forty-five minutes later than scheduled. Wasting time was a luxury I couldn't afford.

'Take a seat, Mrs O'Connor,' a planning officer said, gesturing to a chair.

The tired-looking man wearing a grey polyester suit and pink tie walked around the table and sat opposite me. He opened a file and took out drawings, licensing applications, and other legal documents bearing the name Mulligans. 'We've had multiple objections. There are concerns about the level of noise, the increase in traffic and parking problems due to the pub's operation, and a petition about community disruption,' the man said.

I raised an eyebrow, but inside I was boiling mad. Beneath my calm exterior, something darker lurked. Fury clawed at my ribs, begging to be let loose.

'They're all valid complaints, Mrs O'Connor.'

'Are they? It seems very strange that nobody had any issues when Mr Bennett ran the premises as a late-night casino. Surely all of those objections applied before,' I fired back, glaring at the man in the grey suit.

'I can't comment on anything other than this application.'

'That's handy. So who raised the complaints? I'd like to see a list of the names.' My fingers twitched. I was desperate to lash out at something.

'I'm afraid I can't disclose information like that. Planning objections are strictly confidential,' the man said. Then he scooped the paperwork into a pile and put it back in the file.

'So where does this leave my application?' My voice cracked the air like a whip.

'It will be discussed at a committee meeting where councillors will decide the outcome.'

'This is ridiculous. How long is this going to take?' I snapped, slamming the heel of my hand on the desk. The planning officer seemed appalled by my outburst, which prompted me to rein in my anger. I clasped my hands together tightly in my lap so I wouldn't be tempted to wrap them around his throat.

'We aim to reach a decision within eight weeks of receiving a case.' The man pushed his chair back and got to his feet, signalling that our meeting was over.

'I'm only trying to refurbish an eyesore of a building. I really don't understand what the problem is. I'll be doing the local community a favour, but if my application is rejected, you can tell Mr Bennett from me that I'll be appealing the decision. If it's a fight he wants, a fight he'll get,' I said, leaning forward. My voice was calm but steely.

The man looked startled by what I'd just said. He didn't bother to reply or deny Reggie's involvement as he ushered me towards the door. I should have known Bennett would try to sabotage the refurbishment of Mulligans. But he wasn't the only person who could grease palms.

* * *

The front door slammed hard enough to rattle the glass in its frame. As I looked up from where I was peeling potatoes at the kitchen table, my eyes were drawn to the window. It was already dark outside, and the street was glistening with London drizzle. Orla marched in a moment later. There was no sign of her blazer, it was no doubt stuffed into her bag. The black hoodie she was wearing was soaked, and her auburn curls hung in rats' tails over her shoulders. 'You're soaked to the skin. Get out of those wet clothes before you catch your death,' I said.

Orla tossed her bag on to the floor and glared at me with defiance seeping out of every pore. Her black eyeliner was smudged all over her face. She looked a mess.

'Stop bossing me around! I'm not a child,' Orla roared and then she stormed out of the room.

I'd had the day from hell. The last thing I wanted was a run-in with her, so I kept my mouth shut and went back to the spuds. I put the peeler and the potato on the table, pushed my chair back and walked over to the doorway when I heard Orla stomping down the stairs a short while later. She'd changed out of her wet clothes and scraped her damp hair into a high ponytail. She'd applied a coat of deep wine lipstick and drawn a small black heart near her eye with a kohl pencil, but she hadn't bothered to fix the smudges under her lower lashes. Orla was wearing an oversized Siouxsie and the Banshees T-shirt and a black pleated mini skirt with ripped tights and Dr. Martens boots. A large crucifix hung around her neck. Once she got to the last step, she reached for her long black coat hanging on the rack.

'Where the hell do you think you're going?' My voice cut across the room. It was low and controlled, although my insides were in turmoil as anger surged through me.

'Out,' Orla replied.

'No way. Not on a school night.' I stood in front of her to block her path, but she shoved past me. My daughter was tall like her father, although she didn't have his build. She was as thin as a reed, with long arms and legs. There was nothing I could do to stop her. She towered over me.

'I'll do what I want. I'm not five,' she yelled as she slammed the front door behind her.

I grabbed my coat and keys and flew out the door after her, but Orla had already disappeared into the night. She was nowhere to be seen, so I paced down the road and turned on to the next street.

'Josie, what are you doing here?' my sister-in-law, Philomena, asked, raising her sculpted eyebrows when she answered the door to me.

She looked me up and down while she waited for me to reply. I knew I didn't meet her exacting standards. Her nails were always painted, her lipstick always on. She was always doused in perfume and wouldn't be seen dead without her gold jewellery. It amazed me how a mother of two small children had the time to be so glamorous.

'I need to speak to Niall urgently,' I replied without bothering with pleasantries, which would have been wasted on her.

'You'd better come in then.'

Philomena stepped back, and I walked into her immaculate home. She showed me into the good room and went to get her husband. I should have felt honoured as the space, which was in pristine condition, was reserved for special guests and special occasions, but I knew she just wanted to show off; it wasn't because she held me in high esteem.

Philomena resented my close relationship with Niall. Our mutual hatred ran deep. It had built up over decades, but it had worsened since Sean's death had seen a shift in power. She despised what I represented and was bitter that she held a lower rank in the family than I did.

Niall appeared a few moments later with a frown settled on his forehead. 'Hi, Josie. Is everything all right?' he asked, then he sat opposite me and placed his elbows on his knees.

'I had words with Orla and she's taken off. I don't know what to do.' I swallowed the lump in my throat as I searched my brother-in-law's eyes for the answer.

'She'll come back,' he said in a gentle voice. 'She always does.'

I tore my eyes away from his and stared into nothing. 'I don't know how much more of this I can take.' The words hitched in my chest as tears stabbed at my eyes.

'You're stronger than you give yourself credit for. You've held the business together—'

'This isn't a business. It's my daughter.' My voice cracked when I interrupted Niall. 'I'm losing her. Bit by bit. Day by day. She looks at me with such hatred, like I'm the enemy.' My shoulders slumped. It was too much to bear. The problems with the council. With Reggie. And now with Orla. I was struggling to manage it all. Why was life so difficult?

Niall leaned forward and reached for my hands, knotted in my lap. 'You've both been through hell. She's angry. She's hurt. She doesn't hate you, Josie. She loves you. She just lashes out at you because she doesn't know how to handle her emotions. She's a teenager. Her hormones are all over the place.'

I wanted to believe Niall, but I had to face facts, and the truth was ugly. 'She's slipping through my fingers, and I don't know how to reach her.' My voice dropped to a whisper. 'I hoped she'd have everything I didn't have growing up. We were poor, but we were content. I wouldn't have chosen this life for her.' A long silence passed. 'I'm scared, Niall. Not of Reggie. Not of Declan. Of what she'll become if I don't stop her…' For the first time in a long while, I let the tears fall freely without trying to hold them in, even though I could see Philomena hovering in the doorway, watching and listening, storing the information to throw back at me at a later stage. Niall didn't say a word, but he stayed with me, holding my hand as he did his best to comfort me.

9

DECLAN

London, May 1985

I'd been summoned to a meeting by Gavin Davis. He wanted to discuss a change to the arms deal before the shipment set sail. Conversations like these couldn't happen over the phone, and he was refusing to come to Dublin to agree on the terms, so if I wanted the business, I had no choice but to head over to the Big Smoke. I had bad memories of the place. The thought of bumping into Josie put the fear of God into me, but Fergal had agreed to come with me, which put my mind at rest a small bit.

The venue, a private back room above a seedy snooker club in Bethnal Green, was easy enough to find and low-key enough to keep me off the radar. As soon as we arrived, we were ushered into a space where fluorescent light flickered overhead. I stepped into the room first and scanned it with sharp eyes. The carpet was sticky underfoot – years of grime and stale beer were woven into the pattern. Fergal shuffled in behind me, keeping his head low. A set of heavy red curtains was drawn tight, blocking out the world beyond the window, and a battered wooden table was in the middle of the room. Gavin was sitting up one end of it, legs spread, tapping ash into a chipped saucer. He looked relaxed, but there was an edge to him. Two of his men, shaven-headed muscle, stood against the far wall.

'About fucking time too,' he said, beckoning us towards him. His voice was low and scratchy. He had the kind of East End accent that sounded like his vocal cords were regularly marinated in cigarettes and late-night lock-ins to preserve the raspy sound. 'You bastards know how to keep a man waiting, don't you? Sit the fuck down, I haven't got all night!'

I felt myself bristle, but I followed his instructions, sinking into the chair opposite. Fergal hovered behind me. He kept his hands in his pockets. I knew he was reading the room.

'Neither have we. You dragged us across the water for a reason. Let's get on with it.' I didn't want to stay in London a moment longer than necessary. There were eyes everywhere and I couldn't afford to let my guard down. I didn't want Josie to get wind that I was back on the scene. I had a lasting souvenir from the night the O'Connors had got hold of me. I never spoke of it, but the limp was there in every step I took. The injury was old, but it had never fully healed – a permanent reminder of a moment I wouldn't forgive or forget.

Gavin stubbed out his cigarette and leaned forward. He had an appetite for trouble. 'That's the problem with you country boys. When you're born in a bog, no fucker teaches you manners.' His face broke into a crooked smile.

Gavin was as ignorant as shit. He knew full well I was born in Dublin and grew up in the city. He was just trying to goad me, but if I mouthed off at him, I'd blow the deal, so I had to hold my tongue. I'd make sure he paid for the insult one way or another.

'My contact wants to add more toys to the order – a lot more. Proper gear, no rusty leftover farm shit. I'm talking Uzis, MAC-

10s, rifles, crates of ammo…' Gavin handed me a list of his requirements.

'You realise what you're asking for won't come cheap. This is serious kit.' I fully intended to put a hefty markup on the extras to recoup the money Gavin had done me out of.

'Serious kit? You don't say! Are you suggesting I don't know this game? I know exactly what I want, and I know exactly what I'm going to pay. And before you start bleating on about risky shipping routes or Republican eyes, let me tell you something: I don't give a fuck how you get it here; if you want my money, you get it here ASAP.'

Gavin's grin returned. It was cunning, wolfish. There was no denying the calculation behind his beady, dark brown eyes. He wore the steely glint of a man who knew loyalty only went as far as the next deal. For a long moment, I considered his proposal. I didn't take my eyes off Davis while I mulled things over. He saw himself in the power seat, but if he thought he was going to call all the shots, he was very much mistaken.

'That's a big ask. I'll need a bit of notice to get an order like that together.' I was having to think on my feet. I could threaten to walk away from the deal, but I knew the stakes were high. Having said that, I wasn't about to let Gavin tell me how much he was prepared to pay for the weapons. That wasn't good business sense, especially as he'd already shafted me once. It wasn't going to happen a second time.

'How come your buyer needs so many toys?'

'His patch is expanding rapidly, not that it's any of your fucking business. What is this? Prime Minister's Questions?' Gavin let out an exaggerated sigh and then threw his eyes to heaven.

'Would he accept partial shipments?' Smaller drops were

easier to disguise within cargo and posed less risk than a large consignment.

'If you're not up to the job, Kelly, just say!' Gavin's face was like thunder.

'I'm up for the job, all right. I'm just trying to work out the logistics. I'd need to check with my contact and see how quickly he can get the stock you're after.'

'My buyer is planning to start pushing cocaine through neighbourhoods in Whitechapel and Bethnal Green that don't belong to him. Before he can do that, he needs weapons, reliable ones to establish dominance over the old-guard firms. The Turkish and Albanian gangs have had footholds in those areas up until now, but things are about to change.'

Gavin looked so smug. Anyone would think nothing could go wrong. But I'd have to come up with a new way to send the weapons. I wouldn't get away with hiding a shipment this size among the fishing gear on *Storm Chaser*, the trawler I used to move my bootlegged whiskey, which was a shame because I knew Duffy, the skipper, well. He'd been transporting my cargo for as long as I could remember and knew everything there was to know about the smuggling game.

I'd been hoping this meeting would be a formality, to finalise arrangements, but the face-to-face negotiations were tense. Gavin had been cocky from the moment we'd walked in, assuming he could push me around. Accepting the change in terms of the order hadn't done me any favours, and now he saw me as weak and was trying to exploit the situation. I wasn't going to stick my neck on the block for chicken feed. His buyer would be raking in the money selling class A drugs, so he could afford to pay the going rate. Awkward as it was going to be, I'd have to insist on a decent cut and control over the logistics.

'You've gone very quiet on me.' Gavin started drumming his

ring-adorned fingers on the pitted table. His impatience was palpable. 'For fuck's sake. I haven't got time for you to go all thoughtful on me. I need a decision. My buyer is hungry. His patch is growing by the day, but he needs more than muscle and supply lines. He needs firepower to survive the coming wars. Are you in, or are you out?'

I could hear Fergal shifting his weight from foot to foot behind me, but I didn't turn around. I kept my eyes fixed on Gavin.

'I'm in, but I'm not discussing the price until I speak to my supplier. And I'm going to need the cash up front. I can't afford to make another loss.' I stood my ground, refusing to budge an inch.

'You'll have to come and collect it in person. I'm not bringing the dosh to you,' Gavin replied, then he leaned over the table and patted my cheek like a proud father.

'I'll be in touch,' I said, pushing my chair back.

'Make it snappy. The Camden crew won't tolerate a delay. And word will spread fast if you let them down. I'll make sure of that,' Gavin warned.

This shipment couldn't afford to fail. It could put me on the map. My days as a whiskey kingpin were over. I'd been looking for other ventures for a while now. Ones that didn't cross paths with Josie. I had every confidence that this was going to be the making of me. If it meant I had to go to London to seal the deal occasionally, so be it.

10

JOSIE

I stepped into the stale, overheated office, dressed in my most expensive power suit. My oversized shoulder pads were engaged, and I was ready to fight. I was here to do battle, and I wasn't leaving the building until I got what I wanted.

My stiletto heels clicked against the lino as I made my way to the reception desk. A surly teenage girl with electric blue eyeliner and mascara caked all over her eyes eventually acknowledged my presence, so I stopped drumming my fingertips on the folder I'd placed on the counter.

'Name?' she asked, shuffling papers to make herself look busy.

'Josephine O'Connor. I've got an appointment at eleven o'clock with Mr Carver.'

'Take a seat. I'll let him know you're here.'

I eased myself on to the nearest plastic chair, which hadn't been designed for comfort, and waited to be called. I'd arrived ten minutes early, so I'd been expecting to be sitting there for some time, but to my surprise, the girl told me to go straight through.

'Mr Carver will see you now. His office is down that corridor. It's the second door on the left,' she said, pointing towards a set of double doors.

'Thank you,' I replied, to illustrate the fact that I had manners.

I ran my hand over my red hair, which was swept into a chignon, to check it was still in place, then knocked on the door and pushed it open. The office was cramped. The walls were lined with peeling municipal notices, and a portrait of the Queen hung at a wonky angle above a cluttered desk. Mr Carver, the head of planning, was wedged behind it. He was a big man with a bald head, which appeared sweaty despite the chill outside. He looked up from a pile of paperwork and forced out a smile.

'Mrs O'Connor, please take a seat. What can I do for you?' he asked.

I sat down opposite him and placed the folder on the desk. 'You keep finding reasons to delay my application, which is unacceptable. I'm losing a lot of money,' I replied as my stare pinned him to his chair.

He cleared his throat and shuffled the papers in front of him. 'Firstly, I'm not deliberately delaying the process. The licensing board has strict codes that I have to adhere to, especially after what happened to the property previously. There are safety measures to review, local objections—'

'Let's not put obstacles in the way, shall we?' My voice was steely when I interrupted him. 'I want to open before Christmas. It will be the perfect time of year to launch Mulligans. You know as well as I do, Mr Carver, people will line up around the block to have a drink in a pub where the staff know how to pull a pint of Guinness properly.'

'Christmas, you say!' His eyes were wide as he blew out a breath.

Then he slipped a chubby hand inside the pocket of his navy pinstriped suit, pulled out a brown checked handkerchief and started dabbing his forehead with it. 'I'm afraid it's not that simple, Mrs O'Connor. A December opening is rather optimistic. There are forms to be completed, inspections to undertake, criteria to be met...'

I slid the folder across to him, having flipped it open. The only thing inside was a thick envelope. My eyes didn't leave his face as I gauged his reaction. 'I wondered if that might help to speed up the process,' I said, leaning forward. 'And there'll be another envelope coming your way when you sign off the final inspection without any more delays.'

Mr Carver's eyes darted to the closed door, then back to me. 'I'm a council official. Are you asking me to accept a bribe, Mrs O'Connor?'

'Of course not. I'm just asking you to do your job a little faster, that's all.'

He licked his lips as he looked at the envelope. I could see he was tempted. Then he wiped the perspiration from his face and peered inside the folder. He seemed scared to touch the wad of cash in case it burned his fingers. 'Someone could report this. What you're asking me to do is highly illegal.' Mr Carver's voice was barely above a whisper.

'We both know it's nothing you haven't done before. You've accepted money from a lot worse people than me in the past. I'm just a mother, a widow, trying to make a living and provide for my child. I need to get the pub open. If you want a quiet life, you'll get the necessary paperwork signed off today.' I kept my breathing steady, but inside me a storm was brewing.

Mr Carver swallowed hard, then he ran his index finger around the collar of his shirt. His hand was trembling as he reached into the folder and took out the envelope. He stared at it for the longest moment before he slid it into the top drawer of his desk. 'You'll have your papers by the end of the week.'

I leaned across the desk and glared at him. 'I can't wait that long. I need the paperwork today.'

'Very well,' he replied without meeting my gaze. He picked up a pen and opened the file on his desk marked Mulligans. A short while later, he handed the planning permission to me.

I smoothed down my pencil skirt as I rose. 'Good man. You'll have an extra bonus coming your way very soon. And I'll send you a bottle of the finest Irish whiskey as well.'

He nodded, but he didn't look up from his desk.

As I left the office, my lips curled into a satisfied smile. Once I was in the corridor, I drew in a long breath and blew it out. To say I was relieved that the renovations could finally start was an understatement. I'd poured my heart and soul into this venture, working long hours to try and get it off the ground. Mulligans was going to open on time. I didn't care who I had to pay off; nobody was going to stand in my way.

11

JOSIE

The hammering had stopped for the day, but the dust still hung in the air like a ghost. I slammed the ledger shut and pressed my fingers to my temples. My head was throbbing. The smell of paint and damp plaster clung to my hair and clothes like a second skin. Every inch of me felt grubby.

Niall suddenly appeared in the doorway, his face tight with stress. 'Josie, I'm sorry to disturb you, but there's a call for you from Dublin.'

My head snapped up from the closed book. This had to be about the shipment. I stormed out of the makeshift room and over to where the phone was mounted on the wall in a section of the building that had escaped the fire.

'Hello,' I said. My voice was sharp.

'Josie, it's Eamonn. There's a problem with the whiskey,' he said.

'What's going on?' I snapped. I could picture Eamonn's cheeks flushing, but I wasn't going to apologise for being abrupt.

'Customs have been poking around more than usual. They've somehow got wind of the shipment, and they're holding two of the containers at the docks. They're planning to carry out a thorough search of the cargo in the morning.'

I closed my eyes for a second and allowed his words to sink in, but they started swirling around in my mind. 'Have they seized the whole lot?'

'No, half of it.'

My hands were steady as I held the phone, but my stomach was in a knot. This was a disaster. The whiskey was my lifeline. It bankrolled everything. I needed the money from the sale of it to keep the builders paid. If my supply dried up, I'd lose loyal customers. And Declan would be only too happy to poach them from me.

'How did this happen?' I didn't try to disguise the anger in my voice.

'I don't know. Someone must have tipped them off. What do you want me to do?' Eamonn asked.

My insides churned as a wave of nausea washed over me. His reply was too quick. Too rehearsed. That was a bad sign. A man in his position should be frantic. Apologetic. He sounded composed. Almost like this wasn't a surprise.

'I don't know if it'll work, it depends on the inspector, but do you want me to try slipping them a few quid to look the other way?'

My mind whirred as I pieced things together at speed. Then I swallowed something sour at the back of my mouth – the taste of being lied to.

'I've diverted the other half of the shipment to a different warehouse, so you'll still get that, but if you want the containers that are being held, it's going to cost you.'

I felt my temper spike. 'Cost me? Why is it going to cost me? I pay you to ensure stuff like this doesn't happen.'

'I risk my job every time I handle your shipments. But things are getting tighter. If you want your cargo to pass through smoothly, you'll need to give me more grease for the wheels.' Eamonn didn't apologise. Instead, his tone was stroppy. I didn't appreciate the way he'd spoken to me.

'If you're not up to the job, I'll find somebody else to take your place.'

'You can try, but I doubt very much you'll find anyone willing to put their neck on the block like I do,' Eamonn fired back.

'Don't flatter yourself. Everyone's replaceable,' I replied through gritted teeth.

I could see Niall shifting from foot to foot out of the corner of my eye while chewing the nails on his right hand. He wasn't the only one who was nervous, but Eamonn needed to be taken down a peg or two.

'Move whatever you can tonight. Hide it on outbound trucks. We'll have to take the hit on the other containers. I've parted with enough of my hard-earned cash for one shipment. I'm not lining any more pockets. I want this mess sorted out. I've got enough on my plate without your dithering.'

Niall pulled a face, but this situation was crying out for a no-nonsense approach. If I didn't come down hard, Eamonn was going to run rings around me.

'I'll do my best to make things right. I always do. I know every dark corner of the port and how to move contraband past watchful eyes.'

Now that I'd stood up to him, Eamonn seemed to be backing down. He'd been loyal enough to keep the whiskey shipments flowing, but ultimately, he had only his best interests at heart. He was willing to help me as long as it didn't land him in hot water.

'Let me know what happens with the quarantined containers. Do your best to push them through unchecked. But I'm not paying anyone else off to facilitate their movement. Do I make myself clear?'

'Yes, Josie. I'll keep you posted,' Eamonn replied.

I slammed the phone down and stood staring at the wall, breathing heavily. Niall didn't move from the doorway, but I could feel his eyes boring into the back of my skull.

'Trouble with customs?' he asked.

'Half the load is stuck. We might lose it all if they start digging deeper,' I replied, shaking my head as I turned to face my brother-in-law. I didn't shout. I went quiet. I had a pressure cooker kind of temper.

Niall blew out a low whistle. 'Christ, that'll be a huge loss to the—'

I cut him off with a sharp wave of my hand. 'Don't say it. Don't tempt fate.'

The business couldn't afford to take a hit like that. At the moment, bills were coming from every angle. The refurbishment was costing a fortune. Far more than I'd expected or budgeted for. I didn't want Niall to know that, as he'd never given me his blessing to go ahead with the venture. He'd just resigned himself to the fact that I was doing it whether he liked it or not. To preserve our relationship, he'd taken a step back and kept his opinions to himself. I respected him for that. He didn't agree with me, but he wasn't trying to interfere with my plans either.

The walls suddenly seemed too close, as if they were pressing in on me. I took a step and staggered. I felt dizzy. Lightheaded. I thought I was going to faint. Niall rushed over and put his arm around me to steady me.

'Are you OK? You're as white as a sheet.'

'I'm fine,' I lied.

My legs were wobbling like jelly as Niall ushered me back to my desk. He pulled out the chair with one hand and then guided me on to it.

'Would you like some water?' he asked.

'No, thanks. I don't know what it is, but something feels off. Eamonn's always been sharp. He never used to be so sloppy.'

Niall frowned. 'Do you think he's turning on you?'

'I don't know.' I took a deep breath and exhaled it slowly. 'I can't prove anything. He's in Dublin, and I'm in London. The distance gives him power. It would be easy for someone to whisper the right number in his ear and make his loyalty evaporate into thin air.'

I felt violated to think that Eamonn would betray me, in a bone-level way that confirmed every fear I'd tried to silence since stepping into Sean's shoes. The idea of the masses lining up to watch me fail bothered me. It burned more than the financial loss.

'It's worrying to think Eamonn's shafting us.' Niall's dark brown eyebrows knitted together. 'He could be telling the truth, though.'

'I'm not convinced. Why would customs only seize half of the shipment if they were following a tip-off? That doesn't make any sense.'

Niall rubbed his jaw while he considered what I'd just said. 'I suppose he could be pulling a fast one, hoping to squeeze more cash out of you by pretending to grease more palms,' he replied after a pause.

'That's what I'm worried about. Or he's got involved with Declan and they're trying to scam me. But I haven't got time to play guessing games.'

'Surely Declan wouldn't be stupid enough to do that.'

'Who knows what's going on. I hate to say it, but I'm not sure I trust Eamonn any more.' I let out a loud sigh, and a heavy silence settled between us.

The whiskey wasn't just a product – it was my credibility. If Eamonn had sold me out, he'd made a fool out of me. Thinking people were laughing at me behind closed doors made rage well up inside.

'Do you want me to put someone on him? Quiet-like?' Niall asked.

I shook my head. 'No. Not yet. If I'm wrong and he's not playing us, we can't afford to scare him off. If he folds, the whole line will collapse, and we'll be finished. For now, we watch and wait.' Outside, a car horn blasted, and I jumped out of my skin. 'I don't get it. I've proved myself over and over, and yet some of the men still don't accept me as their leader. They see me as a figure-head. Someone who keeps them in work and the cash flowing, but they don't respect me the way they did Sean.' I swallowed hard. My throat was raw.

'Ahh, Josie, that's just the way of the world. Smuggling whiskey is a man's game. Some of the old boys are set in their ways and very narrow-minded,' Niall replied.

That comment ignited a fire in my belly. I'd been reluctantly holding the reins for the last ten years, and the company had flourished. I did things differently from my late husband. I wasn't as reckless. I was more calculated and the business was thriving under my leadership. 'I think I'm doing a good job.'

'You are. I was only trying to explain why some of the men treat you differently to Sean.' Niall's dark brown eyes washed over me. 'Don't let the bastards break you. You're running yourself ragged, Josie. You're trying to juggle too many things. The renovations, Orla, the shipments...'

I knew I'd taken on too much, but it was hard to admit I'd

made a mistake. I didn't want to lose face. Niall was looking for any excuse to get me to abandon the refurbishment. 'I'm slowly getting to grips with the business, but Orla's a different kettle of fish altogether. She's out of control, and I don't know how to bring her back into line.' When my voice cracked with emotion, Niall placed his large hand on the top of my shoulder and gave it a reassuring squeeze.

'She's going through the terrible teens, that's all.' Niall tried his best to convince me.

'You reckon? She clears off without telling me where she's going, and then she comes home hours later reeking of cigarettes and booze...' My voice faltered, so I pressed a hand to my chest. I could feel the thundering beat of my heart through my silk blouse. Orla got her fiery nature from her father, but I was the one left to battle her recklessness and bad attitude, and they were wearing me down. 'I'm at my wits' end!' Tears pricked my eyes as I stared into my brother-in-law's face.

'I know you are. But you're not on your own, you know that, don't you?'

I shook my head. 'I might as well be. Sean's dead. And you've got your own family to look after. You've been a great support, but I can't keep leaning on you...'

'You can lean on me as much as you want to. I've got your back, Josie. I'll always be there for you.' Niall's expression softened.

'You're a good man, Niall. I wonder what Sean would say if he could see the way Orla's behaving. She's got no respect for me. She hates me!'

'She doesn't hate you. She's just a teenager trying to figure out where the boundaries are. She's been such a good kid up until now. She'll settle down again. I'm sure of it. And as for Sean, he'd be so proud of you, Josie. Never doubt that for a second.' Niall offered me a sympathetic smile.

The tears I'd been holding back slid down my face as I clamped my trembling lips in place with my teeth, my emotions finally getting the better of me.

12

DECLAN

Dublin, June 1985

The corrugated shutters rattled as Cormac kicked them shut behind him. The air in the lock-up smelled of oil and damp concrete, and every movement echoed. I stalked forward and glanced at the crates stacked haphazardly against the far wall. I flicked open the nearest one, then ran my fingers over the AK-47. I let out a loud sigh and shook my head. I wanted Cormac to know I was unimpressed by the condition of the assault rifle. He was leaning against a pillar, watching me with his arms crossed over his chest. His gaunt face was half-shadowed, but his eyes were sharp and unblinking. 'You expect me to pay good money for these shite knock-offs?' I scoffed, slamming the lid shut. 'I could get a better batch in Hamburg for half what you're asking.'

Cormac didn't flinch. 'Go to Germany then. But you came to me because you didn't want eyes on them. These came straight from the North, so you're paying for discretion.'

My lip curled. 'I get that, but the barrels are rusted. My client wants top quality. If I send him these, he'll string me up in a back alley.'

Cormac stepped forward slowly to close the gap between us. His boots scraped the concrete as he moved. His face was inches from mine, and I could smell cigarettes on his breath. 'You should go back to shifting crates of whiskey. You're not cut out for this game. You don't get to pick and choose. The best weapons are reserved for our brothers fighting the cause.'

My eyes narrowed. I couldn't gauge the measure of this young man. Cormac was unsettling. He had an aura of restraint about him, combined with the stillness of a loaded trap. He was half my age, but he had more knowledge of moving arms than I could ever hope to possess.

'I don't give a shit about the cause. I'm not here to support the fight. I'm here for the money. And if I fail to supply this shipment, I'll lose my standing in London. I won't be made a fool of. What about the rest of my order? Where are the Uzis, the MAC-10s and the crates of ammo?'

Cormac scoffed. 'You're not the kind of man I want to do business with. The fight is bigger than you. It's bigger than all of us.' He fired me a look that could kill. I could sense the deal was about to slip through my fingers. If that happened, my new venture would be dead in the water and my hopes of distancing myself from Josie would sink into the depths.

'I'm sorry if I offended you,' I said, holding my hands up in front of me. 'But if I don't come up with the weapons quickly, I'm going to be in shit up to my neck.'

Cormac tilted his head and studied me like a hawk. 'The difference between you and me, Declan, is I know when to keep my trap shut. You won't find a better facilitator. I'm trusted enough to mediate between active service units and foreign suppliers, but far enough removed to avoid being targeted by

Special Branch or MI5. You're the one who needs me, and yet you speak to me like I'm some kind of fucking arsehole you can push around. I'm not having it,' he said.

'And I've apologised for my outburst. What more can I do?' I kept my voice steady, but inside I was raging. Cormac was a jumped-up little prick, and he was enjoying making me sweat, but enough was enough. I didn't have time for this bullshit. 'How soon can you get the rest of my order?'

Cormac took the cigarette from behind his ear and placed it in his mouth. Then he put his hand in his pocket, pulled out a box of matches and lit it. I held his stare for a long, tense moment. 'I'll phone you when it's ready, not a moment sooner. Now do me a favour and fuck off. I've got work to do,' he said.

Cormac Walsh needed a good hiding. Being in a position of power at his age had gone straight to the cocky bastard's head.

13

ORLA

London, June 1985

Majella and I were holed up in her tiny box room with the curtains half-pulled.

'You've been acting weird all day. What's up?' Majella asked. I chewed my lip, but didn't answer, so she nudged my knee. 'Come on. Spill it.'

'I've done something stupid.' I kept my voice low, even though we were alone in the house.

'What?'

I hesitated, then mumbled, 'I slept with Shay.'

Majella's mouth dropped open. 'When? At the house party?'

I nodded. My cheeks were burning.

'Holy shit, Orla!'

My eyes filled with tears.

'Hey, don't cry. I'm not judging. I'm just surprised you didn't tell me sooner.'

I shrugged. 'And now I'm late.' The words sounded strangled. My throat was tight.

Majella blinked rapidly. 'How late?'

'Two weeks. Maybe three. I don't know. I'm scared to count.' I felt sick just thinking about it. I didn't want to be a teenage mum.

Majella grabbed a pillow and squeezed it like a stress ball. 'Jesus, Orla. Does anyone else know?'

I shook my head. 'No. God, no. And you can't say anything, Jella. Not to your mum, not to anyone.'

Majella raised both hands. 'Course not.'

The tension thickened as silence stretched out between us.

'Have you done a test?'

'No. I'm scared to.'

Majella reached for my hand. 'You can't deal with this on your own. You need to tell someone.'

'I can't tell my mum. She'll kill me.' My head started pounding as I imagined her reaction. I was stressed out of my mind.

'What about Philomena? She's sound. I'm sure she'd help you.'

'I guess.' Tears started rolling down my cheeks. 'I've fucked everything up.'

Majella pulled me into a hug. 'You have to confide in Philomena. She'll know what to do.'

'I will, but not today. I just want to forget about it. I fancy a night out to take my mind off things.'

* * *

From the minute we'd stepped off the bus, Camden was alive. It was a humid Friday evening, and the smell of fried food drifted from the few remaining market stalls that hadn't closed for the evening. Garlic, chilli and other unidentified spices tangled together, forming an aromatic cloud that wafted through the air.

I paced ahead of my best friend, eager to get to the venue. My Dr. Martens boots splashed through the puddles left behind after the downpour, as my dark auburn curls bobbed up and down, wild and defiant, a bit like myself. My hair was hard to control at the best of times, but it always took on a life of its own in this weather. I glanced over my shoulder and saw Majella trotting behind me, doing her best to keep up with my long strides. Even from this distance, I could see her eyeliner was smudged like bruises under her dark brown eyes. It looked cool with her bright purple lipstick. If I hadn't known better, I would have thought she'd done it deliberately.

'For fuck's sake, Orla, slow down! My feet are killing me already,' Majella whined.

I rolled my eyes and stopped for a beat to allow her to close the gap between us. She tugged her fishnet tights back into place as she tried to catch up. My fingers were twitching for a cigarette. I went to reach into my pocket, but Majella shoved one into my hand without me even having to ask as she reached my side. Then she offered me her neon green plastic lighter.

We had our fake IDs ready for inspection, as proof of age was required to get into the Electric Ballroom. Once we were inside, the place was heaving. Strobe lights pulsed in time with the band on the stage. We were already half-cut as we'd shared a two-litre bottle of cheap cider while we'd been on the bus.

We pushed through the crowd and took up position in front of the band. I was wearing a ripped black mesh top over a black vest, a short red tartan skirt covered with different-sized safety pins, and laddered tights, while Majella wore a second-hand black slip dress, which she'd deliberately torn, big platform boots to give herself some extra height and a leather jacket. Our make-up was identical, apart from the fact that she had purple lipstick, while mine was black. Jella's dyed jet-black hair was scraped into a messy ponytail. The top layer had streaks of blue running through it, which looked really cool, like spilt ink.

We'd been having the time of our lives. Laughing so hard we'd nearly choked on the smoke from the endless cigarettes we'd been lighting up. The bass in the Electric Ballroom felt like it was coming up through my bones as we'd danced and sang along. My hair was stuck to the sides of my face, all messed up from twirling around, but I didn't care. No one cared. That was why we loved Camden so much.

Majella had just shouted something in my ear. I couldn't hear what she'd said over the music, but it must have been something funny about the bloke on stage, I think, as she was pointing at him before she doubled over laughing, clutching her chest. That was when I saw them. A gang of skinheads, twenty at least, had entered the hall and were shoving their way through the crowd like they owned the place, their bald heads gleaming under the stage lights. They were all dressed the same, Fred Perry shirts buttoned all the way up, Harrington jackets and jeans.

'Jesus Christ!' I yelled, grabbing hold of Majella's hand as they drew closer.

They moved forward as one terrifying unit. People tried to get out of the way, but the group just knocked them down, kicking innocent members of the public with steel-toed boots. They started throwing punches and beating up the audience and in under a minute, they had brought chaos to the building. The music stopped and it was like someone had yanked the plug on the whole night. I felt Majella's hand slip out of mine.

'Majella!' I screamed, but my voice got swallowed by the crush.

A fist flew past my cheek, and I ducked to avoid it. My heart was hammering in my chest. I was petrified and the air had turned sour with fear. Somebody slammed into my back. I stumbled forward and dropped to my knees, skidding on the booze-drenched floor. I pushed myself up and craned my neck to see if I could spot my best friend. But she was nowhere to be seen.

The skinheads were relentless, laying into anyone who crossed their path. Blood splashed against the speakers. Girls were screaming as they tried to shield each other, but nobody was out of bounds. Panic rose like bile. I knew I had to get out of there and although I tried to push through the sea of bodies, it was like swimming in concrete. A boot connected with my calf, making me yelp. Tears sprang to my eyes, and I fell again. I was being trampled on the ground, so I covered my head with one arm as I clawed my way back on to my feet. Every inch of me was aching.

People suddenly surged towards the exit, so I let them carry me along like driftwood on the tide. I wouldn't have been able to resist the pull even if I'd wanted to; my legs were barely working. I couldn't think straight. Everything around me blurred.

I was halfway to the door when a big man in a bomber jacket crashed into me, sending me sideways into the wall. A pain shot through my shoulder, and I felt something wet run down my arm. Was it blood or sweat? I wasn't sure.

'Jella... Majella...' I whimpered. Where the fuck had she gone?

I gasped for air when I made it outside. My hair was plastered to my forehead, and my body was covered in perspiration. When my knees buckled, I nearly threw up on the pavement. I turned around, searching for my best friend in the mass of panicked people who'd spilt on to the street. But she was gone. I had no idea what to do. Camden High Street was a neon blur, wet with drizzle and littered with chip wrappers. It had suddenly lost its appeal. I felt vulnerable. Alone. All I wanted to do was go home to my mum.

I had to fight back tears as my emotions began spiralling. Tonight was meant to be fun, not dangerous. What the fuck was I doing here? Mum was right. I was going to destroy myself if I carried on like this. I'd been craving independence, but I was in way over my head. I had to sort my life out and stop getting into trouble, but I didn't know how to break the cycle. I needed my mum's help, but she was so distant these days, I didn't know how to reach her.

14

JOSIE

I untangled my fingers from my rosary and rushed out to the hall when I heard the phone ringing. Was it Orla? Was it the police? I had a bad feeling that something terrible had happened to her. I cleared my throat as I picked up the receiver, battling to extend the spiral cord. 'Hello?' I tried to keep my voice steady so I wouldn't give away the panic I felt.

'Hi, Josie, it's Eamonn,' the voice on the other end replied.

I felt my heart sink. 'I take it you've got news for me?' Talk about stating the obvious. He wouldn't be calling otherwise.

'I thought you'd want to know that I've pulled a few strings and called in a favour with a lad I know at customs. Your shipment will be landing in Liverpool tomorrow.'

'Tomorrow?' I wasn't sure I'd heard him right.

'Yes.'

'What's happening with the cargo in the quarantined containers?'

'He's agreed to push that through, too, without any more checks.'

I could tell Eamonn was grinning from ear to ear, even

though I couldn't see his smug face. Don't get me wrong, I was happy to hear the shipment was on its way, but I was sure there would be a hefty price to pay for his trouble.

'It's good news, isn't it?' Eamonn piped up when I said nothing.

'It's great news,' I replied, but something still seemed off.

'And best of all, it's not going to cost you an extra penny,' Eamonn chirped.

That didn't make any sense. Why wasn't he trying to bleed me for more cash? He was known for his greed. 'How come?' My tone was suspicious.

'A favour for a favour.'

'You'd do that for me?' I raised my eyebrows.

'Of course. You bring a lot of business my way, Josie, so I wanted to help you out.'

'Thank you. I appreciate what you've done,' I said before I ended the call.

I went back to the table and pulled out a chair. Orla still wasn't home. I didn't know what to do. Waiting was torture, but there was no point in going out to look for her. I wouldn't know where to start. I tried to distract myself from worrying by mulling over my conversation with Eamonn while attempting to keep my rising panic at bay when the sound of the front door closing snapped me to attention. I looked up from the rosary entwined in my fingers. My prayers had been answered. My daughter was home safe and sound. I stood quickly, and my chair scraped against the floor as I hurried to the doorway. Orla's footsteps were uneven and dragging. My heart skipped a beat when I caught sight of her in the hall. 'Orla? What happened?' I asked, clamping my hand over my mouth.

She didn't answer, but she let out a groan. She was steadying herself against the wall with one hand while the other was clutching her side. Blood was matting her hair, her face was bruised, and both of her knees were grazed and bleeding. I could tell by the rivers of mascara running down her cheeks that she'd been crying. I rushed over to where she was propped.

'You're hurt! What in God's name happened to you?'

'Nothing. I'm fine,' Orla snapped as she stared at me, glassy-eyed.

I could see she was in pain. 'You're not fine. You're bleeding!' I tried to stay calm, but my voice cracked with emotion as rage and fear battled against each other. I stretched my arm up to touch my daughter's face, but Orla flinched.

'Please, Mum, I just want to go and lie down.'

I wasn't prepared to let her go until I got to the bottom of this. I couldn't ignore the blood, the bruise blooming along her cheekbone and the tremble in her hands. 'Who did this to you? Was it a boy?' I demanded. I suddenly felt unhinged. I wanted to lash out at the person who'd done this to my girl and make them suffer.

Orla was doing her best to avoid my gaze as I trained my eyes on her. 'Just leave it.'

That wasn't going to happen, so I ignored her request. 'Tell me what happened. Were you mugged? If you don't start talking, I'm calling the police.'

Orla slipped down the wall and sat on the hall floor like the fight had drained from her. 'There was a riot.'

'Merciful God in heaven! Where?' My hand flew up to my chest.

'At the Electric Ballroom.'

Orla wasn't old enough to get in there, but I'd have to save that fight for another day.

'A group of skinheads came in looking for trouble and all hell broke loose.' Her voice cracked, but she collected herself and began speaking again. 'Majella got out before me, I think. I don't know for sure. It all happened so fast.'

I crouched in front of her, trying to be strong for her. Trying not to let my hands shake. I wanted to scream. I wanted to shake her. I wanted to ask her why she was there in the first place. But instead, I reached forward and gently cupped Orla's face. 'You're home now, love. You're safe.'

Orla nodded, but her eyes stayed blank. She was somewhere else. I could only imagine she was still in that building. Still hearing the screams. Still scared out of her mind.

I stood up and then helped Orla to her feet. 'Let's get you upstairs and get you cleaned up,' I said. As I guided her along the hall, she stopped next to the phone on the table.

'Can I give Majella a call?'

'It's after midnight, Orla.'

'I know, but I need to know she got home safely...'

I backed down when tears sprang to her eyes. 'OK, but make it quick,' I replied, taking myself off to the kitchen. I was more rattled than I cared to admit and had a gut-level dread I couldn't shake. I'd faced threats. Men with guns. But none of that compared to the fear of losing control of my daughter. I was disgusted with myself. I was failing at the only job that mattered.

15

ORLA

My heart was hammering in my chest as I inserted my finger into the circular holes of each number and turned the dial clockwise until it stopped, then let it spin back. The process was long-winded, but I was taking my time. If I made a mistake halfway through, I'd have to hang up and start all over again. After I dialled the last digit, the phone rang twice before somebody snatched it up.

'Orla?' Majella sounded breathless. Panicky.

A wave of relief crashed through my body. I was so delighted to hear her voice. 'Thank God, you made it home. I've been so worried about you.' A beat of silence followed, and my mood took a nosedive. 'Where the hell did you go? One minute I was holding your hand, and the next thing I knew, you were nowhere to be seen.' My voice cracked, ragged with emotion. 'I got shoved onto the floor. Everyone around me was screaming, and you'd disappeared into thin air.' I only realised I was shouting when Mum stuck her head around the doorframe.

'I didn't run out on you, if that's what you think.' Majella snapped, cranking things up a notch, too. 'I was looking for you. I swear I was. I'm not sure what happened, but I reckon we got pushed in different directions when the crowd surged forward. I stayed inside as long as I could. I saw a bloke get bottled right in front of me, his face was sliced open, chunks of flesh were hanging off...' Majella sobbed. 'I knew I had to get out. I'm sorry, Orla. I was shitting myself. I wasn't thinking straight.'

I didn't say anything at first. The silence stretched on between us. The unspoken words felt heavy. Oppressive. 'I was shitting myself, too,' I muttered. 'I didn't know if you were hurt or worse.'

'I wouldn't have left you on purpose. Camden was fucking mayhem. I waited outside the Ballroom for ages, but then a copper moved me on. He told me to leave the area and go home. I walked down to the bus stop. I thought maybe I'd bump into you there. About ten minutes later, one pulled up, so I got on it. I didn't know what else to do...'

'Are you OK? Were you hurt?' Majella eventually asked.

I exhaled a long, slow breath. 'I got trampled. Knocked to the floor twice. I've hurt my shoulder. My knees. I've got a lot of cuts and bruises...'

'Jesus Christ! Did you go to A & E?'

'No.'

'Do you think you should?'

'Nah, I'll be all right. I feel better already now that I know you made it home.' I sniffed back my tears and swiped the ones that had fallen away with the back of my hand. There was no point in being angry with each other. We'd been through a terrible ordeal. We were both shaken. But we'd got through it.

'Next time, we don't let go. No matter what!' Majella laughed to make light of the situation.

'Next time? I don't think there'll be a next time. I've had enough of Camden to last me a lifetime.' What happened tonight would stay with me for a long time. I'd been terrified, and I never wanted to experience fear like that ever again. Mum stepped into the hall, so I knew that was my cue to say goodbye. 'We'd better get some sleep,' I said.

'Yeah. Sweet dreams,' Majella replied.

Our friendship had been momentarily bruised, but now that we'd cleared the air, the squabble was a thing of the past.

'Orla, come on,' Mum said, bringing me back to reality.

'Night, Jella.'

'Night,' she replied.

16

DECLAN

Dublin, July 1985

'Where the fuck are the toys?' Gavin's voice boomed down the receiver, which was no big surprise as I'd been expecting his call.

'You knew it was going to take time to assemble the order. I told you that up front.'

'And I told you we needed the stuff in a hurry. Patience isn't my customer's strong suit, Kelly. He's tired of dealing with middlemen. He wants me to cut you out of the equation and deal with the supplier directly.'

My jaw clenched. 'Is that so? If you try to break our agreement, I'll make sure you live to regret that decision.'

'That sounds like a threat!' Gavin laughed, mocking me.

'You haven't paid me a penny yet towards the drop. I've already told you, I want the money in full this time. I'm not being shafted again.'

'But here's the thing, my customer doesn't want to pay what you're asking...'

I knew that was coming. 'I can't lower the price. There are a lot of overheads on an order this size. Logistics, security, extra payoffs. You know the score.'

'You'll have to take the hit at your end to account for that.' Gavin was trying to drive a hard bargain, but I wasn't going to let him catch me twice.

'No can do. The amount we agreed isn't open to negotiation,' I replied.

'I think you'll find it is. You can't afford to upset me, Kelly. You need my cash. And if you fuck me around, don't think I won't go straight to your boy in Belfast and just cut you out,' Gavin warned.

He knew nothing about my source and Cormac was based in Dublin. 'You threaten me again, Davis, and you'll get fuck all.' I felt my nostrils flare. Gavin was pushing my buttons to provoke a reaction, but shouting and roaring wasn't my style.

'You should remember who's holding the purse strings. You want a seat at my table? You accept my terms. And don't speak to me like I'm an arsehole. I won't tolerate it,' Gavin bellowed.

I held the phone away from my ear. The tension was palpable. 'You want the toys, you need to bring the cash to me. I'm not going to London to get it,' I said.

'And as I've already told you, I'm not setting foot in that shithole you call home ever again,' Gavin snapped.

I had no intention of being locked in a Mexican standoff with Gavin over this. 'Send the cash with a runner then. The sooner you get it to me, the sooner I'll fulfil your order,' I said before I ended the call.

* * *

I'd arranged to meet Cormac at The Three Chimneys in the heart of Dublin's criminal underbelly. The Liberties was a gritty, working-class neighbourhood known for its tight-knit communities, black-market dealings and illegal activities. It was easy to stay under the radar amid derelict buildings, shuttered storefronts, and crumbling tenements.

The old pub was tucked down a narrow, cobbled lane off Meath Street and didn't advertise itself. No sign hung above the door. Locals knew it by the three soot-darkened brick stacks that rose unevenly from its crumbling slate roof. Outsiders wouldn't dare to step inside the place.

When I pushed open the door, a waft of stale porter and coal smoke barrelled towards me. They were embedded in the fabric of the building, and no amount of airing would get rid of them. The walls were yellowed from time and tobacco and the low-level lighting overhead cast shadows around the room. Empty pint glasses lay discarded on the round tables, and cigarette butts flowed from overfull ashtrays.

The front bar was claustrophobic, too warm, and the patterned carpet was sticky. But people didn't come here for the ambience. They came here because no one asked questions. The old boys from the flats and the lads fresh from Mountjoy kept themselves to themselves. It was a place where favours were traded, deals were brokered, secrets were shared, and a man's silence could be bought with pints.

The back room was accessible through a scarred wooden door. There were whispers that the IRA once used this space for clandestine operations. More recently, it had become neutral ground for smugglers and gunrunners to do business. Nobody turned to look when I twisted the doorknob and stepped inside, clicking the door shut behind me. A single bulb hung in the centre of the room, which was lined with warped tables and mismatched chairs. A set of heavy curtains covered the window, blocking the light and the outside world from view. The thick layer of dust which had settled on the fabric indicated that they hadn't been opened in a decade. Cormac was sitting with his back against the far wall with a half-drunk pint of Guinness before him when I arrived.

'That's for you,' he said, gesturing to the other glass as I walked towards him.

My shoulders were tense beneath my overcoat as I dropped into the chair opposite him. 'Thanks for the drink,' I said, lifting the pint of stout to my lips.

Cormac drummed his fingers against the table. He seemed wound up. Coiled. He didn't take his eyes off me. 'You're late,' he said as I put the glass down on the wonky table.

'You're a fine one to talk about time-keeping,' I threw back. The only sound was the bulb overhead humming like a bad omen. 'Let's get down to business. I'm here to talk about the price and what's causing the delay.'

Cormac's eyes narrowed. 'What do you want me to say? The weapons are scattered all over the place. They're not stored in a central warehouse. They're hidden in locations across Ireland, both North and South, to avoid detection. I can't just walk in with a trolley and pick them off the shelves,' he replied unapologetically.

'What I want is a straight answer. And a better price. These delays are unacceptable.' I glared at Cormac as I reached for my pint. He leaned back in his chair, trying to act casually, but I could see he wasn't relaxed.

'I've had to bleed the weapons into Dublin in small batches. The Gardaí look for big hauls, but they never suspect small drips.'

'Spare me the crap. My buyer's putting the thumbscrews on. When will the order be ready to ship?' I felt like I was flogging a dead horse. We were going around in circles. I was beginning to wish I'd stuck with whiskey smuggling. Dealing arms was a nightmare.

'You'll be notified when the shipment is at the docks. But it won't be leaving unless you bring every penny I'm owed. And the price is what we agreed. Do you have any idea what it costs to smuggle this gear past the eyes I pay to stay shut?'

Cormac's words hung between us as we stared at each other. The only sound was the low rumble of conversation from beyond the wall.

'If I agree to your terms, can you do something for me?' I owed it to myself to try to negotiate something out of this mess.

'That depends on what you're asking?' Cormac eyed me with suspicion.

'I need to use your IRA supply lines to move the guns to the UK.'

Cormac blew out a loud breath. 'I don't know about that,' he replied, then he took the lid off the tin in front of him and calmly rolled a cigarette.

'You want my money, don't you? For the cause? For a united Ireland?'

Cormac nodded once, then he stood up and walked out of the room without saying another word. He didn't smile or shake my hand. After the door creaked shut, I stayed seated and lit a cigarette with a trembling hand. Not from fear. Not from weakness. From the adrenaline that came from dancing too close to the flame.

17

ORLA

London, July 1985

The July sun was pressing down hard, making the pavement shimmer as I walked the length of the street. Sweat clung to my temples, but the clamminess was due to my nerves more than the heat. My chest felt tight. My stomach was twisting and turning, as though my intestines were tying themselves in knots. I paused when I reached the gate. Then I pushed it open and dragged myself across the gravel. My hand was shaking as I rang the bell.

Philomena answered a moment later, fanning herself with her manicured hand. 'Christ, Orla, what's the matter? You look like a ghost.' Her heavily made-up eyes scanned my face. 'You'd better come in,' she said when my face crumpled and my tears began to flow.

Philomena looked effortlessly elegant, despite the heat. She was wearing a nautical-style white dress with navy bows and puffed sleeves. Whereas I was a hot mess. My clothes were sticking to me, I was sweating like a pig, and my hair had gone all frizzy from the humidity.

Philomena led me into her glitzy kitchen, which had glossy red cabinets, shiny black tiles and was the height of modern sophistication. She pulled out a metal-framed chair for me and sat down on the one next to it. 'Would you like some water?' she asked, pulling a tissue from the box of Kleenex on the counter behind her.

'No thanks,' I replied, even though my throat was parched. I wanted to get this over and done with before I changed my mind. Then I put my elbows on the smoked glass table and buried my face in my hands.

'What's wrong, love. You know you can tell me anything. Whatever it is, I'll listen.'

I'd come here because I trusted her and knew she wouldn't judge me like Mum did. We got on well together because she treated me like her little sister, not her niece. Philomena was being so kind, but I was struggling to open up to her. 'Have you had another fight with your mum?' Philomena rubbed my back with the palm of her hand.

I lifted my head. My eyes were already brimming. 'I didn't know where else to go,' I whispered. My knees were bouncing. I couldn't control them. It was like my body was trying to shake the news out of me.

'You know you're always welcome here. Your mother can be an awful bitch sometimes.' Philomena sounded bitter as she drew her hand away.

For once, Mum wasn't to blame for my tears. 'I'm late.' My voice was small and feeble, but those two words were powerful enough to rock the house. They filled the room like a thunderclap.

'Oh, Jesus,' Philomena gasped. 'I didn't know you had a boyfriend.'

I let her response hang in the air for a heartbeat, hoping to swallow the shame along with the fear, before I broke down in tears. I wrapped my arms tightly around myself as I tried to pluck up the courage to speak, but the words clung stubbornly to the inside of my mouth until I finally managed to force them out. 'We're not officially an item.'

Philomena's hand was on my back in an instant, rubbing slow circles, offering me some comfort. 'Oh, love, you poor thing. How late is your period?'

'I've missed two now. I think I might be pregnant,' I suddenly blurted out. The words seemed to echo around the room, and once they were out, I folded in on myself.

'So you haven't done a test?'

I shook my head.

'The first thing we need to do is find out for certain before you worry yourself to death.' Philomena got up. 'Come with me. I always keep a test in the bathroom cabinet. I like to have one handy.'

My heart thudded louder as a feeling of dread washed over me. The idea of actually knowing – of seeing the proof in black and white – made my stomach turn.

'Here you go,' she said when I caught up with her. 'We'll know soon enough. And then we can deal with it.'

I took the box with trembling fingers and stared at the print on the cardboard as if it was written in a foreign language. The words were swimming before me.

'Honestly, love. You need to find out. I'll be just outside the door in case you need me.'

The air was as thick as soup in the room. It pressed down on me as my hands fumbled with the box. By the time I managed to coax some urine out of my bladder, my stomach was doing somersaults.

'I've done it. How long do I have to wait?'

'A couple of minutes. I'll time it for you.'

I placed the test on the edge of the sink and backed away as if it was something dangerous. It seemed to be stealing all the oxygen, and I felt like I was suffocating as I paced the room with my arms wrapped around myself. My heart was hammering in my chest. It sounded too loud in the silence. Each second stretched into eternity as I whispered under my breath, *Please, God, don't let it be positive. Please. Please. Please.*

'The time's up,' Philomena called, and I thought I was going to be sick.

I cautiously approached the sink as though it were a wild animal. My palms were slick when I lifted the test. I almost dropped it again when I saw two blue lines staring up at me. 'Oh God,' I yelled, and Philomena burst through the door. She wrapped her arms around me before my sobs tore me apart. 'I've ruined everything. I can't believe I let this happen. I've been so bloody stupid.' My voice cracked, so I buried my face into her shoulder.

'Don't cry, sweetheart. You're not stupid. You're young and you made a mistake, that's all. You're not the first girl this has happened to, and you won't be the last.'

I clung to her like she was stopping me from drowning as the reality sank in. One drunken fumble was all it had taken to change the course of my life. My heartbeat spiked as panic set in. Chaotic thoughts ran through my mind. I didn't want to have a baby. I wasn't ready to be a mother. I was too young. Too irresponsible. I cried without holding back until my throat was raw. Big, racking sobs that shook my chest. Philomena just held me, without lecturing, until the storm passed. 'I'm sorry to burden you with this,' I croaked.

'Don't be silly. You did the right thing coming here,' Philomena soothed. 'Let's go and sit down and talk this through.'

I pulled back from Philomena, and she towed me down the hallway.

'Do you want me to have a word with your mum?'

'No way! She'll go mental. She'll never forgive me for disgracing the family.' My voice cracked on the last word as shame knifed me through the chest. My cheeks were burning hotter than the July sun. I was mortified to be in this position.

Philomena hushed me and took hold of my hands. 'Don't you dare talk like that. You've nothing to be ashamed of, do you hear me?'

I nodded, but I wasn't convinced. 'It only happened once. We were at a party. We were drunk and we got carried away...' Tears welled up and tumbled from my eyes. 'I'm scared.'

Philomena brushed the damp hair from my face. 'I know you are, but I'm here for you.'

'I don't know what to do. I'm not sure I can go through with the pregnancy. Everyone will be talking about me. Whispering behind my back. And what about Shay? I haven't seen him since. He never promised me anything. I don't want him to think I tried to trap him.' More tears spilt down my cheeks.

'Now that you know for certain, you need to give yourself time to think things over. It's a big decision to make, so don't rush it. But you're not alone in this. If you want to talk, you know where to find me. Whatever you choose to do, we'll face it together.'

I didn't give a shit what my mum's opinion of Philomena was; I thought she was amazing! I was glad I'd listened to Majella and confided in her now.

18

ORLA

When the doctor confirmed I was pregnant, her words hit me like a fist, even though I'd already known what she was going to say. She'd offered to arrange antenatal care for me, but how could I go through with this? Mum would shit a brick if she found out. Shay wouldn't be delighted either. We were too young to be parents. I really liked him, and I didn't want him to run for the hills, so I wasn't going to let him in on the secret and asked my GP to refer me for a termination.

She sent me to Marie Stopes in Ealing, a specialist centre, to have counselling and a complete evaluation because of my age. The clinic was quiet. The air was heavy and sterile. I sat hunched on a plastic chair while the pale green walls closed in on me. I still hadn't told my mum because I was worried how she'd react. Philomena was next to me, looking the height of sophistication in her cobalt blue double-breasted power suit, white pussy bow blouse and black patent court shoes. She'd tonged her long blonde hair into a mass of curls and was flicking through an old *Woman's Own* magazine. I wasn't convinced she was reading it, though, as her eyes weren't moving over the page. I tugged at the hem of my black Dead or Alive T-shirt, trying to ignore the posters emblazoned on every wall about the importance of contraception. The word made my stomach churn as silence hung over us like a shroud. The only sound was the clock on the wall ticking.

'Orla O'Connor?' a nurse called.

Relief and dread rose in equal measure now that my turn had arrived. Philomena reached across and gave my hand a quick squeeze before we got to our feet. I clenched my jaw as we followed the nurse down the corridor with the sound of my pulse echoing loudly in my ears.

'Please go straight in. The doctor's expecting you,' the nurse said, offering me a sympathetic smile.

Philomena went in first. I was two steps behind her, and I glanced at the woman in the white coat who was sitting behind the desk opposite the door. A pile of papers was neatly stacked on one side while a plastic anatomical model of the female reproductive system perched on the other.

'Please take a seat,' the doctor said, gesturing to the two chairs in front of her.

I followed her instructions as my eyes scanned the room. It was plain and functional. The only other piece of furniture was a filing cabinet in the far corner next to a window with a street view.

'I'm Doctor Russell. Pleased to meet you, Orla,' she said, giving me a warm smile. 'And you are?'

'Mrs O'Connor,' Philomena replied, which was a brilliant answer as the doctor now presumed she was my mother.

'Orla, I know this must feel overwhelming. But I need to ask you some questions. Are you sure you want to go through with a termination?' Doctor Russell asked, tilting her head.

'Yes,' I replied without missing a beat.

'I can see from your notes that you're eleven weeks pregnant. Do you understand what the procedure involves? Not just the physical part. The emotional part, too?'

I nodded. Although the truth was, I was blocking out my emotions. I wouldn't allow myself to think of it as a baby. It was a mistake I was correcting. And once it was sorted, I could put it behind me. But I was terrified I was making the wrong choice, even though I didn't want to be trapped in a life I wasn't ready for.

'I need to be sure this is your decision and that nobody's pressuring you into it.'

Doctor Russell glanced at Philomena, who reached for my hand in a show of support and gave it a squeeze. My fingers were clammy in hers.

'Nobody's pressured me into this.' My voice cracked with emotion, and tears welled up in my eyes.

'I've seen a lot of girls over the years in your position. Some end up regretting the decision. Some don't. But terminating a pregnancy never really leaves you. Not fully.'

I swallowed the lump in my throat. I hadn't expected her to say that. I didn't want to spend the rest of my life weighed down by Catholic guilt, but I didn't want to be a teenage mum either.

'Would you like more time to think things over?' The doctor must have sensed my unease.

'No.' I fired the word out firm and strong without any hesitation.

'Would you mind waiting outside for a moment, please?' Doctor Russell asked Philomena.

'OK,' she replied, turning towards me with a smile of encouragement.

Doctor Russell waited until Philomena had closed the door before she spoke again. 'Choosing to end a pregnancy is never an easy decision. You need to be certain. I know I've already asked you this, but do you feel under any pressure from anyone to make this choice?'

I shook my head. 'No. It's my decision.'

The doctor nodded and made a note on the sheet of paper in front of her. 'Mrs O'Connor, you can come back in now,' she called, and Philomena reappeared in a heartbeat. 'Would you like me to arrange a counselling session for you?'

'No, thank you.' The last thing I wanted was to discuss my situation with a stranger.

'The procedure will be carried out here at the clinic. All being well, you'll be released the same day. We'll take good care of you, but you might experience some discomfort afterwards. Do you have any questions?'

'No.' I shook my head.

The doctor slid a form and a pen across the desk. 'I'll need your signature to confirm you're consenting to the termination.'

My hand trembled as I lifted the biro and scrawled my name on the line next to the cross. Then I pushed the paper back to the doctor.

'We'll book you in for the next available appointment. It should be in the next week or two.'

The double doors opened, and I stepped outside, feeling lighter than I had in weeks. Worry was a heavy burden to carry, and now that a date had been set, a sense of calm had washed over me, but it was short-lived. As Philomena and I left the grounds, the pavement outside the clinic was lined with people with banners. Handwritten cardboard placards with slogans that read, 'Abortion is murder!' and 'Choose life!' mixed with glossy posters of aborted foetuses. A nun in a habit clutched her rosary to her chest. Her eyes were closed and her lips moved soundlessly in prayer. I flinched, my stomach flipped, and my heartbeat went into overdrive as my tears threatened to spill. I willed myself not to cry, but the hostility coming from total strangers blindsided me.

Philomena slipped her hand into mine, steady and firm. 'Ignore them. They don't get a say in this. It's none of their business.'

I nodded, but my chest was tight. I lowered my gaze, fixing it on the pavement as I walked, trying not to look at any of their faces. But a woman with hard eyes thrust a pamphlet in front of me, which made me stop in my tracks as I read the words, 'Murderer! Don't kill your baby!' I felt my cheeks flush, and my knees went weak.

'You'll regret this for the rest of your life!' she said as I shoved it aside.

'Leave her alone!' Philomena's voice snapped as hard as iron. She kept her arm around me as we made our way through the protesters. 'Keep walking, Orla. Don't give them the satisfaction of breaking down.'

'They don't know me and they don't know a thing about my situation,' I said once we'd reached the safety of Philomena's Vauxhall Cavalier.

Philomena cupped my face and forced me to meet her gaze. 'No, love, they don't. But I do. And I'm proud of you. End of story. Now let's get you home.'

My eyes brimmed with tears, so I leaned into Philomena for a moment. 'Thanks for being so supportive. I honestly don't know how I'd have got through this without you.'

'You're brave, girl,' Philomena whispered before she planted a kiss on my cheek.

My stomach twisted with a mix of fear and relief.

19

JOSIE

The house was quiet when I came back from Mulligans after another long day. At first, I'd thought Orla was out, given that it was the school summer holidays. I'd gone upstairs to get changed when something made me open Orla's door without knocking, which was out of the ordinary for me, but I hadn't expected her to be sitting cross-legged on the bed with a stack of folded leaflets in her lap.

'Orla? I didn't realise you were here,' I said.

The curtains were half-drawn. The room was dim, except for a thin strip of early evening light cutting across the bed. She was listening to her Walkman. The tinny music was bleeding from the foam-padded headphones, so she hadn't heard me coming up the stairs. She almost jumped out of her skin when she looked up and saw me standing in the doorway. She froze, and then she shoved the papers under her pillow.

It was clear she didn't want me to see what she'd been looking at, which prompted me into action. Her jaw was tight. Her eyes were wild and shimmering with unshed tears as I paced towards her with my heart beating like a drum. The corner of one of the leaflets was sticking out from where she'd stashed it, so I pulled it free. I felt my face contort when I read the words, 'What to Expect During a Termination.' Heat clawed up my spine like the devil himself was blazing a trail. 'Jesus, Mary and Joseph! What the hell is this?' I roared, waving the pamphlet at her.

Orla looked away, muttering something inaudible under her breath, so I reached under her pillow, grabbed the rest of the pile and fanned them across my hand. My breath hitched when I realised all of them were from Marie Stopes. My head felt like it was going to explode.

'What's going on? Is this some kind of joke? You're fifteen years old! You can't be preg—'

'Don't be so naive. I can. And I am!' Orla fired back, cutting me off mid-flow.

My features darkened as the words hit like a slap. 'Don't you dare use that tone with me. What the hell were you thinking? You're too young to be having sex! Who's the father?' All manner of ideas were running through my head as my thoughts spewed out of my mouth. My blood was boiling. What kind of bastard took advantage of an underage girl?

'Nobody you know.'

'I have a right to know who you've been sneaking around with behind my back!'

'I'm not keeping it, so it doesn't matter.'

'Doesn't matter? Of course it matters! You think this is just about you?' I threw my hands up to heaven.

'It *is* about me! It's my life, not yours. Stop trying to control me and everything I do,' Orla shouted.

Her words stung because they were loaded with meaning. I took a deep breath to steady myself as I fought back tears.

'Jesus Christ, Orla, what you've done is wrong. It's illegal.

Immoral. You're still a child.' My voice cracked, not with rage but with disbelief.

'I'm not a child! It's my body and my choice, so spare me the lecture!' Orla yelled.

'You're too young to make a decision like this.' I held the booklets with trembling hands. My eyes skimmed over them, making my vision swim as muddled thoughts raced around in my brain.

'I know what I'm doing.'

The silence that followed was thick. The air was charged. I stared at my daughter and saw the fear behind the bravado. My chest ached with a mix of anger, sorrow and fierce protectiveness. I was partly to blame for this situation. I'd been so preoccupied with work that I'd let her get away with too much recently and now I was going to have to face the consequences.

'You think you know what's best for everyone. You love bossing people around. Bossing me around. Well, I'm fed up with it. I can't have the baby. It'll ruin everything.'

'And you don't think you'll ruin yourself by going through with this. Abortion is a sin!' My tone was sharp.

Orla wavered and stared at her lap. 'This is why I didn't want you to find out. I knew you'd say that. I knew you'd make me feel like a murderer! Why don't you understand I'd rather stick my hand in a blender than go through with this pregnancy? I made a stupid mistake, but you want me to pay for it for the rest of my life!'

The words hung between us, their jagged edges sharper than glass. They made me flinch, but my anger pushed through the hurt. I swallowed hard and gripped the leaflets so tightly that the paper bent. Then I threw them down on the floor. My chest was heaving. 'You can't go through with this, Orla.' My voice was shaking. 'You'll never forgive yourself for ending the life of an innocent child. That kind of choice never leaves you. It eats away at you and gnaws at your conscience.'

Orla shifted, but she didn't look up. 'Don't start trying to make me feel guilty. You've got no idea what it's like, Mum. You've got no idea how I'm feeling. You can't stop me from keeping the appointment, so keep your nose out of my business!'

Orla scrambled off the bed. She was trembling now, and her fists were balled at her sides. Her chest was heaving. I stared at my daughter. I was furious with her, but we were going around in circles. Arguing was getting us nowhere, so I turned on my heel, paced across the floor and slammed the door hard enough to rattle the frame.

20

JOSIE

I pounded on the door with my fist and repeatedly rang the bell with my forefinger to convey the urgency. Philomena flung the entrance to her domain open and greeted me with a face like thunder. She was dolled up to the nines as usual, even though she probably wouldn't be leaving the house all day.

'I need to speak to Niall urgently,' I said without exchanging pleasantries.

'Hello, Philomena. How lovely to see you,' the stupid bitch replied.

'I haven't got time to play games.' I pushed past her and tore down her hall like an evil spirit was in pursuit of me. 'Where is he?' I asked when I realised nobody was in the kitchen.

'He's out. But I can guess why you're here. Have you just found out that Orla's got herself into trouble?' Philomena's glossy red lips stretched into a smirk.

Her words shocked me to the core, and a stack of emotions hit me at once – fast and unforgiving. The ground shifted under me. I felt betrayed that my daughter had turned to someone else. Then hurt, anger, fear and guilt bombarded me from every angle. I wanted to scratch her heavily made-up eyes out. 'You knew?'

'Aww, Josie, it must pain you to realise she chose to confide in me and not you.' Philomena laughed.

The sound rumbled through me, shaking me to the core. I felt my face flush as fury simmered just below the surface. 'She's my daughter. You had no right to get involved.'

Philomena leaned towards me and jabbed her manicured finger at me. 'Maybe if you weren't so high and mighty, she'd have trusted you with the news. She came to me because she knew you'd be ramming the Catholic church down her throat. I didn't judge her or make things harder for her, I just supported her when she went to the clinic.'

'So you're the one who's been filling her brain with…' I stopped myself mid-flow.

'With what, Josie? Sense?' Philomena looked smug.

'With poison,' I continued. I was riled up, so I wasn't going to hold back. 'How dare you put notions in her head? She's only fifteen, and now she thinks she can wipe this away like it never happened.' I spoke low and sharp in a tone of voice that carried more threat than if I'd shouted.

Philomena folded her arms and glared at me. 'Notions? She was terrified. What should I have done? Turn my back on her and tell her to pray the fear away?'

Abortion was a sin, morally wrong. I couldn't condone it. I wanted no part of it. Although I couldn't help feeling for Orla and the fear she must be facing. My jaw was working, but the words were caught somewhere between my faith and my conscience and refused to pass my lips.

'It's Orla's decision. Not yours. Not mine. And definitely not the Church's.'

My eyes were blazing. 'You're meddling in this to get back at me. Stay out of it. Orla needs her mother, not you!' I slammed my hand on the table.

Philomena barked out a laugh. 'Christ, Josie, doesn't it tell you something that she'd rather pour her heart out to me than to you?'

Her words stung and made me blink. 'All it tells me is that you've poisoned her mind. You love trying to turn everyone I care about against me, don't you? But this latest stunt is in a different league altogether. You're actively undermining my authority as her mother and encouraging her to go against my values!' I couldn't help lashing out at the evil bitch. Orla was young and impressionable, and Philomena was taking advantage of her.

'Think what you like, but the truth is, she didn't want you knowing she was in the family way. You weren't the one she trusted. How does that feel, Josie?' Philomena was openly gloating at my despair.

I felt my bottom lip start to quiver, so I clamped down on it with my teeth. I wouldn't give her the satisfaction of reducing me to tears. The air was sharp with spite. A cloud of hatred hovered above us. My hands curled into fists as I glared at my sister-in-law. 'Stop sticking your claws in my family, or I'll make sure you regret the day you got involved.'

The back door creaked, and Niall stepped in. He froze, clocking the tension and sensing the storm he'd walked into. His eyes darted from me to his wife. 'What's going on?'

'Orla's pregnant!' I blurted out.

'Jesus,' Niall replied with a horrified look on his face.

I wasn't sure whether he'd been let in on the secret or not, but judging by his reaction, it was news to him.

'I'll kill the bastard,' Niall growled.

'You'll do no such thing,' Philomena replied.

'Your wife has arranged for her to have an abortion behind my back!' My voice was shaking with rage.

Niall's gaze flicked over to Philomena as he shifted uneasily.

'It was Orla's decision. I just went to the appointment with her.'

'Orla's about to murder her own flesh and blood, and your wife's supporting her!' I threw my palms up as I looked up at Niall. Desperate for an ally. Desperate for him to take my side.

'Murder? You've no right to throw that word about.' His voice was quiet, but the words cut me like broken glass.

I felt myself stiffen with the fear that he was about to expose me in front of the mouth almighty. 'What's that supposed to mean?'

'Don't start preaching like you're squeaky clean. You can stop the moral posturing. You're no saint. We both know you've had blood on your hands. More than once!' Niall's dark brown eyes were blazing.

My lips parted, but nothing came out. His betrayal wounded me, but he was right. I was a hypocrite. I'd taken a man's life before.

Niall shook his head. His disgust was plain to see. 'Don't you dare call Orla a murderer. Not when you've done worse and slept at night!'

I was shocked by the way he'd turned on me when I'd come here for his help, but his delivery was like a cold, surgical jab. A wake-up call. I suddenly felt caught between my faith, my guilt and my daughter's choice. I'd been counting on him to take my side when he'd got caught in the crossfire. But I should have known he'd always back Philomena. She was grinning from ear to ear, revelling in my discomfort. The victory was hers. I couldn't take any more. I had to get away from them. My throat tightened as I stormed out of the house without saying another word, slamming the door behind me for good measure.

21

JOSIE

I sat alone in the kitchen as the muffled sound of Orla crying upstairs seeped through the ceiling. I was having trouble digesting the fact that my fifteen-year-old daughter was carrying a baby. It seemed like only yesterday Sean and I had brought her home from the hospital. How could she be pregnant herself? She was still a child.

How would I be able to live with the guilt if she ended the life of my unborn grandchild? It would destroy what was left of our relationship. The weight of my rosary beads felt heavy in my hand as I prayed for guidance, but the hopelessness of the situation made me feel abandoned.

Everyone else was focused on supporting my daughter, apart from me. But how could I accept her decision when it clashed with my faith and everything I believed in? It was breaking my heart listening to her sobbing, and now that I'd got over the initial shock, I was scared that if I forced my opinions down her throat, I would drive her further away. I suddenly felt the need to reach out to her.

'Go away,' Orla shouted when I knocked on her bedroom door a moment later.

It was the response I'd been expecting, but I carried on regardless. I turned the handle and stood in the open doorway. 'I don't want to argue with you, love. I just want to talk. Philomena told me that she went to the clinic with you...'

Orla had been lying on her side, facing away from me, but she scrambled off the bed and stared at me. Her face was pale, and there was panic in her eyes.

'I wish you'd come to me first.' My words wobbled. I felt wounded by her rejection.

'I knew you'd try to stop me. I'm not ready to be a mother!' She swiped her tears away with the back of her hand. The air vibrated with her despair.

I felt like I was being pulled in different directions. 'I carried you, Orla. I raised you. Don't shut me out now.' My voice sounded brittle. I could feel my eyes well up, but I blinked back the tears. 'I'm not the enemy, but I can't stand by and watch you make a decision you might end up regretting.'

'There you go again. Why can't you try to see things from my perspective? It's my life! Not yours!' Orla shouted and sank back on to the bed, shaking with rage and frustration. Her shoulders were drawn tight, as if she was bracing herself for another fight.

I was torn between my faith and my daughter. She needed my help, not my judgement. My love, not my rules. As I absorbed her outburst, I began questioning whether I had the right to impose my beliefs on her. She was the one facing the unplanned pregnancy. A wave of guilt crashed down on me when I saw her tears start to fall again. We were at breaking point. It was time to offer an olive branch. 'We might not always see eye to eye, but I'm not ready to watch you go through hell without me.'

Orla's lips parted, but no words came out. Her defiance had

slipped. She looked scared. Vulnerable. I stepped closer to her. It wasn't going to be easy, but I'd have to put my own principles aside to preserve our fragile relationship.

I sat down on the edge of the mattress. 'I want you to know, whatever comes next, you won't face it alone. If you want to go ahead with a termination, I'll support your decision.' My tone was soft. For once, I'd taken a different approach. I hadn't barked orders, made demands or tried to seize control.

I disagreed with Orla's decision, but if I pushed her too far, she might cut me out of her life for good. Philomena would love that. She'd be more than happy to step into my shoes. She was looking for any opportunity to turn my daughter against me, so this felt like the right thing to do. I wanted to shield Orla from pain, and that desire outweighed my unease about the path she was planning to take. But my chest still ached with the weight of it all.

22

ORLA

My mouth dropped open, and I stared at her as her words drifted in the air like smoke. My ears were ringing. I couldn't seem to make sense of what she'd just said. We'd been at war over this since Mum found out. I never thought we'd be having this conversation in a million years.

Mum was sitting on the edge of my bed with her hands folded in her lap, as if she was pondering what to have for tea. The sudden U-turn seemed too good to be true, and a ripple of suspicion passed through me. 'Do you really mean that? You're not going to throw me out, or send me off to live with an elderly relative?' My voice cracked halfway through.

Mum's jaw worked as she prepared to speak. A red flush had broken out on her milky skin. I could see that she felt uncomfortable, but she managed to hold herself together. 'Of course not. I'm going to hold your hand every step of the way. I've buried too many people I love. You're all I've got left, Orla. I don't want to lose you, too.' Her green eyes didn't flicker. They stayed fixed on mine.

I couldn't look at her. I tore my gaze away and let it settle on the carpet. My throat felt tight, as if a stone was lodged in it, and my stomach had twisted itself into a knot. I still couldn't take it in. What I was planning to do went against everything she believed in, but she'd promised to support me.

I was stunned. I never thought Mum would back down and put my wishes above her religion. I was blown away by the sacrifice she was making. It was clear how much affection lay behind her decision. She'd never told me she loved me. She never said the L-word out loud. That wasn't her way. But actions spoke louder than words, didn't they?

Mum reached out and brushed my hair back from my face. She hadn't done that since I was little, and I felt tears stab at my eyes as guilt clawed at me. I'd put her through hell. Rebelled at every opportunity. But now that I needed her, she'd pushed all of that to one side to be there for me. She was tiny, but fierce. The type of woman who could cut a person in half with one look – which would come in handy if the protestors were outside the clinic when I went back for my appointment. Since my dad had died, she'd had to run the business while taking on the role of being a single parent. She'd been amazing and hadn't shied away from anything. I was lucky to have her. It was time to show her some appreciation. 'I'm blown away by your offer, but I can't picture you standing beside me when it's time to go to Marie Stopes.' The image of the women with the placards forced its way into my brain. The experience had been traumatic.

Mum reached for my hand. Her grip was warm and solid. 'Picture it. I mean it, Orla, I'll be there for you.'

Now that Mum was on my side, a complicated mix of emotions swirled inside me. I didn't feel good about what I was doing either. But because of one stupid mistake, I was going to have to live with the consequences. This felt like a turning point, and I was ready to share my fears with her.

'I feel so conflicted. I don't know if I can go through with it,' I whispered. The words had barely made it out of my mouth before I broke down in floods of tears.

Mum let go of my hand and put her arm around my waist. Neither of us spoke for what felt like an eternity. I felt drained. Hollow. My head was spinning. I was starting to unravel.

'I'll be here for you, whatever you decide,' she said.

'It makes me feel sick thinking about the appointment but what's the alternative? I become a teenage mum? Either way, I lose. Either way, it's a disaster.' I'd been keeping my worries to myself for weeks, but once I started to speak, everything came tumbling out. My whole future was ahead of me. I never wanted this to happen. I folded in on myself and buried my face in my hands.

Mum didn't say a word. She just sat beside me, rubbing my back. Her touch steadied me in a way that words couldn't. I'd half expected her to take the opportunity to force-feed me her opinion now that she realised I was struggling with the decision I'd made. I respected her for keeping quiet. I knew it was stupid and childish, but when she tried to badger me into something, my natural instinct was to do the opposite. The more she pushed, the more I'd pull away.

'I'm so scared of what lies ahead of me. I'm scared of having the anaesthetic. I'm scared of falling apart. I'm scared of living with the guilt. But most of all, I'm scared of what people will say if they find out.' My voice cracked as the confession spewed out, so I bit down on the inside of my cheek until it stung. Then the floodgates opened again. They always did when there was too much to hold inside.

'I know you are, love, but I'll do everything I can to help you,' Mum soothed.

'I'm not sure I can go through with it. But I'm also not sure I can keep it.' Shame sat in my chest like a stone.

'You don't have to decide now.'

Mum's eyes scanned over me like she was cataloguing my pain and fear. Her silence was a promise in itself. No speeches. No lectures. She was listening to me pour my heart and soul out without trying to lay down the law. The truce between us felt good. I hoped it would last.

'I can't put it off much longer. I'm already eleven weeks pregnant and the termination is set for next week.' My room felt smaller, like the walls were closing in as the words hung between us. The silence was louder than any argument we'd ever had.

'You could always keep it.' Mum's tone was cautious, like she was testing the temperature of the water with her toe. 'We'd manage. I'd help you.'

My chest tightened. Her words felt like a hand closing around my neck. I pressed the heels of my hand into my forehead. 'No way!' I curled my fingers into the edge of the duvet until my knuckles went white.

Mum's mouth twitched, but she stayed tight-lipped. I felt bad for being so spiteful when no lecture followed, but I was venting my emotions and needed her to listen without commenting.

'I'm sorry I snapped at you, but I can't handle the pressure. I don't want to be a pregnant schoolgirl and have everyone gossiping about me. I also don't want to do something that I might regret for the rest of my life. I don't know which choice is heavier. Please don't try to push me in a certain direction. You should know by now that I don't like being corralled.' The confession sat between us like the elephant in the room. Big. Weighty. Impossible to ignore.

'You've got until next week to decide. Why don't you sleep on it? You look exhausted,' Mum suggested, getting to her feet.

I nodded, and she walked out of the room, which was the best thing she could have done. I knew she was struggling not to interfere, but that restraint was exactly what I needed, and then I'd be able to make up my mind without triggering my built-in reflex to rebel.

23

JOSIE

The kettle was just starting to boil when I heard Orla come down the stairs. Her steps were dragging, so I didn't turn around. I set about making the tea, adding leaves first and then pouring the boiling water into the pot. I let the steam cloud up my face while I waited for her to find her voice, but she said nothing.

'Morning, love.' I smiled as I carried the breakfast things over to the table.

Orla was standing in the kitchen doorway. Her red hair was a mass of wild curls, and her face was deathly pale. Without all the heavy make-up, she looked younger than fifteen – the little girl who used to crawl into my bed after Sean died, woken by nightmares, was watching me intently. I didn't ask her how she slept. The dark circles nestled under her eyes told me everything I needed to know.

'I want to keep it.' Orla was trembling.

As I put the cups and the pot down, the air stilled, and a sense of relief washed over me. I wanted to ask her why she'd had a sudden change of heart, but I thought better of it in case I talked her out of it. Orla's blue eyes were wide. She looked terrified, but

I could see a thread of steel in her spine – that same bloody-minded streak her father had, which never wavered.

Orla's lip wobbled. I could see she was holding back tears. I was too, but I kept my face steady, the way I always did when the ground shifted under me. If she was brave enough to face the backlash and the consequences, then she was brave enough to face anything. I had to stay strong for her and be the person she leaned on.

'I can't go through with the termination, but I know people are going to gossip about me. Everyone will have an opinion, the teachers, the girls from school, the strangers who'll whisper and stare at me like I'm an exhibit behind glass.'

'Listen to me. I won't let anyone make you feel ashamed of this.'

'That's easy for you to say, but I'm not sure I'll be able to cope with the snide remarks.'

'We'll handle whatever comes our way.' I offered her a sympathetic smile.

'You're probably wondering what made me change my mind.'

'Like you said, it's your decision.'

'The more I thought about it, the more I knew you were right, I'd...' Orla paused. 'I'd never forgive myself...' She sobbed as she blurted the words out. I could hear that her throat was raw.

I rushed over to my daughter, fighting back tears myself and pulled her into a protective hug. As I held her tightly, my mind was already spinning with plans for the future.

24

JOSIE

London, August 1985

My hands were wrapped around a cup of tea I hadn't touched for hours. I felt hollowed out like I was barely able to keep my spine straight. I hated it when Orla went out. I dreaded to think what she was getting up to. I just hoped that she'd learned her lesson where drink was concerned, especially now that she was carrying a baby. This was a nightmare situation. I was worried sick about my girl. Damn you, Sean. Damn you for leaving me. And damn you for giving our daughter your rebellious streak.

The kitchen was dark except for the yellow glow of the small lamp on the counter. The silence was oppressive. I couldn't bear it any longer, so I pushed back my chair and walked over to the sink, inserted the rubber plug, and opened the hot tap. I began scrubbing a single glass for what felt like hours. My head was spinning. I couldn't focus on anything other than Orla.

I heard footsteps outside, so I glanced up at the clock. It was half past midnight. My heart galloped in my chest. I tossed the glass on to the drainer and quickly dried my hands on the kitchen towel. I was waiting in the hall when she inched the front door open, trying not to make a sound. She should have known I'd be waiting up for her.

Orla's auburn hair was a tangled mess. Her eyeliner was smudged halfway down her cheeks. There was no denying she was drunk, but there was a wildness in her eyes I didn't recognise, or perhaps I did. Perhaps I didn't want to admit that my underage daughter had also taken drugs. The thought was too awful to contemplate. The fear of the unknown was what terrified me the most.

'Do you know what time it is? Where the hell have you been?' I demanded. My voice was sharp and too loud. I knew my outburst would damage our fragile relationship, but I couldn't help myself.

Orla didn't stop. She shoved past me, heading towards the stairs. 'I was out. What's it to you?'

'Don't you dare talk to me like that!' Her defiance ignited a fire in my belly, so I grabbed her arm, harder than I meant to, but Orla was much taller than I was, and I needed to do something to stop her in her tracks before she walked off. She ripped her arm away, glaring at me with a hatred that felt like a knife to my gut.

'Get your hands off me! Don't you dare touch me. You think you're a big shot running the firm, keeping the boys in line, but you can't even handle your own teenage daughter. You're pathetic,' Orla spat.

I felt my lips start to tremble, so I clamped them with my teeth. Every word she'd said was true. I'd been thrust into this existence, but I didn't feel equipped to deal with it. I'd tried to lay down the law, but I was putting on a front. And Orla could see right through it. 'You might not like my rules, but you're fifteen and you're living under my roof! The last thing you should be doing is drinking. It's bad for the baby!'

Orla laughed in my face. 'I might be fifteen, but I'm not a child and sod the baby! I'll do what I want! You think because you say a few Hail Marys and wear your cross around your neck like a badge of honour that you're some kind of saint? You're not. You're a liar and a hypocrite!'

My hand twitched. I was so angry that I was tempted to slap her, but that would only escalate the situation. I forced it down by my side, allowing my nails to bite into my palm as I tried to restrain myself.

'Don't you dare talk to me about lies,' I choked out. 'You think I don't stay awake at night, terrified for you? Terrified for my unborn grandchild? And you still haven't answered my question. Where were you until this time?'

'I told you. I was out.'

'Out where? You were meant to be home by ten.' I put my hands on my hips and glared at my daughter.

'Nowhere you'd approve of.' Orla shrugged and headed for the stairs.

'Don't walk away from me.'

'Why not? I've got nothing to say to you.' Orla spat the words out as though they were burning the inside of her mouth.

'Well, I've got plenty to say to you, young lady, so don't bother storming off until I've finished. Your behaviour is unacceptable. You have to take responsibility for the life you're carrying. The life you created.' She still hadn't told me who the father was, which was adding to my stress and anger.

'Give it a rest, will you? Anyone would think I planned this.' Orla put her hands on her flat stomach.

'You need to start taking responsibility for your actions. After your dad died, I had to pick myself up and carry on. Do you think I'd have chosen this life for myself? I felt like I was swimming against the tide. I had no idea how to run a business.'

'Maybe not, but now it's all you ever think about. You're obsessed with the fucking pub, aren't you?'

'Don't you dare use language like that in my house,' I warned.

'I'm sick to death of your rules. I can't wait to move out,' Orla shouted.

'Where would you go? You won't be able to stand on your own two feet.' She might not realise it, but she needed me. Her blue eyes were blazing as the weight of my words hung in the air. 'Your stubbornness will get you nowhere. You're too much like your father for your own good,' I eventually said.

'Do you think I want to be like him? It's his fault we're in this mess. I hate him.'

Her words hit me like a punch to the gut, and I felt my heart crumple inside my chest. Orla had always been a daddy's girl. She'd adored her father, and he'd worshipped the ground she walked on. She didn't mean what she'd just said. She was hurt and was lashing out.

Orla's nostrils were flaring, and her eyes were brimming with unshed tears. I could see her emotions were at war when she pushed past me and stormed upstairs. Her boots pounded on each step, and the sound echoed around the hallway like gunshots.

I stood alone, gripping the edge of the table so hard that my knuckles turned white. My shoulders were shaking, and my breath rattled. Tears stung my eyes as I stared at the photo of us at the beach, taken when Orla was little. We'd been a normal, happy, carefree family. Sean's arm was snaked around my waist as I held our girl in my arms. We were smiling because we'd had no idea what lay ahead for us. How could such a wonderful memory cause me this much pain?

I sank to the floor and pressed my forehead to my knees. 'Dear God... please help me. I don't know how to reach her. I don't know how to save her,' I whispered, with tears streaming down my face.

But the only answer was the sound of Orla slamming the bathroom door. I'd never felt more alone. I'd had to fight tooth and nail to earn respect from Sean's men and keep a roof over our heads. To survive the betrayals and the bloodshed. But this fight, with my daughter, was the hardest battle I'd had so far. And I was scared to admit I was losing it.

A knock at the door made me jump out of my skin. Who would be calling at this time of night? I tightened the belt on my dressing gown and inched down the hall.

'Josie, it's me,' Niall said as I drew closer.

I flung the door open. 'Is everything OK?'

'No. Do you mind if I come in?'

I stepped aside and then closed the door behind him. He was already sitting at the table when I walked into the kitchen. Worry was etched into his features.

'I'm sorry to call so late, but I thought you'd want to know there's a problem with the shipment...'

'I knew it!' I replied, then let out a loud sigh and sat on the chair opposite him.

'It looks like some of the crates have been tampered with. After we'd unloaded the shipment, I noticed a few of the seals were broken. I quizzed the driver, but he swore blind they were like that when he loaded the van in Dublin. What do you want me to do? Do you want me to go through the boxes to see if any of the whiskey is missing?'

'No. Leave it until the morning, and I'll come with you. There's nothing we can do about it tonight,' I replied.

'I'm sorry, Josie. I shouldn't have bothered you with this. I know it's late, but I saw your lights were on...' Niall gazed at me with a guilty look on his face.

'I'm glad you told me, but you'd best get home. I don't want to face the wrath of Philomena for keeping you away from your bed,' I joked.

But it was no laughing matter. Philomena was insanely jealous of my relationship with Niall, and that caused untold problems. She threw hissy fits over the slightest thing, even though Niall would stand on his head to please her. The woman was a nightmare. Rotten to the core. May God forgive me, but I couldn't find a nice thing to say about her. Sean had never liked her either. And I detested her even more since she'd gone behind my back and taken Orla to the clinic. She'd well and truly overstepped the mark. Nobody should ever try to come between a mother and a daughter. That wasn't the way the world worked.

Niall was too good for her, everyone knew that, but she'd cast a spell over him the minute he'd laid eyes on her, and the novelty hadn't worn off. He was just as smitten with her today as he had been all those years ago. She was a permanent fixture in our family, whether I liked it or not. If Sean had lived, I was sure he'd have sent her packing before things got this far. He'd seen through her from the first moment he'd met her. He knew how manipulative she was and what a hold she had over his younger brother. But Philomena had got her claws into Niall, and she wasn't going to let go.

25

JOSIE

The air inside the speakeasy's cellar was musty and stale from the layer of dust resting on the oak barrels. Niall and the men had lined the shipment along the back wall. It all appeared to be in order at first glance, but I stepped closer to take a better look. The click of my heels against the concrete echoed around the low-ceilinged space. When I crouched down by the nearest crate, I saw why my brother-in-law had been concerned.

'Get me the crowbar,' I said.

The cases should have been sealed when they left the distillery, but there were telltale scrape marks around the lid. Somebody had tampered with the shipment, and my money was on Eamonn. Anger flared inside me. My fingers flexed, I wanted to grab him by the throat.

I worked the nails loose, and the lid creaked open. The rows of whiskey bottles glinted like amber jewels under the light. All of them were there. I'd expected some of them to be missing, but that wasn't the case.

'That's weird,' Niall said.

I carefully lifted one out, and as I did, I felt something else, a heavy, compact shape wedged in between the bottles. I turned to look at Niall.

'What's wrong?' he asked, peering into the crate. He hovered next to me with his arms folded, trying to read my expression.

I put the whiskey down on the floor and then pulled out the object. It was a clear-plastic-wrapped brick. I didn't need to open it to know the white powder was cocaine. My jaw tightened. 'I knew that bastard was up to something.'

Niall swore under his breath. 'Do you think it was Eamonn?'

'Who else?'

'He's got some cheek using our shipment to move his gear.'

I shoved the brick back into the crate like it was filth contaminating my hands. 'I wondered what was going on when Eamonn said he'd got the shipment pushed through as a favour. When have you ever known him to do anything for free?'

'He's a greedy fucker, that's for sure,' Niall agreed.

'He told me he wanted to help me out because I brought a lot of business his way. But all he's done is show me total disrespect! Does he take me for a fool?' I was under so much pressure and struggling to manage everything. This was the last thing I needed. My blood was boiling. It was hard to contain my fury.

Niall blew out a breath.

'Eamonn must have had an ally in our camp to be able to pull this off. Someone who'd have access to the shipment must have been in on this.' I tapped my lips with my fingertips as I mulled over the options. It galled me to think a trusted employee had betrayed me.

Niall tilted his head. 'Can you think of anyone?'

'Mossy Flaherty,' I replied without missing a beat. He'd worked for our firm for years, but he didn't like taking orders from a woman.

Niall looked startled by my suggestion. 'I don't know about that, Josie.'

'He was here yesterday when the shipment was delivered, wasn't he?'

'Yes, but—'

I cut him off with a sharp wave of my hand. 'But nothing. I've never trusted the man.' He was cocky and thought he was God's gift to women, wearing his leather jacket open with a thick spill of chest hair on display like a badge of confidence. It made perfect sense to me that he was the snake. He had a reptilian stillness about him and was always watching from the shadows. There was something cold-blooded and calculated in the way he observed my every move. It gave me the impression that he was waiting, coiled and patient, until it was time to strike.

Niall frowned. 'That doesn't mean he's the guilty party. Mossy's been with us since Sean's day, and he's never put a foot wrong.'

'That's why he'd be the perfect man for the job. No one would ever suspect him. He's dependable. Part of the inner circle. It would be easy for him to slip something past us,' I shot back. Men like Mossy shed their skin when it suited them.

'I'm sorry, Josie, I don't buy it.' Niall's tone was challenging.

'Who checked the crates and signed them off when the lorry was unloaded?' I countered.

'Mossy did.'

'Did he notice the shipment had been tampered with?'

Niall cast his eyes to the floor. 'No.'

'And you don't think that's odd?' Alarm bells were ringing in my ears.

Niall shrugged.

'For God's sake! The man needs to get his eyes tested if he missed the seals being broken. That's something you'd look for before accepting the delivery, isn't it?' My question was met by a wall of silence. 'Why are you covering for him? Please tell me you weren't involved?' My heart was in my mouth while I waited for a reply.

'Of course I wasn't!' Niall was outraged, which put my mind at rest. 'I was the one who spotted the damage. I told you last night that I quizzed the driver, and he insisted the crates were in that condition when he loaded the van in Dublin. Unless he was lying.'

'I suppose that's a possibility. But that doesn't explain why Mossy signed off on the delivery.'

Niall clenched his jaw. 'What are you suggesting we do?'

'We bait him. We'll set a trap and let him walk straight into it. When I've got proof, Mossy will be wishing he'd never crossed me.' My voice went flat. My gaze flicked to Sean's old chair in the corner, and a thought slipped uninvited into my head. Would Mossy have dared to do this to my husband? I knew the answer, so I pushed the unpleasant notion away as anger started burning inside me. When would these men learn to respect me? Hadn't I proved myself over and over? Yet they still thought they could take the piss out of me.

26

JOSIE

The delay at the speakeasy had cost me precious time, so I wasn't best pleased to hear the sound of chit-chat greeting me as I pushed open the front door. Seeing my builders standing around idle made my anger flare up again. We were on a tight deadline. We didn't have time to waste. So why had their power tools ground to a halt? I was wearing a padded-shouldered navy power suit and had a wide belt cinching my small waist. My hair was swept into a neat bun, and my lipstick was bold. I'd chosen everything deliberately. I wanted my appearance to announce that I meant business as I'd come here to inspect progress, but the foreman's face dropped when he caught sight of me, which said it all. 'What's going on? I'm not paying you to have a mothers' meeting.' I didn't try to keep the sarcasm out of my voice.

'Good morning, Josie,' the foreman said.

But there'd been nothing good about it so far. Orla and I had been at each other's throats, my shipment had been tampered with, and now my workforce was on a go-slow.

'I'm glad you're here. I was just about to phone you. We've got a bit of a problem...'

'What sort of problem?' I asked, narrowing my eyes. 'Not the council again?'

'No. I'm afraid it's worse than that. You'd better come with me. You're going to want to see this.'

He held his hard hat under one arm as he led the way. My heels clicked against the dusty floor as I trailed two steps behind through the empty shell of the pub. The smell of fresh paint was overwhelming. My mind whirred as I imagined what the issue could be, but nothing could have prepared me for what I saw when I walked into the recently refurbished area. The foreman pushed open the saloon doors, which led to the glass-fronted bar, and I stopped dead. My breath caught in my chest at the sight of the destruction.

Red paint was splattered across the newly laid black-and-white checkerboard tiles. Some of them were cracked and had been prised up in places like somebody had taken a crowbar to them. The bar fittings, installed last week, were smashed. The brass rail, which ran the length of the countertop, was twisted and had been wrenched off at one end. The beer taps were damaged, and the huge mirror behind the bar was shattered into a spiderweb of shards. Broken glass glittered on the floor beneath where it had hung.

'Oh my God!' I gasped before covering my mouth with my hands. I willed myself to stay in control, but it was hard to hold back my tears. All the hard work had been undone in an instant.

The foreman let out a loud sigh as his eyes scanned the room. 'It was like this when we got here. Someone broke in last night.'

'How'd they get in?'

The foreman gestured towards the back. 'Through the service door. The lock was popped clean off. The back alley's muddy, so whoever did this left footprints behind.'

As I surveyed the mess, my hands tightened into fists. I knew who the culprit was. I stepped towards the bar and fragments of tile crunched beneath my feet. When I ran my fingers over the buckled brass, a lump formed in my throat. 'Was anything taken?'

'Nah. This wasn't theft,' the foreman replied.

Thousands of pounds worth of stock was in the basement. Luckily, we hadn't got around to lining the shelves with the expensive bottles of spirits yet. I should be grateful for small mercies, but it seemed like little consolation at this stage.

'Whoever did this just wanted to wreck the place. It's like they wanted to send you a message.'

My eyes flicked toward the broken mirror as his words registered. Twelve versions of the same furious woman stared back at me, so I turned away. My heart was hammering in my chest. My head was pounding as thoughts raced through my brain at a hundred miles an hour while my pulse whooshed in my ears. It was all too much. I discreetly gripped the mahogany counter when I felt my knees start to give way. The mindless vandalism was designed to break me. But I wouldn't let it. I had to stay strong. I couldn't afford to show weakness.

'Someone's got it in for you. Can you think of anyone?'

Reggie's face flashed into my mind although I kept that to myself. I knew he was behind this without a shadow of a doubt, but I couldn't prove it. He thought he was one step ahead of me. I wasn't going to let him win this battle, no matter how hard he tried.

'I didn't mention this to you before because I didn't want to stress you out, but some geezer tried to pay the lads to walk off the job last week. If you ask me, somebody definitely doesn't want this place reopening,' the foreman said with a grim look on his face.

Reggie could try to sabotage the redevelopment all he liked. He'd thrown everything he had to block my plans, but I didn't have the time or energy to waste on his petty power games. I'd vowed to launch Mulligans in time for Christmas, and I had no intention of going back on my word.

'Get the men to sweep up in here and then salvage what you can. Start laying the broken tiles again and repairing the damage. I want this area back to the way it was by the end of the week.'

The foreman raised his eyebrows in alarm, but he said nothing.

'Bolt the back door shut from the inside and board up the windows so people can't see in. I'll hire a nightwatchman with a dog to keep an eye on things while we're not here.'

The foreman nodded. He was already moving back to where the builders were assembled.

The entire front of Mulligans had tall panes running from waist to ceiling height. I'd been making a statement when I'd chosen them. I wanted everyone to think I had nothing to hide. I was already regretting that decision. The clear view into my domain made me feel vulnerable.

I stayed behind, drinking in the wreckage for a moment as the silence buzzed around me. There was a stillness that often came before something violent, before a storm was unleashed. My jaw was clenched so tightly it ached. My fingers were balled into fists at my sides. I was livid, but I felt more determined than ever that my name would hang above the door. 'You want to rattle me, Reggie?' I said to the empty room. 'You'll have to do better than this!' Then I adjusted the cuffs of my suit jacket, straightened my shoulders and walked out of the building with my head held high. On the outside, I was calm. Controlled. Cold. But in my heart, a fire was burning, so I made myself a promise without saying a word. Bennett was going to pay for this in blood.

27

REGGIE

The air inside the derelict building opposite The Velvet Ace, where I'd set up home so that I could keep an eye on things, stank of damp and old piss. I was crouched behind a broken window panel, peering through a gap in the warped plywood, carrying out surveillance.

My heart sped up when I spotted Josie O'Connor, dressed to the nines, strutting along the pavement like she owned the place. Stupid bitch. The padded shoulders of her suit jacket doubled the size of her natural frame, making the rest of her body look out of proportion.

I could see her expression darken when she walked into the room next to the front door and discovered her workforce standing around chatting. I studied her the way you would fish in a tank. She was exposed, openly visible, glassed in on all sides. She looked as though she was about to blow a gasket, which had me grinning from ear to ear. She had a face like thunder as she followed the foreman through the building. I rushed over to the next set of windows so that I wouldn't miss the big reveal.

From the shadows, I watched her freeze. Her head tilted, from one side to the other, like she didn't trust what she was seeing. Like her brain needed a few extra seconds to process what was in front of her. Josie's eyes bulged and nearly popped out of her skull when the sight finally registered. I thought her head was going to start spinning around on her neck.

I couldn't hear the conversation. The only sound in the room was the wind rattling through the rafters behind me. But I could read between the lines. Her reaction was priceless. Pure gold. At first, Josie looked panicked, but then she tried to shake it off and put on a brave face.

I laughed out loud. My handiwork had hit the spot. I deserved a pat on the back. Josie didn't scream or cry. She just stared straight ahead with her eyes locked on the devastation. I'd shattered her dreams, which made my day – my year. She'd taken my pride and joy, but I'd make sure she lived to regret that decision. Pretty soon, she'd wish she'd never stepped on my toes and taken on the refurbishment.

I shifted slightly, angling myself to get a better view, and a rat scurried near my foot, but I didn't flinch. I was so used to sharing my living quarters with the furry bastards at this stage that we were practically on first-name terms. Josie walked up to the bar. Her shoulders were rigid. Her jaw was set. I'd known her a long time. Long enough to read her even from this distance. She was shocked and angry, but that wouldn't stop her determination. She was calculating. I bet her mind was working overtime.

She said something to the foreman, he nodded, and then he headed for the door. Josie took one more look at the damage before she walked towards the street. Her gaze scanned left, then right, from the doorway as if she was searching for something. I stepped back from the crack in the plywood instinctively as her stare sliced through the air like a razor. For a second, I wondered if she'd seen me. Then logic told me there was no way she could have, but she seemed to sense my presence. Sense the fact that she was being watched, which should have unsettled her. Josie steeled herself like a queen preparing for battle. Then she stepped on to the pavement, and a moment later, she disappeared from view.

28

JOSIE

'Thankfully, the shipment's intact. We were worried about nothing,' I said, trying to keep my voice light and airy when a ball of rage was bouncing around in my stomach. I'd decided to pretend we hadn't found the drugs, as they were buried inside the crate and not visible on first inspection.

'That's great news, Josie.' Mossy beamed.

Seeing him grinning from ear to ear made my anger spike. We'd been good to the man. Given him a well-paid job and treated him with respect, and this was how he repaid us. 'Niall and I have got to pop over to Mulligans. I know there are fifty cases to deal with, but do you think you'd be able to unload the shipment while we're gone?'

'Not a bother,' Mossy replied, flashing me a wide smile.

If my hunch was correct, I'd soon wipe that smirk off his face. 'Before you get to work on the shipment, can you have a look behind the bar to see what needs replacing?'

'Will do,' Mossy replied.

'We'll see you later,' I said as he walked away.

I thought he'd question why I'd asked him to check the stock, as we didn't usually bother, but he seemed happy to follow my orders for once. I needed to get him out of the way so Niall and I could get to our vantage point without him seeing. I wanted to catch him red-handed by observing his movements with an old-fashioned stake-out.

The open-fronted loft was built over part of the basement and was used to store empties. It was enclosed on three sides by rough panelling and accessed via a narrow wooden staircase tucked behind the beer kegs, so Mossy wouldn't notice anyone was there unless he looked directly up. We'd be able to spy on him without him realising.

As soon as he was out of sight, I scampered up the stairs. My nose twitched from the smell of dust and stale beer. I stood in the half-dark, pressed against the rough timber wall with my heart hammering in my ears as I waited for Niall to join me. When he appeared beside me, we crouched low, making sure we were far enough back from the edge to remain undetected. The hum of the fridge in the far corner would cover the sound of our breathing.

From our perch, I could see the central open space of the speakeasy's basement with ease. The whiskey crates were stacked like a fort in the middle of the room. I'd chosen the vantage point because the mezzanine level had a good line of sight to where Mossy would unload the crates, so we'd soon see whether he was innocent or not.

'Mossy's coming,' Niall whispered, and my pulse started galloping at the side of my neck.

A moment later, the heavyset Irishman, who was pushing fifty, stepped into view. He had two strangers with him, whose collars were turned up against the cold, and their faces were half-hidden in shadow. From what I could make out, one of them was in his mid-thirties. The other looked to be around sixteen or seventeen. Their shoes echoed off the damp concrete as they strode across the room. Mossy glanced around before he picked up the crowbar. His broad back hunched as he worked it under the lid of the first crate. The squeal of nails pulling free drifted up through the slats in the floorboards as he levered it off. Beads of sweat broke out on my upper lip as I tried to keep my breathing steady.

The first layer of straw came out. Then Mossy reached in deeper and lifted out a bottle of whiskey. He placed it down on the ground and delved back inside. He pulled out a plastic-wrapped brick and passed it to the older man without a word. As he turned it around in his hand, giving it a thorough inspection, my breath caught in my throat. Niall shifted to get a better look. His movement made the old planks under us creak faintly. I shot him a sharp look, put my hand on his arm and dug my nails into the fabric of his coat. Mossy glanced around the room before his eyes flicked toward the ceiling. When he looked in our direction, I thought our cover was blown. His eyes swept the shadows and lingered near our hiding place. I didn't dare to breathe. The fridge motor's low thrum suddenly sounded deafening. When he looked away, relief surged through me.

Mossy turned his attention back to the crate. He pulled out another bottle of whiskey and set it down so that he could get to the cocaine concealed beneath it. When he handed another brick to the man, I felt the heat rise in my chest. It wasn't the fire that came with sudden rage, but the steady boil of disappointment that a loyal member of staff had betrayed me. I'd suspected Mossy's involvement right from the start. Now that the awful truth had been confirmed, it was a bittersweet moment knowing that my hunch had been correct.

I felt sick to my stomach when the man handed Mossy a large wad of cash. I desperately wanted to storm down the stairs, but I couldn't afford to sabotage the deal, so I forced myself to stay still and not break cover as my pulse hammered in my neck. Every muscle was locked as I watched Mossy like a hawk.

Once the two men had left, he went through all of the crates, lined the bottles of whiskey up on the shelves and stashed the bricks of cocaine in a large black holdall, which he hid in an access hatch below ground level. Nobody would notice it if they weren't looking for it. It sat flush with the concrete floor, near the back wall – boot scuffs had dulled its edges, making it look like nothing more than a faint square in the floor.

Mossy knew exactly where to leave the stash, which suggested this wasn't the first time he'd done this. The loft felt smaller by the second as my fury pressed down on me. I was getting a cramp in my leg and wanted to move position. I was desperate to stand up and stretch. But I didn't want Flaherty to find out he'd unknowingly walked into my trap. I wouldn't let him in on the secret. Not yet. I'd confront him in the not-too-distant future. I needed to gather my thoughts first before I dealt with him. But deal with him I would.

29

JOSIE

I was absolutely livid with Mossy and Eamonn for putting my business at risk by hijacking my shipment, and then Flaherty went one step further by dealing drugs on my premises. I couldn't bear to look at the turncoat, so I'd closed the speakeasy early and dismissed him for the day. Niall and I had things to discuss that couldn't wait.

The floor was still tacky from the day's trade, but that was the least of my concerns. I sat opposite Niall at a corner table. He was watching me while a cigarette burned low between his fingers.

'Go on then, say it,' he muttered with a scowl on his face. Then he took a drag on the cigarette, making the end flare before he crushed it into the ashtray with deliberate pressure.

I wouldn't say I told you so. This wasn't about gloating. It wasn't about who was right and who was wrong. It was about loyalty and betrayal. No good would come from me rubbing his nose in it. Niall was as gutted as I was, probably more so. He'd been the one singing Mossy's praises and fighting his corner. But knowing somebody for years didn't mean a thing when temptation came their way. 'I'm disgusted with them for filling my shipment with shite.' I shook my head as thoughts skittered wildly around my mind.

'I never had Mossy down for a traitor, but cocaine's worth a hell of a lot more than the whiskey, so his greed must have got the better of him,' Niall said, and his jaw tightened.

'Not to me, it's not. But I won't be left out of the deal. When will the men I deal with learn to take me seriously? They think that because I don't swing my fists like Sean used to, they can take advantage of me. I've proved myself time and again, yet I still have to put up with their crap. Enough's enough,' I replied.

'What are you planning to do?' Niall asked.

'I'm going in hard on both of them. They won't be double-crossing me again!'

'I guessed as much. Which one of them is first in line?'

'Mossy. We'll need to keep a close eye on him. When he moves the stash, we'll follow him. I want to know who the last link in the chain is.' I intended to go straight for the jugular.

'He's not likely to go near it while one of us is around,' Niall pointed out.

'We'll keep the speakeasy closed for the next few days, which will give him plenty of opportunity to move it. One or the other of us is going to have to spy on him from the loft hatch. We'll have to man it day and night, so we don't miss him.'

Niall let out a loud sigh. 'Philomena's going to love that!'

I rolled my eyes to heaven. She was the bane of my life. 'Don't worry. I'll do the first watch. I reckon he'll shift it quickly. He won't want to risk getting caught with it, will he?'

'I suppose you're right. Have you checked out how much is down there?'

'Let's take a look.'

30

JOSIE

The basement was cold and damp. Niall followed me down the staircase and over to the access hatch. I crouched down in front of it. It was made from reinforced steel and painted the same mottled grey as the concrete to disguise it, although it was hardly noticeable. The hinges were sunk, invisible from the top side. There was no handle; a small, recessed lip had to be hooked with a crowbar or strong fingers.

'Let me get that for you,' Niall offered, wrenching it open with his large hand.

The hatch concealed a narrow, coffin-like cavity that had been dug out below the floor. It was bigger than I'd expected. I could only imagine what it had been used for in the past. Sean had many a secret I didn't know about.

I lifted out the black holdall and unzipped it. The cocaine bricks were wrapped in thick layers of plastic and had been stacked with neat precision. The air inside the cavity smelled faintly of earth and mildew. A small wooden pallet at the bottom lifted the contents away from moisture.

Niall loomed over me with his arms folded across his chest. 'There's more than I thought,' he muttered, peering into the bag.

I opened my mouth to speak, but before I could answer, the low crunch of tyres sounded outside. Both Niall and I froze. We exchanged a look, then quickly put the holdall back in its hiding place. We rushed over to the far side of the basement and climbed the wooden steps up to the loft space. Dust rattled as the boards shifted beneath our shoes. My muscles were rigid. My pulse was racing. My heart was in my mouth.

The car door shut – not a slam, more of a gentle clunk so as not to attract attention. I heard a key scraping the speakeasy's lock, and the metal shutter rose. The sound echoed in my chest, and my lips pressed into a thin line. When footsteps creaked down the stairs, my pulse spiked. As Mossy came into view, his shoulders were hunched, and his chin was lowered. He was moving like a tiger stalking its prey. He kept looking around, scanning the room like a man who knew he was running errands for the devil.

Mossy went straight to the hatch, opened it and pulled out the holdall, then he turned and left. Once he reached the top of the stairs, Niall and I crept out of our hiding place and rushed after him. He hadn't hung about. He'd moved like the wind with deliberate speed. We didn't follow him out the front; we used the back entrance. We heard him starting his car as we jumped into Niall's Ford Escort parked around the back.

Niall kept two lengths behind him so he wouldn't realise he was being tailed. We sat in tense silence as we headed along Kilburn High Road past the pubs, pawn shops, betting shops, second-hand furniture stores, greasy spoons, and minicab offices.

My eyes were focused on Mossy's Austin Allegro up ahead. One of my hands was tapping my thigh restlessly as my impatience got the better of me. Niall leaned forward in his seat, as if he was watching a scary movie. As we headed towards West Hampstead, Victorian terraces and small local shops sprang up, and by the time we drove past the Swiss Cottage pub, I was wondering where we were going.

'Where do you think he's off to?' I asked.

'Who the fuck knows. It could be Timbuktu at this rate,' Niall replied, shaking his head.

When we reached Chalk Farm Road, I couldn't help thinking it felt grimier and edgier, full of litter and graffiti. A group of skinheads on the corner momentarily drew my attention; they looked like trouble and appeared to be up to no good.

While we were driving, Mossy occasionally glanced in the mirror, but he didn't seem to clock Niall's Escort. As we headed along Parkway, the Dublin Castle caught my eye, and my thoughts turned briefly to Sean. I wondered what he'd make of all of this before I banished him to the back of my mind. The road stretched ahead. It was a scruffy area, lined with a mix of run-down shops; kids in uniforms who should have been at school loitered by the window of a Wimpy.

At the junction, Mossy turned right onto Camden High Street, and instantly the traffic thickened. Red Routemasters belched black smoke into the air as we tried to pass discarded vans double-parked with their hazard warning lights flashing. Posters advertising The Clash and UB40 gigs, as well as pirate radio stations and anti-Thatcher protests, were pasted deep on every hoarding. Their edges had peeled from being out in the rain.

As we passed Camden Town tube, it became even more chaotic as a crowd spilt out of the station. Everyone was moving fast, shoulders bumping one another in the rush to be somewhere else. A busker hammered out a tune on a battered guitar, hoping to earn something for his trouble, but in all honesty, his case was more likely filled with pennies and fag ends.

The pavements were packed. A Rasta was selling cassettes out of a suitcase while reggae blared from the boom box next to him. A group of goths, cloaked in black lace, huddled outside a second-hand clothes shop while punks with hair in every colour of the rainbow, styled in spikes, roamed the streets. A couple of down-and-outs were slumped outside a newsagents with cans of Special Brew gripped in their hands. You had to see it to believe it. Camden was a different world altogether – a magnet for the alternatives.

The car crawled forward in the heavy traffic. Mossy swung left into Inverness Street and the noise and buzz dimmed a little, though not by much. Market traders yelled at the passers-by as they hawked fruit and dodgy watches under sagging tarpaulins, their voices echoing off the terrace walls. The further we drove down the street, the quieter it became. The shopfronts were dilapidated. Some had broken windows, others were boarded up. The atmosphere had shifted. We were only a stone's throw from the hustle and bustle of the high street, but the place felt run-down. Forgotten. It had a squatter vibe about it. An air of danger seemed to be lurking behind the neglected properties.

Mossy stopped his Allegro outside a narrow shopfront. A sign above it, in faded Gothic lettering, bore the name, The Ink Pit. The tattoo parlour was squeezed between a shuttered green-grocer and a minicab office. A couple of teenagers were smoking outside, eyeing the car as though they were weighing up who was inside.

'Looks like this is where he's going to make the drop,' Niall said.

Mossy stepped out of the car. I studied him as he walked

around to the boot. His dark, slick-backed hair was greying at the temples, and his bushy moustache sat heavily on his lip, giving him a slightly seedy, seventies porn star look. His brown leather wide-lapelled jacket was well-worn and outdated. It was as though he was stuck in the last decade and hadn't moved with the times, although I imagined he thought he looked sharp. He seemed out of place among the more rebellious Camden crowd. He had too much chest hair and not enough edge.

Before he'd had time to lift the holdall out of the boot, Niall and I had crept up behind him. 'Hello, Mossy...'

He had a look of horror on his face when his head snapped around and he saw us standing behind him. His eyes flicked towards the iron bar Niall was holding in his fist. Mossy froze with one hand on the bag.

'Jesus, Josie... you scared the shit out of me,' he said, slamming the boot shut before turning to face us. 'What brings you to Camden?'

'I was just about to ask you the same thing.'

Mossy's Adam's apple bobbed up and down. He looked as guilty as sin.

'Are you getting a tattoo, Moss?' Niall laughed.

'Umm. Umm...'

'What's in the boot?' I asked, irritated by his stalling.

'The boot?' Mossy echoed, trying to act all innocent.

I pushed past him, opened it and then pointed to the holdall. His shoulders slumped. 'Don't bother trying to fob me off, I know exactly what's in the bag,' I said, my voice low and controlled.

'I'm sorry, Josie,' Mossy said, glancing towards the pavement. He wouldn't look me in the eye.

'I bet you are. I can't believe you'd double-cross me like this. You're not doing this without me, Mossy. Not when you used my cargo to carry your powder over the water. You thought you could cut me out? Well, that's not happening.'

Mossy's face drained of colour and his lips trembled, but he nodded. He knew there was no point in arguing. Not while Niall was inches away from him with an iron bar hanging easily in his hand.

'Are you sure about this? Are you sure you want to get involved? These men are dangerous, Josie,' Mossy said.

I let out a laugh. 'I'm already involved. I got involved the minute you stashed kilos of cocaine in between my bottles of whiskey.' My words were laced with venom. 'So who's your buyer?' I didn't mention that Niall and I had seen him hand over two bricks already because I didn't want to give away our hiding place in case we needed it at a later stage.

'Lewis Slater.' Mossy replied.

'Is he taking the lot?'

'Yes.'

Either the transaction Niall and I witnessed was a sample purchase or Mossy was still lying to me. It didn't really matter either way. I didn't trust the man as far as I could throw him. And he was going to pay for his treachery when he was no longer useful to me.

'So let's get on with it,' I said, gesturing to Niall to pick up the bag. It must have weighed a ton, but Niall was a strapping man, so he lifted it with ease.

'Are y-you s-sure you want to do this?' Mossy stammered.

'I've never been more certain about anything.' My voice was as hard as flint.

The noise of the Camden street dulled for a moment, like it was holding its breath as Mossy glanced toward the tattoo parlour's door then back at myself and Niall.

'I don't know how they're going to react if we all walk in. I'm just being honest with you, Josie,' Mossy said, which made me laugh out loud.

'Honest with me? You don't know the meaning of the word! There's only one way to find out. Shall we?'

31

JOSIE

I could see movement inside The Ink Pit. Lewis Slater was waiting, so Niall gave Mossy a shove with the iron bar to prompt him to move. The teenagers had finished their cigarettes, but they were still hanging around, eyeing us with more than a casual interest. It suddenly occurred to me that they were lookouts, making their presence felt to anyone who walked past the shop's vicinity.

The tattoo parlour looked shabby and grimy from the outside. It didn't have much kerb appeal and was the kind of place you'd question whether the needles were ever cleaned. It definitely appeared to be a real business Lewis was using as a front. It was a good choice; accessible to customers yet hidden in plain sight. I'd been expecting the exchange to take place in a disused warehouse.

Mossy led the way. He didn't hesitate when he pushed the door open, and I got the distinct impression that he'd been here before. A bell rang out, announcing our arrival. A mix of stale smoke, disinfectant and alcohol hit me as I stepped inside.

A small reception counter was by the door. It wasn't very

welcoming. The appointment book lying on the counter was dog-eared, and an ashtray was overflowing with cigarette butts. A girl with back-combed hair and heavy black eyeliner sat behind it, filing her fingernails. She gave Mossy a once-over as he approached her.

'Have you got an appointment?' she asked in a cockney accent.

'Yes. I'm here to see Lewis Slater.'

'Are they with you?' she cocked her head in our direction.

Mossy nodded.

'Take a seat.'

The only place, a cheap sofa, was already occupied. A couple of teenagers, about Orla's age, who I presumed were part of Lewis's crew, were sitting on it smoking roll-ups and passing a bottle between themselves while watching the door. They were all attitude and bravado, but a puff of wind would blow them over.

As we waited for Lewis to appear, I took in the measure of the place. The room had two buzzing fluorescent strips overhead, which flickered and blinked. A selection of pre-made tattoo designs, including pin-up girls, crucifixes, Union Jacks and skulls, were taped on to the yellowed wallpaper.

The tattoo chair was positioned on the right-hand side of the space, behind a hanging beaded curtain that partially obscured the workspace. A big man with a shaved head was working on a tattoo while drinking lager from a can. He was barely paying attention to the customer in his chair. The young lad was wincing, but nobody in the shop seemed to care that he was in pain.

A man in his mid-thirties appeared in a doorway opposite the entrance, smoking a cigarette. He was dressed in a black leather jacket, a white T-shirt, tight jeans and had a gold chain glinting at his neck. His brown hair was starting to thin slightly on top. He had a wiry build and drawn features, with a sharp nose, tired eyes and a mouth that looked as if it rarely smiled.

'How's it going, Lewis?' Mossy asked with a familiarity in his tone that confirmed this wasn't the first time they'd met. He was trying too hard to look like he belonged as he swaggered over, wearing a half-smile with his hand outstretched.

Lewis didn't answer right away. He just dragged on his cigarette, glanced at the teenager in the Fila tracksuit who was closest to him and then back at Mossy.

'Who've you brought along for the ride?' Lewis's eyes narrowed as they flicked between Niall and myself.

He was English, as expected, young enough to be seen as brash and ambitious, but old enough to carry authority.

Mossy's grin faltered.

'I'm the reason your cocaine got here in the first place,' I said, stepping forward, my voice as hard as steel.

Lewis tilted his head, and the corners of his mouth lifted in amusement. 'Fuck me, you're a bit mouthy, ain't ya? Talking to me like you own the place.' He spoke like an express train with a London accent that cut through the room like broken glass.

'I'm Josephine O'Connor. I came to tell you, if you're going to stow cocaine in my shipment, you'll pay me for my trouble,' I shot back.

The tracksuit-clad teenager smirked. He had an edge to him, but that was no concern of mine. I'd come here to negotiate with his boss.

'In that case, you'd better come through,' Lewis said, gesturing to the teen to follow as he turned on his heel. Slater carried himself with the confidence of someone who knew he was getting somewhere. He was on the climb. He wasn't at the top of the tree yet, but I could see he was going to be. He was carving a name for himself running Camden.

Beyond the parlour was where the real business happened. The cramped back room doubled as an office. There was an old table in the centre which was bare apart from a phone on one side. Its spiral cable hung over the edge in a tangled mess.

'Take a pew.' Lewis sat on the edge of the table and gestured to a couple of crates that were acting as chairs.

'I'd prefer to stand, thank you.'

Niall and Mossy followed my lead.

My eyes did a quick scan of the room. A rusting motorbike was propped against the far wall, next to a half-glazed door that led to a backyard full of overflowing rubbish bins. It was no doubt handy for quick getaways or dodgy deliveries, although it seemed strange to keep it inside.

'I'm not here to close the deal down. I'm here to muscle in on it,' I said, pushing my shoulders back and straightening my posture.

Lewis and his teenage sidekick, a tall, wiry lad with dark, floppy hair and watchful eyes, burst out laughing, which made anger rise up in me.

'No offence, love, but the idea of you muscling in on anything is hilarious,' Lewis said, with a big grin on his face.

If this jumped-up London gobshite thought I was going to stand here while he mocked me, he could think again. I turned towards Niall. 'It's time to go,' I said through gritted teeth.

Lewis glanced at Mossy, then back at me, weighing up the situation. 'Let's not do anything hasty,' he said, getting to his feet. 'I'm sorry if I offended you. It wasn't intentional.'

He put his hand on his chest in an effort to make his apology heartfelt, but I could see straight through him. He could save his breath. It wouldn't wash with me. He didn't regret what he'd said. He was just worried he wouldn't get his hands on the coke, so he was turning on the charm. His words were convincing to the untrained ear, but I was an expert at spotting bullshit when I heard it. I'd had years of practice thanks to Sean.

'So, can we have a truce? I'd wave a white flag if I had one.' Lewis winked as charisma seeped out of every pore.

I had to stop my lip from curling into a snarl. Lewis was the kind of man who could sell you a stolen watch at a hugely inflated price and make it sound like a bargain. He had a hustler's confidence combined with enough menace that people didn't question him.

'I won't be spoken to like that. Show me the respect I deserve, or the deal's off.' My words were slow. Deliberate.

Lewis kept shifting his weight from one foot to the other while he scanned the room. The movement was subtle, but the nervous tic betrayed his underlying ambition. I could tell he thought he was destined for greatness.

Slater put his hands up in front of himself in surrender. 'I've learned my lesson. I promise I'll be on my best behaviour from now on. OK?'

I nodded my head.

'Any chance I can see the gear now?' He smiled.

I gestured to Niall, who obliged by putting the holdall on the desk. Lewis unzipped it and delved his hand inside. A moment later, he pulled out one of the blocks. Then he took a flick knife out of his jacket pocket and stabbed it into the plastic wrap. Being careful not to spill any of the white powder balancing on the knife's blade, he dipped his finger into it and rubbed it on to his gums.

'That's good shit,' he announced once he'd had time to savour the flavour.

I wouldn't have known whether it was or not, so that was music to my ears.

Lewis lifted out the bricks, counting them as he did. There

were twenty-three in total. 'So we said eighty thousand a kilo, right?'

I thought my eyes were going to pop out of my head. I suddenly felt flustered. My pulse was galloping in my neck, but I tried not to let it show as I battled to compose myself.

'That's right,' I replied, opting to say as little as possible.

'Any chance of a discount as I'm buying in bulk?' Lewis grinned, chancing his arm.

'No.' My tone was stern.

'I thought you might say that. Fair enough. I won't argue with a woman who's got the balls to walk into my shop and call the shots.' He stepped behind the desk, pulled open one of the drawers and started stacking piles of notes next to the cocaine.

I was frantically trying to multiply eighty by twenty-three to work out how much he owed.

'There should be one million, eight hundred and forty thousand there. I take it you want to check it,' Lewis said, pulling out a calculator from one of the other drawers along with a device I'd only ever seen in a bank before. 'The money is in bundles of ten thousand. If you count and weigh one of them, you can then check the others against it. It saves a lot of time when you're dealing with a large sum.'

It was clear Lewis was used to handling big volumes of cash. All I could think about was the windfall that had landed at my feet as Niall got to work checking the notes.

'It's all there,' Niall said, putting the cash into the black holdall.

'It's been a pleasure doing business with you, Josephine,' Lewis said, offering me his hand.

I shook it out of politeness, but I didn't reply. As I turned to leave, I felt the teenager's eyes fix on me, and something unspoken passed between us. He was only young, but he was already hardened by Camden life. I marched out of the tattoo parlour on my stiletto heels with my head held high and a smile on my face. I let out a sigh of relief when I stepped out of The Ink Pit, knowing I had more than enough money to finance the redevelopment of Mulligans.

'Where do you think you're going?' I asked, stopping Mossy in his tracks. He was heading towards his Allegro, but he turned around to face me, wearing a guilty look. 'Get in the back.' I gestured to Niall's car. I wasn't done with him yet. Not by a long shot.

Niall kept a hand on his shoulder like a warder until he was safely in the Ford. Mossy looked pale; sweat had settled in a layer across his forehead. The real fun was about to start, and I was going to enjoy watching him squirm.

32

JOSIE

When Niall and I had witnessed Mossy handing over two other bricks of cocaine, I hadn't realised the transaction was worth one hundred and sixty thousand pounds. It was a huge amount of money, by anyone's standards. There was no way I was going to allow him to keep a penny of it. I wasn't greedy by nature, but he needed to learn the lesson the hard way that double-crossing me was a big mistake. So I'd hit him where it hurt the most: in his pocket. He didn't deserve a piece of the action. He'd broken my trust and betrayed me in the worst way possible.

I might have taken a different stand on the matter if I'd been consulted beforehand, but he'd had no intention of sharing whatever his cut was with me, which was why I was going to take the lot. I didn't care if that landed him in hot water. Mossy was lucky he was still breathing. I'd let him live for now. He was a useful pawn, and I still needed to confirm that Eamonn was the supplier.

Mossy slumped in the chair in the speakeasy's office with his eyes glued to the floor. He looked broken already, and the interrogation hadn't even started. But he wasn't going to get an ounce of sympathy from me. I was leaning against the edge of the desk with my arms folded across my chest, preparing myself for what was to come as Niall lingered by my side.

'You thought you were being so clever, didn't you? What have you got to show for it?' My voice was calm but assertive.

Mossy slowly raised his head and looked up at me with a hangdog expression on his face. 'I'm sorry, Josie.'

'Is that all you've got to say for yourself?' I wasn't going to make this easy for him now that I had him boxed in with nowhere to run and proof in my hand. Niall shifted as we waited for Mossy to respond, but he remained silent. 'How many times have you used my cargo to smuggle cocaine across the water?'

'This was the first shipment,' Mossy replied without hesitation.

I narrowed my eyes and scrutinised his features. 'If you're lying to me, you won't see me coming!'

'I swear on my children's lives I'm not,' Mossy said.

'How well do you know Lewis?' I probed.

'I'd met him once before the drop-off. He came to the speakeasy to get a couple of bricks so he could test the quality. I've set aside the money he paid me. I can get it for you now if you want?' Mossy offered.

His admission had gone some way to repairing the broken trust. Not that I was going to tell him that. Niall and I had watched the exchange, but I hadn't known for certain whether Lewis Slater was the man we'd seen or not.

'Can you imagine how devastated I felt when I realised Eamonn had paid off one of my guys to get the cocaine out of the shipment and distribute it to his buyer?'

Mossy looked wounded, like I'd just stabbed him in the gut with a blade. He didn't deny Eamonn's involvement, which was proof enough for me. Guilt was seeping out of him, but that didn't stop the heat from his betrayal burning in my chest. Knowing there was mutiny in the ranks made me feel sick to my stomach.

I took a step closer and jabbed my finger towards him. 'It didn't take us long to work out who the turncoat was, did it, Niall?' My brother-in-law said nothing, so I pressed on. 'Eamonn needed someone dependable, an insider, and you were the perfect fit. No one would think to watch you. I'm disgusted that you've done this to me. Do you know that?'

Mossy's eyes filled with tears. 'Jesus, Josie, what can I say? I made a mistake. I've acted like a feckin' eejit, but I swear to God, I'll do anything you want to put things right between us.'

His apology was lost on me. My gaze drifted to Sean's old chair in the corner. He'd loved it, even though the leather was cracked and the seat sagged. Admittedly, it had seen better days, but I couldn't bear to part with it. I wondered if my late husband would have stopped this fiasco before it happened. If he'd have sniffed out the rot in his own ranks sooner. The thoughts soured quickly. Sean was gone. This mess was mine to fix.

'I hear what you're saying, but I don't trust a word that comes out of your mouth. I can't believe you thought you'd get away with this. Thought you could treat me with so little respect. That tells me two things, Mossy. One, you're stupid. And two, you're desperate.'

Mossy swallowed hard. 'Josie, I—'

'Shut up! You do realise I could have dumped your body in the canal tonight, don't you? I could have made an example of you. But you're worth more to me alive... for now.'

Niall looked at me with a startled expression on his face. 'Really? You're going to let him walk?'

I nodded my head and then leaned closer to Mossy. 'I'm going to let you go, but don't mistake my kindness for weakness. You're only breathing because I said so. If you double-cross me again, that will be the last anyone sees of you. Understand?' My words were as sharp as glass.

Mossy nodded furiously. His lips were trembling. 'Thank you, Josie. I promise I'll never let you down again.'

He sounded genuine, but the trust between us had gone. 'If you do, you won't need money or any worldly possessions where you'll be going,' I warned.

The mention of money must have sparked a thought in Mossy's brain, and the colour drained from his face. 'Eamonn will be expecting me to bring him the cash from the deal. He'll know something's up if I fail to show up as agreed next month.'

'We'd better not disappoint him then,' I said with a wry smile on my face.

33

JOSIE

London, September 1985

The atmosphere inside my kitchen was tense. The air was simmering with the unspoken words I wanted to say to my sister-in-law. Steam rose from the kettle and curled around me as I busied myself making tea, while Niall and Philomena sat side by side at the table. It was my house, and yet she had the look of someone who had the upper hand.

I could hardly stand the sight of the woman. She was carrying on as if nothing had happened, as if she hadn't bundled my girl into her car and taken her to that place behind my back. The thought of the two of them at Marie Stopes still burned a hole in me. I couldn't breathe. The rage in me wanted to tear into her, to shout until she understood what she'd done, but I had to keep a lid on things. Much as I hated to admit it, I needed her help.

'I hope you appreciate the favour I'm doing you. It's a big responsibility looking after somebody else's child,' Philomena said. Her tone was curt.

My jaw ached from how hard I was clenching it. I wanted to

throw her out, to tell her never to come near us again, but instead, I looked at her with a smile on my face. 'I know that and I'd be happy to do the same for you if Shannon and Tyrone ever need watching,' I replied, trying to keep the barb out of my voice.

Philomena laughed. 'That won't be necessary. Unlike yourself, I'm a full-time mother who puts her children's needs first.'

Her insult stung, but I took it on the chin and carried on preparing the drinks as I prayed for patience. If I'd had another option, I wouldn't be leaving Orla with Lady Muck while I went to Dublin with Niall and Mossy. My daughter was at a difficult age; she was a handful, so she needed supervision. My best friend, Biddy, worked long hours, whereas Philomena spent her days applying lipstick and ensuring her nails were perfectly manicured, so she was better placed to keep an eye on my girl. But I was already regretting my decision and had to fight back the anger clawing its way up from the pit of my stomach.

I placed a fresh cup of tea in front of Niall, setting it down a little harder than I meant to. Philomena immediately pulled it towards her, spooned in two sugars and stirred it vigorously. I watched the domestic play, feeling like a guest in my own home, while wondering if it was possible to despise the woman more than I already did. I was having to bite my tongue to avoid a confrontation. This wasn't the time to fall out with her. She was holding all of the cards. The power had gone straight to her blonde head. I needed her help for a few days, but she was going to well and truly make me pay for coming to my assistance.

I'd have to cross that bridge when I came to it. I had bigger prey in my sights. Eamonn was expecting Mossy, so we couldn't afford to miss the ferry, or it might raise his suspicions. I wanted to catch him by surprise. We needed to get on the road, so I picked up my daughter's bag and handed it to Philomena. She clutched it to her chest like it was a trophy. 'Orla will make her way to yours after school. We'll be back the day after tomorrow.'

She nodded in acknowledgement, but she didn't waste a reply on me. 'Drive safely, love,' she said to Niall before pulling him into a passionate embrace, which was no doubt designed to mortify me, so I tried not to let my embarrassment show, even though I could feel my cheeks burning. 'I'll look after Orla. Like I always do.'

The words landed heavily between us. Her tone was syrupy, but her eyes were sharp as nails as she glared at me while smoothing a hand over her skirt. I bit down hard enough on the inside of my cheek to taste blood. For Orla's sake, I let the silence hold. My lips twitched. I was on the verge of telling her to fuck off and mind her own business. Remind her that Orla was my daughter and that she'd never take that place from me, but I kept my thoughts to myself as I showed her to the door.

34

JOSIE

Dublin, September 1985

I kept my hands folded in my lap as we made the short drive to the docks from the ferry terminal. It had been a rough journey across the Irish Sea. I was hoping the weather would be kind to us; that wasn't the case. Flying would have saved us a lot of time, but Eamonn had eyes everywhere, and somebody would have tipped him off if we hadn't been on the crossing. We would never have got through airport security carrying the amount of cash he was expecting, so we had to stick to the plan. I didn't want him to smell a rat and bolt before he got what was coming to him.

Eamonn's men were looking out for the Austin Allegro so they could waive it through without a random customs check. I'd ducked down and thrown my jacket over myself as we'd driven off the boat. Whoever had been paid to turn a blind eye wasn't likely to take any notice of Niall accompanying Mossy; they'd presume he was hired muscle, but they might wonder why a woman was tagging along for the ride. I wasn't taking any chances.

As we drew closer, my nails dug faint crescents into my palms. Niall sat in the front passenger seat next to Mossy. He was as calm as a millpond. It was the kind of calm you learned from years of waiting in dark places with a weapon inside your coat. Mossy, on the other hand, was sweating buckets. His nerves wouldn't alarm Eamonn, though, as the Dublin port worker had complete trust in Flaherty. I was confident he'd assume Mossy was edgy because he was carrying an enormous sum of money. He'd think his payday had come. The sneaky bastard was in for a rude awakening.

Eamonn never knew when to shut his mouth. He was always on the take. Always convinced the world owed him something. He saw me as Sean's widow, nothing more, and treated me as an afterthought. Tonight, he was going to learn that wasn't the case. He was going to pay the price for underestimating me. There was no point keeping him around. He was greedy, disloyal and a threat to my business.

The engine ticked until Mossy cut it. We sat for a beat before we opened the doors and stepped out of the car. Niall and I rushed away and pressed ourselves into the recess of an old loading bay twenty yards back. A mist rolled off the Liffey, clinging to everything in its path: ropes, rusted bollards and the creaking hulls of sleeping ships. The lights along the quay cast shadows over the slick concrete, and the hum of a distant generator made the dock feel alive, like it was breathing. There was a smell of diesel in the air, which made me feel queasy, or maybe that was due to the anxiety burrowing its way into the pit of my stomach.

It was a blustery night, so Mossy stood with his coat collar turned up against the autumn damp. His eyes were fixed on something in the middle distance as we watched from the shadow of a container. Eamonn strode out of the darkness. His hands were jammed in his pockets, and his chin was tucked low to avoid the worst of the wind. His guard dropped when he saw Mossy.

'You're a sight for sore eyes. I'm glad you made it in one piece. I hear the crossing was brutal!' Eamonn said as a grin pulled up the corners of his mouth.

Mossy's gaze darted around the dock as though he was looking for an escape route. If he wasn't careful, his nerves would give the game away. His body language was tense, and Eamonn started eyeing him suspiciously.

'Shall we go somewhere more private?' Mossy suggested, creating the opening for us to move in.

A moment later, they headed towards the dockside property where the handover was due to take place. Niall and I followed at a discreet distance. Eamonn released the padlock, pushed open one of the loading doors, and the two of them stepped inside. Niall and I hovered close to the doorway to give them time to get settled. When we slipped inside, Eamonn was already sitting in a chair with his boots up on a crate. He looked relaxed. He was grinning from ear to ear as a cigarette dangled from the corner of his mouth. His eyes were trained on the bag in Mossy's hand, so he didn't notice us creeping up behind him.

'I knew you'd come through, Moss. You had nothing to worry about. I didn't doubt you for a—' Eamonn swivelled in his seat as though he sensed something, and when he clocked us, his expression froze, and the colour drained from his face. 'Jesus... Josie, what are you doing here?' he asked, jumping to his feet as the cigarette tumbled from his mouth. He'd been caught off guard and tried to power his way through the unwelcome surprise.

I gave Niall a single nod, and he slammed the loading door shut before sliding the bolt home. Mossy had turned a whiter shade of pale and was panting like an animal trapped in a snare.

'What's going on here? What's in the bag?' I asked.

'It's not what it looks like.' Eamonn put his hands out in front of himself.

'Please feel free to enlighten me.' I crossed my arms over my chest and glared at him. I was looking forward to hearing him try to bluff his way out of this.

Niall stormed up to Mossy and grabbed the bag from his hand. Eamonn's eyes darted around the room as sweat broke out on his forehead. Niall unzipped the bag and put on the performance of a lifetime as he pretended he could see piles of money instead of newspapers. I had to clamp my lips together to stop them spreading into a smile. Who knew my brother-in-law was such a great actor?

'Jesus, that's a lot of cash! Did you two rob a bank?' Niall asked.

Mossy trembled from head to toe like he'd been dunked in a sheep dip as Eamonn tried to pull some swagger back on to his face, but the sweat on his upper lip betrayed his confidence. I placed my hand inside my coat pocket and felt the weight of Sean's pistol.

'What's going on?'

Mossy and Eamonn exchanged a glance, but no words passed between them. I was getting tired of Eamonn's refusal to come clean, so I pulled the gun out and aimed it at him. 'Maybe this might help to jog your memory. Where did the money come from?'

'I have no idea. Somebody's set me up,' Eamonn said, trying to act all innocent as he dumped the blame at Mossy's feet.

'Nice try.' I laughed. 'Did you seriously think I wouldn't find out about the cocaine?'

'Cocaine? I don't know what you're talking about.' Eamonn threw his hands up.

His denial was wasted on me. 'Like hell you don't. I know you hijacked my shipment.' I spat the words out like they were burning the inside of my mouth.

'You think I betrayed you? Christ, Josie, after all these years?' Eamonn planted a wounded expression on his face to display how much my accusation had offended him. His jaw tightened, and he spread his arms wide like he was saying Sunday mass. 'Do you really think I'd risk everything we've built for this?' He jabbed a finger towards the bag.

'Yes. You get paid well to turn a blind eye to my whiskey shipments, but what I grease your palm with doesn't compare to the amount of money in there. You stood to make a small fortune just from one drop,' I replied through gritted teeth as I gestured to the holdall that supposedly held his cash. 'I can't believe you thought you could cheat me.' I shook my head as I slowly walked around the desk. My heels clicked on the concrete floor as I circled him like a hawk waiting to swoop on a field mouse.

'I'm sorry, Josie. I got forced into it. You have no idea who you're dealing with. I didn't have a choice, I swear—'

'There's always a choice,' I replied, cutting him off mid-flow. 'But you made the wrong one.'

Eamonn's chest rose and fell fast as his composure crumbled.

'Did you stop to consider what would happen to you if I found out? No, of course you didn't because you were blinded by greed and the weight of the money in your pocket.' My voice was slow and steady as I took a step closer to him. I had the revolver raised, and my finger was on the trigger.

'For God's sake, Josie, it wasn't like that.' Eamonn snapped. 'I was going to hand over the money and tell you about the deal once it was completed.'

'Like hell you were.' Anger simmered inside me. My eyes pinned him to where he stood. I knew he was lying.

'Just think about it for a second. I could have vanished into thin air. But I didn't, did I? I stayed. Doesn't that tell you something? Doesn't that prove my loyalty?' His voice cracked as desperation began to seep through.

'It does nothing of the sort. You only stayed so you could get your grubby hands on the cash, which – in truth – belongs to me. You didn't give me a second thought when you used my cargo as a vessel. You put me at enormous risk. Have you forgotten the shipment was almost seized?' My heart was galloping in my chest. I was seething.

'No. I was the one who got it released! I'm telling you, Josie, you've got the wrong end of the stick. I never intended to keep all of the cash; I only ever wanted a cut.'

'Don't insult my intelligence.' I narrowed my eyes and glared at him. I didn't buy it for a second. All it told me was that he was greedy enough to think he could play me and not clever enough to believe I'd notice.

'It's God's honest truth, but I was sworn to secrecy, that's why I didn't mention it before. This could be a good business arrangement. I'd be happy to act as the middleman for future deals,' Eamonn offered.

'Let me tell you something, you're not getting a penny of the money. And there'll be no future deals. You don't have a future. You're not getting out of this room.'

'Please, Josie. I'm begging you. If you spare my life, I'll make it up to you.' Eamonn's shocked expression and his pathetic attempt to plead for mercy almost made me laugh. Enough was enough.

When I glanced over at Niall, he put the holdall down and paced over to Eamonn. My brother-in-law grabbed the traitor by the scruff of his coat and frogmarched him into the middle of the room.

'Get on your knees,' Niall ordered, pulling a length of rope out of his pocket.

The bluff drained out of Eamonn. His mouth opened and then shut. The room suddenly seemed smaller. The air was thick with tension. Mossy shifted from foot to foot, so I glanced over at him. He'd been quiet all along, but he seemed agitated. Unsettled. I could tell he didn't like where this was going, but he wouldn't dare speak up.

'I expected more from you. You wouldn't have done this if Sean had still been in charge, would you?' I spoke softly, but each word landed heavily.

Eamonn knelt in the middle of the floor. His wrists were bound in front of him, and sweat was running down the sides of his face. His breathing was coming in panicked gasps. His eyes darted around but refused to land on me.

'I can't believe you sold me out.' As I walked over to him, my heels clicked against the floor. I pointed the revolver at him, and its barrel gleamed in my hand. 'There's only one way this can end.'

'Josie, please d-don't d-do th-this,' Eamonn stammered as his words tumbled over each other. 'I t-told you, it w-wasn't like th-that.' His eyes were on stalks, and his mouth dropped open when I released the safety catch from the gun. The look on his face said it all. There was confusion first, then it dawned on him that his time was up. 'What the fuck is this, Josie? Have you lost your mind?' he shouted. Then he went to pieces, bawling his eyes out as his emotions got the better of him. His shoulders were shaking as he tried to compose himself. 'I've known your family for years, Josie. Please. Please. We go way back—' His voice cracked and he began to sob again.

I raised the pistol with steady hands as if I'd done this a hundred times before. He stared up into my face as I aimed the revolver between his eyes. My breath was measured as my eyes locked on his. My heart was beating like a drum. 'It's a shame our long connection meant nothing to you when you were given a better option. I won't stand for disloyalty. It can't go unpunished.'

'I'm sorry, Josie.'

As Eamonn uttered his final words, I squeezed the trigger. The shot rang out in the enclosed space. The bullet landed clean, punching a small, dark hole just above the bridge of his nose. For a split second, his expression froze in shock, then the force made Eamonn's head snap back before he dropped like a puppet would if its strings were cut. His eyes were still open wide when he hit the floor. A trickle of blood ran down his nose. It was stark against the pallor already creeping into his skin. A dark red pool started to spread around his head like a halo, blooming dark against the concrete.

Silence swallowed the space as a shiver ran down my spine. The disused warehouse was cold and damp, but that wasn't what had caused me to shudder. I got no pleasure from this part of the job. It was a means to an end. Survival. Word would soon spread around Dublin that I'd had the nerve to take out a man on his own ground. This was my declaration of war to anyone who doubted my authority. It sent a clear message of how far I was willing to go if anyone wronged me.

The sound of Mossy's ragged breathing caught my attention, so I slowly lowered the gun with my eyes still fixed on the Judas who'd paid the ultimate price. Flaherty had been standing off to the side with his hands buried in his pockets, trying to stay invisible. When I turned to face him, he was staring at the body on the floor with a horrified look on his face. He glanced over at me, and his Adam's apple bobbed in his throat. Watching me put a bullet in someone who'd been one of our own had made the situation very real. If I'd done that to Eamonn, there was no telling what I'd do to him.

'Was there something you wanted to say?' My words came out as sharp as a blade.

Mossy flinched, and his jaw tightened. I could see he was in shock. He knew his betrayal would have consequences, but the weight of what had just happened had hit him all the same.

'Is there a problem?' I asked, drilling into him with my stare when he remained silent.

Mossy shook his head, then he dropped his eyes to the ground to avoid my gaze. He fumbled in his pocket for his cigarettes with trembling fingers. Then he placed one in his mouth. As he cupped his hand around the match, it hid his face momentarily, but I'd registered the fear in his expression before he looked away.

'Good. Then we understand each other. Keep your mouth shut. You know nothing. You saw nothing. You heard nothing. If you think of wavering, you'll end up like Eamonn,' I said flatly as I turned away. If Mossy had a brain in his head, he'd know that following orders was safer than trying to stand against me. 'I'll leave you to organise the clean-up,' I said to Niall.

'No worries,' he replied.

I glanced over at Mossy. He was as pale as chalk. 'You were as much a part of this as he was,' I said, gesturing with a jerk of my head to the corpse on the floor. 'I'm counting on your loyalty from now on. Do you understand?'

Mossy nodded as he swallowed hard. He finally knew better

than to argue with me. I stepped over Eamonn's body and walked towards the loading doors. For the first time since Sean's death, I felt in complete control. My leadership had been tested like never before, but I was more than just a widow. I was the one holding the gun, and everyone else would have to learn to play by my rules.

35

ORLA

London, September 1985

I kicked my boots off and dangled my legs over the arm of Philomena's velvet sofa as I sprawled out on it and stared up at the chandelier. Her house smelled of roses and expensive air fresheners – nothing like ours, which only had an undertone of bleach in the air. Everything was perfect. Not a thing was out of place. The cushions were neat, like they'd been lined up with a ruler. Gleaming crystal sat on polished wood, and porcelain figures with painted faces seemed to watch me every time I moved. I was tempted to break one of them just to see Philomena's reaction, but she glided in from the hallway with her hips swaying, before I'd had the chance.

Philomena was wearing a cream silk blouse, tucked into a black pencil skirt with a wide belt cinching her waist. Her make-up was flawless. She'd teamed electric blue eyeshadow with bright pink lipstick, and had lacquered her blonde hair into place. She looked like she'd stepped out of one of the glossy magazines I sometimes flicked through at the newsagent.

'You must be bored stiff being here with me,' Philomena said, setting a tray with a jug of orange squash and a selection of cream cakes in front of me as though she was hosting royalty instead of her teenage niece.

'Not at all,' I lied, swinging my legs around and sitting up straight. There was a weird vibe going on between us. We usually got on really well, but I could tell she didn't approve of the way I'd made myself at home, not that she'd said anything. She didn't need to. It was written all over her face.

'It's a pleasure having you to stay, but I think it's terrible that your mother shuttles you about here, there and everywhere while she's off gallivanting.'

I felt my stomach knot. I recognised the tone. Philomena never missed an opportunity to stick the knife in, although I was shocked that she was being so open about it. She was waiting patiently for me to help her twist it, but before I could reply, two small whirlwinds tore into the room. Shannon came in first. She was seven and had the same honey-blonde hair as her mother. She was wearing a pale pink dress with puff sleeves and a lace collar, which I thought was a bit dressy for a mid-week afternoon, but she seemed delighted with the way the full skirt fanned out as she twirled around the room while she clutched a plastic doll with its hair hacked off, holding it like a trophy.

Five-year-old Tyrone appeared behind her. He had a round face with a mop of dark, curly hair. His pale blue jumper had a smear of jam across the front. Philomena's eyes widened when she caught sight of it. He had a toy car in one hand, which he promptly drove across the pristine coffee table. The wheels left faint streaks behind, and he grinned at me like he'd scored a point. I had to stop myself from laughing.

'Mind the table!' Philomena snapped as she glared at him. She softened instantly when she turned back to me with a sugary sweet smile on her face. 'You'll have to excuse them. They're very excited. They just adore having their big cousin here. Isn't that right, children?'

Shannon was staring at me in a suspicious manner, like I was an intruder. She was prissy and could be a little brat at times. I much preferred Tyrone. He was cheeky and had way more personality. He was a bit wilder and rougher around the edges. More like me. It didn't matter how well Philomena dressed him; within a short space of time, he'd have grass stains on his knees or mud under his fingernails.

'They're fine,' I said when neither of them replied.

Philomena poured a glass of squash and handed it to me. 'It must be horrible being farmed out while your mother runs off whenever the whim takes her,' she said, with a theatrical sigh as she tried to prise agreement out of me.

But Mum and I were struggling to hold the truce. Once she'd got over the shock, she'd been good about my pregnancy, although the temptation to be at each other's throats never really left us. That didn't mean I felt comfortable bad-mouthing her.

'I'd hardly go that far. This is the first time she's left me, and I'm fifteen. I'm not exactly a child.'

'But that's Josie all over, isn't it? Always thinking of herself. She should be putting your needs before her own, especially in your condition,' Philomena replied, completely ignoring what I'd just said.

I shrugged, but there was something about her tone that made me feel uncomfortable. I sat up a little. 'It's not as though she's jetted off halfway around the world on a month's holiday. She's only working away for two days!' I couldn't help feeling Philomena was making a mountain out of a molehill. She seemed ready to call social services to report my mum for neglecting her child.

Philomena let out a sharp laugh. 'Working? Is that what she told you? She's running around chasing scraps to make it look like she's in charge. But Niall's the one who keeps the business afloat. Josie doesn't know the first thing about how things operate.'

That could very well have been true, so I didn't bother to fight Mum's corner. I didn't give a shit about the business anyway, so I didn't want to get drawn into a lengthy discussion about it. All I knew was that it cost my dad and my uncle Rory their lives. Surely they were good enough reasons to change your line of work.

I let my gaze drift to the coffee table. Then I leaned forward, picked up a chocolate eclair and bit into it. The cream spurted out of the sides, and the sticky glaze clung to my teeth, so I kept my eyes on the French doors, which overlooked the manicured garden, while I tried to free it with my tongue. At first, I didn't notice Philomena waving the side plate in front of me. When I did, I almost rolled my eyes. She looked like she'd been smacked in the face with something horrific. Her blue eyes were on stalks as she hovered below my exploding cream cake with a napkin, ready to catch anything that dropped.

'It might be easier to eat that with a fork,' Philomena said, ramming the plate underneath the eclair.

'Thanks,' I replied. Her smile didn't falter, but she was on such high alert in case I made a mess that she'd put me off the cake. I didn't fancy it now. I just ate it to be polite. My jaw was tight, so I had to chew slowly. It was going to be a long couple of days.

Philomena sat beside me with her hands folded primly in her lap and her knees angled toward me. 'I do worry about you. It can't be easy living at home with just your mother.'

She said it with such compassion, but something else was

lurking beneath her concern. A dig. Or a test. I couldn't be sure. It was probably nothing, I told myself. But the way she was watching me unnerved me. It was as though she was expecting me to pour my heart and soul out to her, and it didn't sit right. Then some unpleasant thoughts crossed my mind. Did she really care about my welfare, or did she want me to pick sides? Was she being nice to me to turn me against my mum?

36

JOSIE

Mossy dropped us at the gates of Niall's house and then drove off as though the devil was on his tail. We exchanged a knowing look, the sort that came from long hours spent in each other's company. I was pretty sure we were thinking the same thing, although we said nothing. Mossy was terrified. He wanted to put as much distance as possible between us. I'd let him go, for now, but his card was marked.

Niall and I walked up the gravel driveway, side by side. Our movements were in step. Practised. My heartbeat sped up when my brother-in-law put the key into the lock and pushed open the front door. I followed him inside and immediately felt out of place. The house wasn't just a home; it was a statement. Philomena had stamped her mark all over it, so I never felt comfortable here.

The warmth was the first thing to hit me, followed by the scent of polish, fresh flowers, and the faint aroma of something simmering on the stove. Niall and Philomena's house was all clean lines. There wasn't a speck of dust in sight, not a scuff on the paintwork. It was amazing to think that two children lived here. It was amazing to think anyone lived here. It was like a show home.

Niall led the way into the living room. Orla was curled up on the sofa, leafing through a glossy magazine. She looked utterly at ease. For a moment, I stood rooted to the spot. My daughter seemed so content that a pang of jealousy stabbed me in the gut. Philomena was sitting next to her with a glass of wine clutched in her red talons, as she glanced at the copy of *Vogue* over Orla's shoulder.

'Hello, love,' Niall said, bounding over to his wife like a well-trained puppy. He stooped down and placed a kiss on her cheek. 'How's it going, Orla?'

'Fine, thanks,' she replied.

Philomena made a point of looking at her watch. Niall and I were later than expected, but the traffic had been murder from the moment we'd got off the ferry. 'So you're back from your little adventure in the big city, then. The pair of you look like you had a rare old time. Laughing all the way home, I'd say.' Philomena's scarlet lips parted into a fake smile.

Her comments made anger rise up inside me, but I wasn't about to give her the satisfaction of letting it show, so I grinned back at her, brushing off her barbed remarks. 'Our business went smoothly enough, didn't it, Niall?'

He gave a nod. 'We got the job done without a hitch.'

Philomena's eyes were sharp as she watched our exchange. She'd always had an issue with the closeness between us and never hid it very well.

'Are the kids in bed?' Niall asked after scanning the room.

'Where else would they be at this time of night?' Philomena snapped.

'I'll go and give them a kiss goodnight,' Niall replied, ignoring his wife's stroppy tone.

'There'll be hell to pay if you wake them,' she said. Her gaze followed him like a hawk's until he disappeared from sight.

'We should get going. It's late and you've got school in the morning,' I said. I had no intention of making small talk with Philomena while Niall was out of the room.

'Don't remind me.' Orla let out a groan, but didn't move right away.

Philomena rested her free hand lightly on Orla's shoulder possessively and smiled. 'It's a shame to drag her away. She can stay here another night. She's been no trouble. We've had a great time, haven't we, love?'

Orla nodded.

'No surprise; we always did get on famously.' Philomena beamed.

The closeness between them was clear. Pain landed like a fist in my ribs, and my gut twisted in response. 'Go and get your bag, please. It's time we went home,' I replied, ignoring my sister-in-law's offer. The words came out sharper than I'd intended, and Philomena's sculpted eyebrows raised like she'd been slapped around the face.

Orla hesitated. Her eyes flicked from me to Philomena as though she wasn't sure who to listen to. The pause was only a heartbeat, but it cut me to the core.

'You'd better do as your mum says.' The blonde witch gave me a sly smile as she rubbed Orla's shoulder.

My jaw tightened. I was silently seething, but I didn't respond.

'You need to take better care of her, Josie. She deserves someone who'll cherish her. Motherhood isn't a part-time job,' Philomena said after Orla left the room, leaning in to me and dropping her voice so we wouldn't be overheard.

My heart hammered in my chest. Philomena was all jagged edges. She didn't waste time with hints. She went straight for the jugular. Even though her words stung, I wasn't going to give her the satisfaction of seeing me crack.

'While you've been off gallivanting with my husband, I've grown even closer to Orla.' Philomena flashed me a wolfish grin sharp enough to cut.

I stiffened, just slightly, then covered it with a laugh. I wanted to scratch her eyes out, but I didn't react because I knew exactly what was happening here. 'I'm glad to hear that,' I replied, but I didn't mean a word of what I'd just said. I should have known better than to leave Orla in her care. The woman was toxic and never missed an opportunity to fill people's heads with poisonous thoughts about me.

'Orla's a young woman who's soon to be a mother. She needs your undivided attention, but you're always too busy. You never have time for her. What kind of example are you setting?'

The way Philomena was talking, she thought she knew my daughter better than I did. Her words landed like a stone dropped in water. I felt the ripple, deep in my gut. I turned my face away for a moment when I felt the stab of tears. Then I looked back at the smiling assassin with my jaw tight.

'I'm never too busy for Orla. She has always been and always will be my number one priority. I don't appreciate you suggesting otherwise,' I said through gritted teeth.

Philomena laughed. 'Children need stability. I'd never leave mine to fend for themselves the way you do with Orla. It's no wonder she's gone off the rails. It's your fault she's wild. There haven't been any slammed doors, rolled eyes, or bitter retorts from her in this house. She's been an absolute delight. You bring out the worst in her.'

As the words left her mouth, they jabbed me like barbed wire. I couldn't hide the hurt I felt, which made my sister-in-law's lips stretch into a triumphant smile. She was really digging the knife in. I tried to keep my expression neutral as my knuckles whitened around my bag's strap.

Philomena and I stood glaring at each other when Orla appeared in the doorway. 'Do you want to get going?' she said. She had her school blazer draped over one arm and her weekend bag clutched in her hand.

The sight of her tugged at my heartstrings. Philomena had really hit a nerve when she'd accused me of neglecting my precious girl. With her ripped tights and her red curls, she conjured up a picture of Little Orphan Annie in my head, and I had to stop myself from bursting into tears. It had been a long and stressful couple of days. I could have done without a run-in with the woman who thought she was the queen bee.

'Take care of yourself, pet. You're welcome here any time,' Philomena said in a sickly-sweet tone. She looked daggers at me before she pulled Orla into a hug.

My chest tightened when I saw the way my daughter leaned into her aunt. The movement looked natural. They were comfortable with each other, which cut me to the quick. Philomena had done real damage in a couple of days. She'd carved me right out of the picture. I swallowed hard. My head was spinning. The room suddenly felt stifling.

'Thanks for having her,' I said to interrupt their hug, masking my hurt with a tight smile. Orla went to pull away, but Philomena's touch lingered just long enough to make it feel like she was laying down a challenge.

'Are you off now?' Niall asked as he walked towards us. His eyes flicked between myself and Philomena. I knew he could feel the tension, but he kept quiet.

I nodded. 'I'm shattered and Orla has school in the morning.'

'Let me show you out.' Philomena's voice came out like silk over steel.

When she wafted past me in her Cadbury's purple long-sleeved jumpsuit, which had large shoulder pads, tapered legs and was cinched in at the waist by a wide belt, I almost choked on the cloud of perfume surrounding her. I couldn't bear the smell of Poison. It was so overpowering, much like my sister-in-law. It was very apt that it was her favourite scent. She was always doused in the stuff.

'I'll give you a lift,' Niall offered.

'There's no need,' I replied. We only lived around the corner.

Orla and I said our goodbyes before we headed out the front door. My pulse was hammering in my wrist when we stepped on to the gravel. The weight of Philomena's words was pressing down on me. I hated how much I'd let her rattle me. I couldn't wait to put some distance between us.

The street lamps hummed faintly overhead as we made the short walk home. Our shadows stretched across the pavement in front of us. There was a chill in the air, so I turned up the collar of my coat.

'So, how was it?' I asked, glancing sideways at my daughter.

The toe of Orla's boot kicked a loose stone as though she was trying to choose her words carefully. 'It was OK,' she eventually replied.

'But Philomena said you'd had a great time...' I was expecting her to be buzzing about the experience.

'We did.' Orla threw me a black look.

'Make up your mind, Orla. Was it OK or great? They're hardly the same thing!' I tried to keep my tone light, but the despair I felt was shining through, and I couldn't disguise it. I wanted her to tell me she'd hated every minute of it and she'd just gone along with pretending to enjoy herself to keep the peace.

'What do you want me to say? It's so obvious it bothers you that I enjoyed myself. I didn't expect to. I thought it would be a nightmare being stuck in a house with a couple of young kids. But it wasn't. I had a ball. Are you happy now?' Orla's face was like thunder.

The last thing I wanted was for us to have an argument, so I linked her arm, but she shrugged me away. Her rejection stung. 'I'm glad you had fun.' I knew I didn't sound convincing.

'Philomena showed me some old photos and told me loads of stories about Dad,' Orla said.

My breath hitched in my chest, and my jaw tightened. 'I have plenty of things I can tell you about him.'

'I'm sure you do, but you don't bother, do you?' Orla shot back.

'What would you like to know?'

Orla shrugged. 'You don't talk about Dad like she does. She made him feel real. Like he wasn't a ghost.'

The wind lifted my hair as though Sean was making his presence felt.

'Do you think she knew him better than I did? She had no right to fill your head with stories. It's not her place—'

'She's got every right!' Orla shouted, cutting me off. Frustration was flaring in her eyes. 'You asked me how it was, so I'm telling you. And yeah, I had a brilliant time, all right? She treated me like I wasn't—' Orla swallowed the rest of her sentence as she turned her face away.

'Like you weren't what?' I demanded. My tone was firmer now.

Orla's expression was sullen again. 'Forget it.'

'I won't forget it. Tell me.'

'Christ, Mum, she made me feel like I wasn't invisible for once.'

My jaw tightened, but Orla wasn't done laying into me yet.

'You're so busy running the business, keeping control of

everyone, you don't have time for me unless I'm in trouble. And you wonder why I'm always out?'

My features hardened as fury simmered beneath the hurt. 'I can't believe you just said that to me. Do you think I'd rather be working than spending time with you? Everything I do is for you,' I said, reeling from the wake-up call.

'Well, don't bother. I don't want any of it. I'm fed up with your constant nagging. As soon as I turn sixteen, I'm moving out, and there's nothing you can do about it!' Orla's voice cracked with rage, but she didn't back down.

'You can't move out. What about the baby? How are you going to manage?'

The silence that followed was heavier than the damp air pressing in around us as the gulf between us widened. We stood under the street lamp, both breathing hard, neither willing to look away first. Finally, I turned and paced up the street. My shoulders were rigid. My lips were pressed into a thin line. Orla trailed behind, scuffing her boots along the pavement. What she'd said had landed hard. But now that it was out in the open, it couldn't be taken back. It had hurt me deeper than I wanted to admit. I couldn't bear to look at the brat I'd raised.

37

ORLA

Fury still simmered inside me after the row with Mum. She thought Philomena was driving a wedge between us when she was the one doing that. The more she put into being a leader, the more I felt motherless. I'd been lying awake all night, staring at the ceiling, mulling things over as the darkness pressed down on me. Every time I closed my eyes, I saw my mum's face. Heard her clipped tone. I'd hoped my pregnancy might repair our broken bond and bring us closer together, but we were still treading on eggshells around each other.

I'd been dreading staying at Philomena's posh house, but after my initial unease, she'd made me feel welcome in a way I never did at home. We'd never really spent much time together as Mum didn't like her. From the unsubtle digs Philomena had made, it was clear the feeling was mutual.

I was buzzing with too much anger to settle. I felt too much hurt to cry. It was pointless just lying here. I threw back the covers, got out of bed and started to pace the room, tearing at my cuticles until they stung. Everything in here felt suffocating. The walls, the posters, even the air. I couldn't sit still. I couldn't shake the anger crawling under my skin. I needed to get out of here.

The curtains were drawn tight against the street below. When I parted them, the sky outside was bruising into daylight. It was almost seven. Mum would be awake soon. I didn't have time to waste, so I didn't bother changing out of yesterday's clothes. I didn't care that I'd slept in them. I yanked my jacket off the chair and grabbed my bag, shoving my uniform inside it. I wanted her to think I'd gone in early when she discovered I wasn't here. School wasn't on my agenda for today. I couldn't sit in a classroom while I felt like this. I wouldn't be able to concentrate, so what was the point?

Without turning on the lights, I crept out of my room and inched across the landing. The house was still. Silent. Mum wasn't up yet. Thank God. I didn't want to see her. Didn't want her to see me. My pulse was thudding in my ears as I slowly went downstairs, holding my breath every time one of the treads creaked. I tiptoed along the hallway and slipped out the front door. I was tempted to slam it shut. I wanted the whole house to feel my rage, but I couldn't afford to raise the alarm.

As I hurried down the path, the cold air hit me, causing me to shudder. I pulled my jacket tighter against the chill as I rushed to the next street. Majella's house loomed ahead. The curtains were still drawn on the windows. She was probably still asleep.

I bent down and picked up a few small stones from the gutter. The damp grit surrounding them clung to my fingers as I aimed. I flicked one of them upwards. It bounced harmlessly against the glass. The sound was too soft to rouse anyone. So I hurled another, harder this time. The clack rang out in the quiet street. For a moment, nothing happened, but then the curtains twitched. The window creaked open, and Majella leaned out. Her hair was messy from sleep. Her bleary eyes were narrowed in confusion. I grinned up at her from the pavement as my breath misted in the cool air.

'What's going on?' she croaked.

'I had a fight with my mum. Can you come down?'

Majella nodded. 'Give me a couple of minutes.'

'For God's sake, hurry up. It's freezing out here.'

The houses in Majella's street seemed to watch us as we fell into step without a word. Some of their lights snapped on like spying eyes, keeping tabs on us. To distract me from it, I pulled a packet of Silk Cut out of my jacket pocket and offered one to Jella. Smoking was bad for the baby, but that wasn't going to stop me. After both of us had lit up, we blew rings into the morning air as we headed to the bus stop. We knew where we were going even though we hadn't discussed it. We were obsessed with Camden and the freedom it gave us.

* * *

When we stepped off the bus, Shay was leaning against the railing. My pulse started galloping at the sight of him. I hadn't seen him for months.

'Are you going to tell him?' Majella whispered.

I shook my head. I'd have to let him in on the secret at some stage. I wouldn't be able to hide my bump much longer, but I was desperate to spend time with him, and I didn't want anything to ruin that.

'What are you two doing here?' he asked.

'Bunking off,' I replied with a grin on my face.

Majella opened her schoolbag and pulled out a bottle of vodka. 'I swiped this from my mum's cupboard. She won't miss it. She was smashed out of her skull again last night. She'll just think she polished it off herself. Care to join us?'

'I know just the place,' Shay replied, leading the way.

The stairwell stank of piss and damp concrete, and huge cobwebs clung to the corners. Shay moved quickly, taking the steps two at a time. I glanced over my shoulder several times as we trailed after him. Every footstep echoed too loudly on the climb to the first floor. By the time he shoved the scuffed door to the flat open with his shoulder, I already knew there'd be no turning around.

The place was bare bones. A couple of stained mattresses lay on the floor next to overflowing ashtrays. The plaster was cracked in jagged veins up the graffiti-covered walls, and the windows were boarded up so the daylight couldn't get in. An old electric heater hummed in the corner, giving off more noise than heat. It felt like a place cut off from the world.

Majella dumped her bag down on the floor. 'Let's get the party started.' She laughed as she pulled the vodka out like a prize in a raffle. The sound of her voice seemed too loud in the small space. She wasted no time unscrewing the cap. She was grinning from ear to ear as she held it up to her lips and took a swig. Her face contorted as the neat alcohol burned its way down her throat.

Majella went to pass the bottle to Shay, but he was busy watching me, not her. His gaze was intense as he fished a bag of pills from his pocket. 'This stuff is better than vodka. These'll take you further. Do you want some?' He smirked.

I felt the weight of the question and hesitated. My eyes flicked to my bestie to gauge her reaction as my stomach twisted into a knot.

She was nodding as she replied. 'Hell, yeah!' Majella already had her arm stretched towards Shay. He dropped a pink pill on to her palm, and she washed it down with a hard gulp of vodka.

Shay followed suit before he turned his attention back to me. 'What about you? You up for it?'

'What is it?' I asked.

'Who cares?' Majella shot back before Shay had a chance to respond.

'It's ecstasy,' Shay replied.

'Go on, Orla. Don't be a killjoy.' Majella's tone was daring.

'Honestly, you'll be fine,' Shay said with a smile on his face.

My heart was hammering. I shouldn't. I knew I should say no, but the word caught in my throat, and I gave Shay a nod instead. My stomach swirled, but I grabbed the pills he handed me anyway. My fingers were clumsy when I picked them up and tossed them into my mouth like I was on autopilot. How much harm could they do? The vodka clawed at my throat as I swallowed the tablets. The taste was sharp, chemical and bitter. They coated my tongue even after they were gone.

There was no doubt I was being reckless, but it felt like the answer. I didn't want to think about my pregnancy. I didn't want to think about the argument or hear Mum's voice in my head any more. The thought of going home, of seeing her, of suffering another lecture made me want to scream. I just wanted to be with Majella and Shay. I wanted to block everything else out. I wanted numbness.

Shay sat down on the mattress, so Majella and I did the same. He propped himself up against the wall, lit a spliff and passed it around. The air filled with the sweet, heavy haze of cannabis. The smoke burned my throat and made my eyes water, but I forced myself to take another drag anyway when it passed my way. I didn't want him to think anything was wrong. I wanted to fit in.

'Can you feel the buzz?' Shay asked, his grin lingering.

Majella started laughing, answering his question with a cackle.

I nodded as the mixture of vodka, ecstasy and weed came creeping in and began to crawl under my skin, making it prickle. As the bottle sank lower, the haze pressed in closer. Our laughter got louder and echoed off the bare plaster.

A near-empty bottle of vodka lay between us, and a bag of pills littered the ground as Shay began rolling another joint. Majella was laughing about something, but I didn't know what. I felt a bit woozy. Everything around me was swimming. Jella and I were lying sprawled across the mattress. Suddenly, everything went quiet. There was something about the silence that felt dangerous – like we'd crossed into a place we couldn't come back from.

'Are you all right, Orla? You look a bit pale.' Shay stopped what he was doing and gazed at me.

I tried to focus on him, but I was seeing double. I was really feeling the effects of the booze, weed and ecstasy.

'I'm fine. I'm just chilling. Floating,' I slurred, looking up at the ceiling. The swirly pattern of the anaglypta made my eyes blink. It was strangely hypnotic.

Majella laughed as Shay handed her the spliff. She took a long drag before shoving it towards me, but I couldn't take it. The edges of everything were blurring. Something was wrong. My limbs were slack, and I felt like I was sweating despite the chill in the room. I started to shake. Felt myself lose control. Felt myself spiralling.

My pulse quickened and started thudding through my veins. My chest was tight, and my heartbeat kept skipping like a scratch on a record. A cold edge seeped in under the rush. The walls seemed to lean and close in on me, making me claustrophobic.

'Orla. Orla. Are you OK?' Majella's voice sounded distant.

I opened my mouth and tried to reply, but no words came out.

'You gave her two, didn't you? The pink ones?' I heard Majella say.

'I thought she could handle it,' Shay replied.

'Babe, are you OK?' I felt Majella touch my hand. 'Her lips are going blue.'

Majella sounded panicked, but I couldn't answer. I couldn't put her mind at rest. My insides were convulsing, so I rolled onto my side. The mattress dipped and shifted beneath us. The movement made me retch, but barely anything came up. I clutched my stomach as the world began spinning around me.

'Shit! Orla. Orla?' Shay called.

I felt Majella's fingertips rub the back of my hand. 'Orla! Can you hear me? Jesus, Shay, she's foaming at the mouth!'

I was aware of the conversation going on around me, but I was too out of it to contribute. My thoughts were sliding into dark corners.

'You told her she'd be fine! She's had an overdose, hasn't she? We need to get help. We need to get her to the hospital. Now.' Majella's voice was frantic.

The last thing I remembered was feeling somebody's hands, most likely Shay's, slip under my body and lift me into their arms. I heard myself let out a faint groan, and then everything went black.

38

JOSIE

'Where is she?' I demanded, storming over to Majella.

She was standing outside the entrance of University College Hospital with her arms wrapped around herself and the weight of the world on her young shoulders.

'She's in A & E,' Majella whimpered as tears began to flow down her face.

But I wasn't about to waste time comforting the girl who was such a bad influence on my daughter. I threw her a black look as I rushed off to find Orla with my half-buttoned coat flapping behind me.

Fluorescent lights flickered overhead as I waited in line at the counter, willing the queue to move faster. 'I'm looking for my daughter, Orla O'Connor,' I said to the woman behind the desk when it was finally my turn.

She tore her eyes away from mine for a moment, and when she looked back at me, she had a worried expression pasted on her face.

'She's in Resus. You can go straight through,' the woman replied, pointing out the direction.

My pulse was pounding in my ears as I crossed the waiting room floor. I gasped at the sight of Orla on a stretcher. Her limbs were limp, her head was lolled to the side, and she was covered in vomit. I quickened my pace to catch up with her.

'Orla,' I called.

She didn't reply, but one of the nurses accompanying her looked over her shoulder at me.

'Are you her mother?' she asked.

'Yes. Is she going to be OK?' The words came out in a panicked gasp as I battled to hold back my tears.

The nurse didn't respond. A doctor barking orders had her full attention.

'We need charcoal. Prepare for gastric lavage,' he said as they wheeled Orla into a cubicle. A moment later, blue drapes drew around it, blocking my precious girl from sight.

The curtain was thin. It was the kind that swayed with every movement and couldn't muffle the chaos behind it. I stood on the other side of it, fighting back tears.

'Her BP's dropping. It's eighty over fifty,' a nurse said, and my heart started hammering in my chest.

'Get another line in. She's dehydrated. Do we know what she took?' the doctor asked.

I held my breath while I waited for the nurse's response.

'Her friends said she'd had vodka, cannabis, and two ecstasy tablets. But you know what teenagers are like. They don't always admit to everything.'

My head felt like it was about to explode. My worry had twisted into something ugly. Something bitter. Why was Orla the only one in this state? How come Majella hadn't been affected? Not that I was wishing her any ill, but it didn't make any sense to me. With the dire situation my daughter was in at the forefront of my mind, something suddenly occurred to me. The nurse had said her friends had brought her in. Plural. Who else was she hanging around with behind my back?

I waited helplessly as the medical team worked on Orla. I felt my features harden as rage consumed me. I slipped my hand into my coat pocket and pulled out my crystal rosary. As I recited a Hail Mary in my head, fear began swirling inside me. I'd never forgive myself if something happened to Orla or my unborn grandchild. Was this God's punishment for all the sins I'd committed?

'Please don't take them,' I whispered as tears rolled down my face.

'We'll prepare to pump her stomach,' the doctor said, and my hand flew up to my mouth as a wail escaped.

'She looks very flushed,' the nurse replied.

'Take her temperature, and someone get some fans and ice packs. What is it?' the doctor asked.

'Forty degrees,' the nurse replied.

I frowned as the number slid around in my head like a loose screw. That meant nothing to me, not really. I hadn't got to grips with the new measurement, but I was fairly certain that thirty-eight degrees Celsius was roughly equivalent to one hundred degrees Fahrenheit, and Orla was hotter than that, so her temperature was dangerously high. Merciful Lord, she was on fire!

I leaned closer until my forehead was nearly touching the curtain as my fingers twisted around the rosary. A metallic clatter made me jump. My heart was pounding. I gripped the curtain edge, but I didn't pull it back. I was scared of what I'd see.

'She's fitting!' the nurse said.

'No, no no no no...' I wailed. 'Don't you dare take them from me,' I said to the crucifix gripped in my hand. Never before had my faith been tested to such a degree. It had been rocked when I'd watched Sean's life slip away, but the thought of losing my child and my grandchild was a new kind of agony. If that happened, I wouldn't be strong enough to bear the pain.

'Get her on to her side and make sure she doesn't fall. Clear the area of hazards. Don't let her aspirate. Keep her airway open,' the doctor ordered.

My head was spinning. I could only imagine what was going on inside the cubicle. I could hear Orla thrashing about, which was so distressing, but then everything went quiet. Everything went still. I thought I'd lost her. I wrenched open the drapes, and the medical team turned to look at me.

'Dear God, is she dea...' I let the word trail off. I couldn't bring myself to say it.

'Mum, I presume,' the doctor replied.

I nodded my head. My hands were covering my mouth. I craned my neck to look past him, but he was blocking my view of Orla.

'Please take a seat in the waiting room. I'll come and talk to you later. Your daughter's very sick and she needs my undivided attention.' He gestured for me to leave before he turned his back on me.

I let the curtain drop and stood rooted to the spot, trying to register what he'd just said. Orla was very sick. She wasn't dead. I blew out a breath, then I lifted the rosary to my lips and placed a kiss on the silver cross. 'Thank you,' I whispered.

'How's her temperature?' the doctor asked.

'Climbing. It's forty-one degrees.'

'Come on, Orla, stay with us,' the doctor said.

I pressed my fist to my mouth to stifle a sob when I heard him say my daughter's name with a sense of urgency. It cut like glass. I felt helpless knowing her fate wasn't in my hands.

'You fight, Orla. Do you hear me? You fight with everything you've got.' My voice was low and desperate.

'Her heart rate's erratic. One hundred and seventy and climbing,' the nurse said.

A long beep. Then another. And another.

'We're losing her. Get the crash cart.'

I gasped and backed away from the curtain like it had scalded me. My breath hitched. My chest tightened. My eyes were wide with terror. Listening to the medical team battling to save them was pure torture.

'Please. Please. Please. I'll do anything. Just don't take them.' I sobbed. My legs had turned to jelly, so I stumbled over to a plastic chair across from the curtain and buried my face in my hands. My shoulders were shaking as tears slipped silently down my cheeks. I dug my fingers into my scalp as I let out a juddering breath.

A tense, awful silence came from behind the curtain. All sorts of horrors were racing through my mind as the seconds ticked by. And then the soft beep of the heart monitor filled the air as it found its rhythm again. I lifted my head. My mouth was open in disbelief.

'Her heart rate is stabilising. One hundred and ten and falling,' the nurse said.

'How's the baby doing?' the doctor asked.

'Better than before.'

I'd never been so relieved in my life. It was so sudden, it nearly knocked the breath from my lungs. I wrapped my arms around myself to try to bring myself some comfort. I wished somebody was here with me, but I'd rushed out of the house as soon as Majella had called to say that Orla was in the hospital. I'd call Niall and Biddy as soon as things settled down. I didn't dare move. I sat staring at the curtain in awe, as if it was a holy relic. The storm hadn't passed, but Orla and the baby were still fighting. Still alive.

A wave of nausea swept over me, so I got to my feet and staggered towards the main entrance. I needed to get some air. Majella was standing awkwardly near the double doors, pale with panic. I could see she was crying, even from a distance. Her black eyeliner was streaked down her face. But I didn't care. The sight of her made rage claw its way up from the pit of my stomach.

'Where did you get the drugs from?' I shouted, powered by fury.

Majella's head snapped up at the sound of my voice. A nurse eyed me suspiciously as I bowled towards the teenage girl with fury pumping out of every pore in my body.

'What did you give her?' My eyes were blazing.

'I didn't give her anything,' Majella replied, shaking her head.

'Don't you fucking lie to me. The nurse said her friends reported she'd had vodka, cannabis, and two ecstasy tablets. She's fifteen. She's pregnant.' My voice cracked with emotion, so I steeled myself and carried on. 'She's had a fit and her heart's been beating way too fast. You'd better hope to God she doesn't die.' Majella looked terrified, but that didn't stop me from jabbing my finger in the little bitch's face. 'What have you got to say for yourself?'

'I'm sorry, Mrs O'Connor.' Majella cast her eyes to the floor. At least she'd had the good grace to look embarrassed.

'I know you're angry, but shouting at her isn't going to make your daughter better,' a woman's voice said.

I turned to see who was speaking to me. It was the nurse who'd been eyeing me when I'd stormed up to Majella.

'I was here when this girl and the young lad brought her in. She was in a bad way, but they did the right thing by getting help. Early intervention can make a big difference to the outcome.

Your daughter's friends looked out for her. You should be thanking them, not berating them.'

I felt my mouth drop open. I was speechless. The last thing I expected was to receive a dressing-down from Florence Nightingale.

'What young lad? Who else were you with?' I asked Majella, turning my attention away from the domineering nurse.

Majella stared at me, but her eyes didn't seem to be focusing on me. It was like she was in another world. I was about to repeat the question when a teenage boy with brown shoulder-length hair stuck his head around the corner.

'She was with me. What's it to you?' the cocky little shit asked. North London's streets had shaped his accent.

There was a flicker of recognition. He looked vaguely familiar, but I was taken aback by his rudeness and sudden appearance and didn't have the brain capacity to try to place him, so I pushed the thought from my head.

'Did you force my daughter to take ecstasy?' I fumed as anger rose up inside me again.

'I didn't force her to do anything. She took the pills of her own free will,' the teenager with the floppy hair replied. I didn't appreciate the way he'd raised his voice and squared up to me. I could see he was the kind of lad who walked through life with a chip on his shoulder and too much weight in his eyes for someone so young.

'This isn't the time or the place to air your differences. Please go and wait in the relatives' room. The doctor will come and speak to you once he's finished treating your daughter,' the nurse said, intervening before anything escalated.

That was a smart move, as I was one step away from battering the young lad. He didn't seem the type to shy away from a fight, even if it was with a woman old enough to be his mother. I stomped off to find the room without saying another word.

39

DECLAN

Dublin, September 1985

I was taking a big risk piggybacking Cormac's system, using the IRA's smuggling routes to import the guns to London, but he knew a lot more about the game than I did, so it made sense to tap into his knowledge. I could tell he resented my motives, that I was purely in it for the profit I'd make supplying the Camden crew. I didn't give a shit about the political struggle, not that I'd openly admit that to a sympathiser.

Cormac and I were holed up in his lock-up in the Liberties while we waited for the shipment to arrive. He was perched on the edge of a crate, watching me like a hawk. Something unreadable was behind his eyes, which was making me nervous. Paranoid. I was beginning to doubt whether he was a reliable source. Was he about to betray me?

'There's nothing easy about any of this. One rat, one checkpoint, and it all turns to ash. The fact that you're shifting guns for money and not for a united Ireland won't sit easily with some. If you piss off the wrong quartermaster, they'll feed you to the pigs,' Cormac warned.

I'd been fed to worse, I thought, as a vision of Josie popped into my head.

Kicking my heels was the worst bit of the whole operation. I couldn't take much more of it. I turned away from Cormac and started to pace the room. The tense atmosphere was making the place feel claustrophobic. The metal walls were sweating with condensation, and the only light was a bare bulb overhead. Boxes of smuggled cigarettes and contraband booze lined the walls.

'What's up, Declan? Is that lot bringing back bad memories and making you feel uncomfortable?' Cormac taunted as he gestured towards the stash.

'Of course not,' I lied, keeping my voice steady. Inside I was riled up, but I didn't want him to know that.

'Looks to me like you're regretting sidestepping into smuggling arms.' Cormac smiled.

'It's not that. I hate hanging around. I'm a busy man,' I said through gritted teeth.

'Busy hiding from Josie O'Connor.' Cormac let out a belly laugh.

'I'm not hiding from anyone.' I felt my features darken. His taunt wasn't just an insult. He'd shone a spotlight on my loss of dignity. Josie's attack had rattled me in a way I didn't want to acknowledge even privately.

'Is that so. Word on the street is you're terrified of the little woman. I'm not surprised. Her size is pretty intimidating. What is she, six stone when she's wet through!'

Cormac was in stitches. I didn't appreciate being laughed at. It bothered me to think people were talking about me behind my back. Talking about my fear of Josie.

'You're so full of crap it's unreal! The reason I've moved to arms smuggling is because there's a lot more profit in this line of work. It's as simple as that!' I snapped, slightly losing control. I rarely raised my voice and was worried I'd overcompensated so I wouldn't appear weak.

That wasn't the case. I'd never admit to anyone that I'd retreated to Dublin following the trouble with Josie in London for my own safety and a chance to rebuild my pride. After she'd instructed her men to give me a near-death pasting, I'd decided the sensible thing to do was to stay out of her way. I was scared to step on her toes after what she'd done to me, and keen to walk down a different path, leaving the whiskey smuggling operation behind. It pained me to think people had seen through my career move.

'You're a feckin' eejit if you think anyone believes that crock of shit. Sit the fuck down. You're getting on my nerves. You're like a dog on heat.' Cormac flashed me a look and then calmly rolled a cigarette.

There was no point in trying to convince him otherwise; his mind was made up. I was only making things worse, insisting the whispers were wrong. It left a bad taste to think that Josie had got one over on me again. It was embarrassing and humiliating. She'd taken away my power and status. Cormac was mocking her size. But he had no idea. He'd do well not to underestimate the little woman, as he put it. Although if the opportunity ever arose for her to put him in his place, I'd love to have a front row seat.

'I don't like being kept waiting. You did it to me on Parnell Square, now this.'

'I'm risking my arse trying to assemble this shipment. I explained to you when we met in The Three Chimneys that I'd have to move the guns in small batches into the city along farm tracks and back lanes in case they're intercepted. The weapons are under constant threat from British and Irish security services, so we have to move them around a lot. Some of the guns you ordered were being hidden in farm outbuildings in Donegal. The stuff's not on the doorstep. My guys are collecting the order from multiple locations. They'll get here when they get here.' Cormac was in a strop. The words had barely left his mouth when the sound of a van pulling into the yard caught our attention.

Cormac stood beside me with his jaw clenched and his black leather jacket zipped up high as we watched the man in the passenger seat jump out. He walked around to the back door and threw it open. Crates were stacked from floor to ceiling inside the van. While we waited for the man to prise open the nearest box with a crowbar, Cormac's eyes flicked to the shadows more than once, although he was trying to be discreet about it. He was suddenly acting suspiciously, which made me nervous. Did I have a reason to be?

'You seem very jumpy,' I pointed out.

'It's a big run. There's a lot on the line. One slip and it's a life sentence,' he replied.

'Are you worried there are eyes on us?'

'I've not seen any.' Cormac's gaze swept around the vicinity again to double-check.

'Do you want to take a look?' the man asked, having removed the lid.

I stepped towards the back of the van, lifted the cloth and peered at the stash of rifles. Then I flicked my eyes back to Cormac and gave him a nod.

'Happy now?' Cormac asked, glaring at me.

The man didn't wait for me to reply before he hammered the lid shut again and closed the van's doors.

'I'll be off now, boss,' he said to Cormac before he slipped out of the yard.

'Did you check all of the crates yourself?' I asked, narrowing my eyes.

'My guys checked them twice. Now let's get out of here,' Cormac replied.

I nodded even though I wasn't sure I could fully trust him.

Cormac wiped his palms on his jeans and then paced over to the cab. He climbed inside to ride up front with the driver. When I took the seat next to him, he didn't look my way. He kept glancing in the side mirror every few minutes, which did nothing to calm my nerves. I wondered what loyalty was worth these days. Very little, I suspected.

Cormac seemed nervous. He kept shifting in his seat as his jaw worked overtime, and his fingers twitched. The driver said nothing. He just shoved the van into gear and drove away from the lock-up. The air inside the cab felt tighter. Smuggling barrels of whiskey was child's play compared to this. A growing dread and sense of unease made me realise I'd underestimated the danger involved, but I was too far down the line to back out now.

40

JOSIE

London, September 1985

Harsh fluorescent lights hummed overhead as Niall, Biddy and I sat huddled together, hands clasped around plastic cups of tea, waiting for news. The walls were a sickly pale colour, and the chairs were hard and uncomfortable. I hunched forward, placed the unpalatable drink on the floor and then rested my elbows on my knees with my hands clasped tightly, staring straight ahead. The room was still and silent. Worried thoughts weighed heavily on all of us.

When I spotted a nurse walking along the corridor, I bolted upright. My eyes followed her, but she didn't stop. Didn't look my way. She just hurried past, and my heart sank. No news. Again.

I put my hand inside my pocket and pulled out my rosary. I pressed the crucifix into the palm of my hand and closed my fist around it as I whispered under my breath, 'Dear Lord, please let Orla and the baby get through this.' I didn't have any right to ask for God's help. To ask for favours. Not after what I'd done. After the sins I'd committed. But I had to try. I had to hope the

Almighty was still listening to my prayers. 'Please don't take them. I'm begging you.' I lifted the silver cross to my lips and kissed it. Then I closed my eyes. My heart was hammering in my chest. My breathing was rapid as I tried to keep it together. Why wasn't Sean watching over Orla like I'd asked him to?

The doors wheezed open and shut as a pair of ambulance men entered with a patient on a stretcher. I looked away and turned my focus back to the corridor where Orla was being treated as time marched on. Why was it taking so long to stabilise her? To stabilise the baby? I clung to the hope that at least they hadn't given up on them.

Emotions started swirling around my body. The rage. The grief. The helplessness. But worst of all, the fear. That was the loudest. It was making its presence felt. Orla meant everything to me. I'd give my life if it meant she could walk out of here. I glanced down at the rosary and silently asked, *You want penance? Take it. Take anything. Just let her live.*

A moment later, footsteps approached. The doctor appeared at the glass. His face was taut. He looked fatigued. I stared at him like he was some kind of ghost. Some sort of apparition.

'Mrs O'Connor?' he asked as he walked into the room.

I leapt out of the chair so fast I almost stumbled. Niall and Biddy jumped to their feet too.

'How is she?' My voice cracked. I swallowed down the panic and clamped my trembling lip between my teeth.

'Mr O'Connor?' The doctor was addressing Niall.

'Yes, but I'm Orla's uncle. Her father's dead,' he replied, and his voice wavered. Even after all this time, he still struggled with the loss of his brother.

'And you are?' the doctor asked Biddy.

'I'm Orla's godmother and a close friend of the family.'

The doctor nodded.

'To answer your question, Mrs O'Connor,' he said, turning his attention back to me, 'we've managed to stabilise your daughter. She's still drowsy, but she's come through the worst of it and is breathing on her own.'

'Thank you.' The words escaped in a ragged sob. My knees buckled, so I gripped the back of the chair. I didn't know who I was thanking more: God or the doctor. Both of them had played a hand in saving Orla's life. 'And the baby?'

He paused just long enough for my heart to start galloping again. 'The baby's heartbeat is strong. For now. But an overdose like this increases the risk of complications.'

'What sort of complications?' I was frantic.

'We can't predict exactly how things will play out, but Orla will need close monitoring for the rest of her pregnancy. The stress and strain of the overdose could trigger premature labour. There might also be placental issues or developmental problems. When is the baby due?'

'January the twenty-ninth. She's twenty weeks pregnant.'

He gave me that cautious doctor's look. 'If she goes into labour in the coming days, the baby will have almost no chance of survival, I'm afraid.'

My hand flew up to my mouth. I was a lousy mother. I'd failed Orla.

'We've flushed most of the substances from Orla's system, but she's still in a critical condition. When ecstasy is absorbed into the bloodstream, it causes the brain to release chemicals, mainly serotonin, but also noradrenaline and dopamine, which produce the pleasurable effects. But if too much is taken, the chemicals can cause the heart to beat too fast. Orla was lucky her friends raised the alarm when they did. Another hour and there may have been a very different outcome.'

I'd heard what the doctor had said, but I still blamed Majella for leading Orla astray in the first place.

'Are you saying she could have died?' Niall asked. The sound of his voice snapped me back to reality.

'Yes. Her temperature rose to forty-one degrees, which meant her organs were in danger of shutting down. Her heart rhythm was also abnormally fast, and that could have led to a cardiac arrest.' The doctor's tone was matter of fact.

His words were bombarding my brain like missiles. There was a moment of tense silence in the room as we absorbed the severity of the situation.

'Do you have any other questions?' the doctor asked.

I opened my mouth, but nothing came out. I was too shocked to speak. I felt like I'd aged ten years in ten seconds. None of this seemed real. How could my teenage daughter be lying in a hospital bed having had a drink and drug overdose? I was struggling to come to terms with everything.

'Is she likely to make a full recovery?' Biddy asked on my behalf.

'We're hopeful. People who end up in A & E in situations like these will usually be back to normal in two or three days,' the doctor replied.

A glimmer of hope rippled through me, but it was short-lived.

'Do you think the overdose was deliberate?' Niall's words stole my breath.

He loved his niece as if she was one of his own children, but his question was blunt. I hadn't considered for one minute that she'd done this deliberately. I felt blindsided, and the contents of my stomach rose. I was scared to hear what the doctor was going to say, but it was better to know the truth so that I could face things head-on.

'We see this kind of thing all too often with young people, so I have no reason to believe Orla tried to take her own life,' the doctor said.

I let out a sob of relief, which made him glance over at me.

'Are you all right, Mrs O'Connor?'

I nodded and knotted my hands together.

'Would you like to see your daughter?'

'Yes,' I blurted out. I didn't need to be asked twice.

'You'll be able to visit her once she's settled on the ward. One of the nurses will come and get you. Now, if you'll excuse me,' the doctor said, before making himself scarce.

He moved down the corridor with the tails of his white coat flapping at his sides like a swan's wings. I sank into the chair and pressed my hands to my lips to stop them from trembling.

'Are you OK, Josie?' Biddy asked, sliding her arms around my waist.

I turned towards her with tears running down my face.

'Aww, come on, love. I know it's hard, but you have to be strong for her,' Biddy said. She took a tissue out of her bag, reached forward and dried my tears.

A short while later, a nurse brought us to the ward. I wasn't sure what I'd been expecting, but the hush was intimidating. Niall and Biddy stood on either side of me as we gazed at Orla, dwarfed by machines. She lay motionless, her back against the stiff pillows, covered by a white sheet. Her face was drawn. Her eyes flickered. There were tubes in her nose. An IV in her arm. Wires trailed from her chest. An oxygen mask covered her face as monitors blinked. She was deathly pale but alive.

I wanted to go to her. To touch her. To tell her that everything was going to be OK. But I did none of that. I froze. A second passed. Then another. And then it hit me. The enormity of what nearly happened came crashing down on me like a landslide. My legs nearly gave out, but I reached forward and gripped the end of the bed to steady myself. I felt Niall's and Biddy's arms around me as my breath hitched in my throat. A sharp, stabbing pain jabbed me in the chest as my face crumpled just for a moment. I bit back my despair, straightened my posture and walked over to Orla.

I sat down next to her and reached out. My hand hovered above Orla's. I was scared to touch her. Scared I'd hurt her. The machines hissed and clicked rhythmically. 'What have you done to yourself, pet?' My voice was barely more than a whisper, and it cracked with emotion.

Orla didn't reply. She didn't stir.

My eyes flicked across her face. On the surface, she looked unharmed. The damage she'd done was hidden from view, which made it harder to accept. I lowered my head and pressed my lips to the side of her head. 'You don't get to leave me. Not like this. Not like he did.' Silent tears started running down my face. I wiped them away, and then I clasped Orla's hand in mine, threading my fingers between the wires. 'I'm going to stay right here with you. I'm not going anywhere. You hear me?'

'We'll come back in the morning. But make sure you call one of us if anything changes,' Niall said.

'I will,' I replied without looking over at Niall and Biddy. I couldn't tear my gaze away from Orla as guilt welled up inside me. I was the person responsible for keeping her safe, and I'd let her down. She was the most precious thing in the world to me, and just like when I lost Sean, my heart was breaking.

41

DECLAN

Dublin, September 1985

The village above Rush Harbour was shuttered tight against the cold as first light bled along the horizon. The stone pier was slick with dew. Lobster pots were stacked at the end, like sleeping sentries, as barnacles beaded their ropes like strings of pearls.

The lights along the quayside cast orange halos over the cobbles. Cormac and I stood by the edge of the water, looking out to sea. The wind was biting my skin like an animal hungry for blood as I watched the fishing trawler glide towards the dock, with its engine humming low. The vessel's name was barely visible, but when I trained my eyes on the faint lettering, I could just about make out her name, *The Pirate Queen*, which brought a smile to my face. Very fitting, I thought.

The tide was creeping in, slow and steady, brushing softly against the slipway, licking higher and higher over the weed-slick stone. As the boat bumped the dock of the isolated port on the Dublin coast, men leaked from the shadows and began to move quickly. No words were exchanged, just hand signals. One crate, then another, was lowered slowly from the van to a dolly. They were wheeled to the trawler and hauled on board by a pulley system. But every slam on the deck felt too loud.

The air was charged with danger, heightening my senses and making my heart gallop. I studied Cormac, but I didn't speak. Something felt off, so I kept my eyes trained on him. I pulled my coat tighter and turned up the collar as my breath clouded in the damp air. The motor was silent for now, but the smell of diesel clung to the harbour like a wet blanket. The boat rocked gently against the worn fenders as a gull called out above us.

'Let's get a move on, lads. We need to leave while the tide's high so the trawler doesn't bottom out in the mud,' Cormac said.

I was keen to get underway, too. I wanted to leave before the sun fully rose to avoid the eyes of the harbour master. Fewer fishing boats headed out at dawn at this time of year, so our departure might draw attention if anyone was watching. But the unseasonal chill in the air meant less people were lingering outdoors.

The men worked in silence. Their boots thudded on the timbers as they moved the crates. The village was just beginning to stir. Beyond the quay, the sea was a sheet of darkness, and the murk hid the narrow passage out of the harbour. It would take a man who knew every sandbank and shifting channel marker to nose a boat out in these conditions without grounding it.

I'd been unsure about Cormac's choice of harbour. I'd presumed we'd leave from Howth, but he'd insisted Rush was a better option if we wanted to avoid patrols. With no radar or permanent customs post due to its small size, I hadn't put up a fight.

There was a stiff north-westerly wind blowing, bringing a bite to the air and a restless chop to the sea. A low mist was blurring the horizon. The cover of bad weather was an asset, though. An angry sea and poor visibility meant fewer customs boats were out looking for trouble. Most of the checks were intelligence-led, so if nobody tipped off the authorities, the water could remain quiet for weeks.

The east coast also had fewer random patrols than the south-west smuggling routes, and smaller harbours like Rush weren't directly monitored. But departures in bad weather could be red flags to law enforcement because they knew smugglers liked to use poor conditions to hide their movements. An unlit boat could slip out in the grey light without being spotted unless it was unlucky enough to pass a patrol vessel lurking nearby with its jaws open like a hungry shark.

I searched the water behind *The Pirate Queen*. No lights were moving offshore. No hum of an engine. A customs cutter with a tip-off could still be waiting, but I was confident that nobody in Rush would risk talking about me. I turned around and my eyes scanned every shadow, every rooftop as if I was suddenly doubting myself. I knew only too well that when you least expected it, people's loyalties shifted. Somebody you thought was an ally turned out to be your worst enemy.

'Come on, lads, shift it up a gear,' Cormac ordered.

They were starting to flag from the exertion. Moving the weapons was hard work for a few pairs of hands, but we'd had to keep the circle tight. One weak link and it would all fall apart. I glanced down at my watch. We'd matched our departure to the rising tide and first light, so we should have been well underway before anyone started morning checks, but it was taking longer to load than I'd anticipated. If we were lucky, we'd have twenty minutes until the harbour came to life.

As the last crate landed on the deck, Cormac and I stepped

onboard. The trawler rocked gently at the end of the dock. Her deck lights were dimmed and barely visible. Two crewmen, one wiry, one broad, began unfastening the mooring ropes.

'Where's the skipper?' I asked.

'Down below,' Cormac replied.

'I'll give Pat a shout,' the wiry deckhand said.

He moved like a ghost; his boots were silent as he disappeared down the stairs. A moment later, he reappeared with a woman in her mid-fifties in tow. I did a double take. I'd been expecting Pat to be male. My eyes blinked rapidly as I stood toe to toe with her. Was this Cormac's idea of a joke?

'You Declan?' she rasped.

'I am.'

'Pat Brogan,' she replied, in a voice so deep anyone would think she had a set of bollocks.

She held out the roughest hand I'd ever known a member of the opposite sex to have, so I followed suit. I almost winced when she crushed my fingers together. She had a grip like iron and a face like a bag of spanners, with a weather-beaten complexion and dark eyes as sharp as flint.

'Is there a problem?' Pat glared at me.

'Are you the skipper?' I asked to clarify the situation.

She nodded. 'Let me guess, you were expecting a man to own the trawler.' Pat laughed. 'Happens every time. I'm more than qualified to be at the helm. You'll have to take my word for it. Although I'll happily vouch for myself. My dad was a fisherman. His father and grandfather before him. They taught me everything I know. You've got nothing to worry about. I've got the sea in my blood.'

'Everything's loaded,' the broad crewman said.

'Then let's get moving. The tide's not going to wait while you size me up.'

'Do you know what's in those crates?'

Pat eyed me, but didn't blink. 'Do you think I'd run a job blind?'

'Lots of people do.'

'I'm not like lots of people. The sooner you realise that, the better.' Pat almost loosened a couple of my teeth when she clapped me on the back before she headed off in the direction of the wheelhouse.

I wasn't sure what to make of the woman. I'd never met anyone quite like her. I stared at her retreating silhouette for a beat, then I went to find where Cormac had scuttled off to.

His eyes narrowed as I drew closer. 'Satisfied?'

'No. Is this some kind of wind-up?' I asked flatly when I stopped next to him.

He was holding on to the railings, looking out to sea. 'I don't know what your problem is. Pat's a great skipper. She knows the sandbanks and currents better than anyone. And she has a knack for vanishing into fog if the need arises. You'd do well not to go upsetting the captain if you want your cargo shifted,' Cormac replied. He finished his cigarette and stubbed it out on the deck.

'Time will tell, but I'm not happy about this,' I replied. Everyone knew being a skipper was a man's job.

'Don't forget who's running the show, Declan. Remember who made these routes possible. Remember whose contacts got you this far? I've risked a hell of a lot to get the weapons on board. If you step out of line, I'll cut you adrift. Understand?'

I nodded, but I was silently seething. 'You're not the only one taking chances. I've stuck my neck out, too. I'll be the one who takes the heat if this doesn't go to plan.'

Cormac flashed me a knowing smile. 'Then maybe you should've stayed in the whiskey trade.'

Once again Josie's shadow loomed over me.

The engine coughed once, twice, then settled into a low, throaty hum. Pat eased the bow around, hugging the north wall of the pier, where the water was deepest, keeping the stone close enough to touch, then she swung wide at the outer marker. I felt the tide grip the hull and pull us east. One wrong move here and we'd be stuck in the mud, stranded in sight of the village.

The channel out of Rush was tight, with sandbanks shifting on both sides. As Pat steered the trawler past the breakwater, the harbour shrank behind us and the open sea stretched ahead, dark and foreboding. A storm was threatening. The wind was howling, whipping up the water. Once we'd cleared the mouth, the boat lurched, its hull groaning with the effort. The channel markers emerged out of the gloom – black shapes, easy to miss if you didn't know these waters.

'Pat will hold a false course, the one the fishermen take out to Lambay Island, for the time being. A ruse in case anyone's watching from shore,' Cormac said, having done this trip before.

Lambay lay ahead like a ghostly figure. Its bulk sliced the horizon and hid us from prying eyes for precious minutes until Pat changed course, skirting Dublin Bay and heading towards deeper water. So far, I'd been impressed by the way she'd handled things. She seemed to be thinking two steps ahead in case a patrol appeared.

The waves crashed against the hull as we cut through the water. Bad weather might be our friend, but I wasn't a fan of the sting of the wind in my face. The gale ripped through my coat, and salt spray stabbed at my skin as I peered into the darkness, looking for signs of pursuit. No approaching lights. No cutter silhouettes. The coast was clear. There was nothing but the vast, restless, inky sea and the hazy horizon.

It had been a smart move to sail from Rush instead of Howth, not that I'd ever admit that to Cormac. He was a little scrote and didn't deserve the compliment. Each knot we travelled put another mile between us and the eyes of Dublin Port and carried us further from the shore, beyond the reach of the small customs cutters and the patrol boats. By the time the city woke, our presence would be nothing but a rumour.

42

ORLA

London, September 1985

The first thing I saw when I opened my eyes was my mum huddled on a stiff plastic chair. Her coat was draped over her like a blanket. There was a deep crease in her brow and a worried look on her face. She was making small jerking movements as she did her best to sleep.

For a moment, I wondered where I was. The world felt muffled. My throat burned. My stomach ached like my insides had been ripped out, and then the horror came back to me. The derelict flat in Camden. The pink pills. The vodka. The weed. I blinked and shook my head to try to dislodge the memories bombarding my brain.

'Mum?' I rasped in a hoarse voice no louder than a whisper, but it was enough to make her stir. 'Mum?'

She jolted awake, and her eyes landed on me. She threw off her coat and rushed over to the bed. She didn't say anything for a beat. She just stared at me like she couldn't believe I was talking to her.

'How are you feeling, pet?' Mum's green eyes bore into mine.

'Awful,' I croaked.

'I'm not surprised. You scared the life out of me.' Mum's voice broke, and a wave of guilt washed over me. But then she composed herself, and her features darkened. 'What in God's name were you thinking? You nearly died, Orla. They had to pump your stomach!'

I turned my head away and stared at the sheet. Guilt rose inside me. It was sharp, uncomfortable. But I swallowed it down. I was ashamed of myself. She didn't need to make me feel worse than I already did.

'Have I lost the baby?' I blurted out before dissolving into floods of tears.

'Shush, don't cry. It's OK. The baby's alive.' Mum's voice was soothing, but I should have known her concern wouldn't last long. 'You've got to buck your ideas up, though. You need to start taking care of yourself. The doctor said that if you go into labour in the coming days, the baby will have a very low chance of survival.'

My relief was short-lived. Since I'd found out I was pregnant, I'd been secretly hoping I'd have a miscarriage so I wouldn't have to face the consequences of my drunken one-night stand. But now that it was a real possibility, I felt devastated that my actions had put the baby's life at risk.

'I've told you before you shouldn't be drinking while you're pregnant, let alone be smoking and taking drugs. You think I'm the enemy, but I was the one sitting in the waiting room, praying the doctor didn't come out and tell me the two of you were dead.' Mum's eyes were brimming with tears, but her jaw was tight.

Her words made me flinch. The monitor beside my bed, beeping a steady rhythm, was the only sound for a few tense seconds. Time seemed to drag on.

'What the hell was going through your head?' Mum was studying me, as if she was trying to decipher a foreign language. As if she was looking at something alien.

I could see she was exasperated, but I couldn't answer her question. I hadn't planned to end up in A & E. One minute we were having fun, and the next thing I knew I was completely out of it. She'd made it clear she didn't approve of what I'd done, so there was no point in confiding in her. She was born middle-aged with a rod up her arse. Her idea of a good time was saying three decades of the rosary followed by a purge of her sins in the confessional box.

'Please talk to me, Orla. I'm trying to understand what made you do something so reckless.'

'I don't know,' I snapped, and then pressed my fingertips to the base of my neck as my throat was hurting.

Mum softened when she realised I was in pain. She sat on the edge of the bed and let out a long sigh. 'You're lucky you came to the hospital when you did. Another hour and it could have been a different outcome...' Mum let her sentence drift off when her voice started to tremble.

'Stop being so dramatic. I'm fine.' My tone was stroppy to hide my guilt.

'You're not fine. Jesus, Orla, you nearly overdosed.' Mum shook her head and exhaled hard through her nose to steady herself. 'Where did you get the pills from?'

I knew that question was going to come up, but I didn't want to answer it, so I folded my arms across my chest and glared at her with a look of defiance on my face.

'You took a class A drug; possession of that could land you in prison. Did you know that?' Mum mirrored my body language. Her posture was rigid.

She always maintained I was my father's daughter, but it

looked to me like the apple didn't fall far from the tree. We were more alike than she cared to admit, which was probably why we were always butting heads.

'Just tell me where you got them, Orla,' Mum pleaded.

'I got them off some bloke at the club,' I replied, hoping to put an end to the inquisition. But I should have known Mum would have other ideas.

'Which club?' Mum's gaze was so intense. It was as though she was trying to see into my soul.

'Does it matter?' I tore my eyes away from hers. I felt uneasy about lying to her face.

'Yes. I have a right to know who's been feeding my daughter poison.'

I glanced back at her. Mum's expression had darkened, so I stared up at the ceiling with my lips pressed together tightly.

'Why are you shutting me out? Why won't you tell me?'

'Because it's none of your business.'

Mum flinched. 'None of my business. You nearly died, Orla...'

I turned my face to the wall. The monitor's beeping filled the silence. Steady. Repetitive. Irritating.

'Maybe I wouldn't be in this position if—' I stopped myself mid-flow, but Mum wasn't going to let that go.

'If what?'

'If Dad was still here.' I knew I shouldn't lash out at her, but I couldn't help myself.

Mum blinked. Her face was taut. Troubled. It was a low blow. The words hung heavy between us. The undercurrent of guilt was still there, but the anger was stronger.

'I know you're struggling without your dad, but I'm trying to give you a good life. A life where you'll want for nothing.'

'Well, you're not doing a very good job, are you?' I fired back.

Mum looked wounded. She stared at me. Her eyes narrowed

as she calculated her next move. 'I'm doing my best. It's not easy being both parents, Orla. I'm trying to keep a roof over our heads while keeping you safe.'

I let out a short, bitter laugh. 'It's a pity you didn't keep Dad safe instead of letting him die.'

My words hit like a punch. Mum's face crumpled, and she flopped down on the hard plastic chair. Her hands were clasped like she was holding herself together by sheer force of will. There was no flare of temper, just the cold stillness of someone who'd been cut deep, but it was her own fault. She'd pushed me to the limit, so I couldn't help twisting the knife.

'Do you think that's a fair comment to sling at me?' Mum's eyes had filled with tears.

The pain in her voice was hard to bear, but I swallowed it down. 'Whether it's fair or not, it's true. It's no wonder he spent so much time away from the house. You never stopped nagging him.' I looked away. For a long, brittle beat, neither of us spoke. I fixed my gaze on a scuff mark on the wall. I could feel the weight of her eyes on me, but I refused to meet them.

'I'll ask you one more time. Where did you get the pills?' Mum asked, brushing what I'd said to one side. Her voice was slow and robotic.

I snapped my head around and glared at her. My anger was flaring, but I stayed tight-lipped.

'Have it your way. If you're not going to tell me, I'll ask Majella. She was there, wasn't she? And who's the lad she's hanging around with? Is that her boyfriend? Or is he the father of your baby?' Mum let off a round of quick-fire questions. By the time she'd finished reeling off the list, I could barely remember anything she'd asked me.

'I don't know,' I said through gritted teeth, hoping she'd get the message.

'Don't lie to me, Orla.' Mum fixed me with one of her looks. They used to scare the shit out of me when I was little, but now I didn't find them the least bit intimidating.

'I'm not lying to you.' I raised my voice. 'You love being in control, don't you? Why do you feel the need to stick your nose into everything I do?'

'Because you're my daughter.'

'That doesn't give you the right to keep meddling in my life. I'm not a kid.'

'You're acting like one.'

My chest tightened as rage took hold.

'It's pathetic that you're suddenly trying to play the doting mother when we both know all you care about is that stupid building!'

Mum's posture stiffened. I saw the hurt flicker across her face. What I'd said had stung, but she refused to back down.

'You want to keep your secrets? Keep them. But don't think for a second I won't find out. And when you get out of here, you're not hanging around with Majella any more.'

'Why not?' My voice came out louder than intended, and a nurse looked over in our direction to see what the issue was.

Mum leaned forward to whisper in my ear so she wouldn't be overheard. 'She's a bad influence on you. The girl courts trouble. And now she's got you mixed up in it too.'

'She hasn't got me mixed up in anything. She didn't force me to take the pills. She didn't pour vodka down my throat. She didn't hold me down and make me smoke the spliff. I chose to do that myself. And do you know why I did it?' I didn't wait for Mum to respond before I carried on with my rant. 'Because my life sucks. Because I wanted to have some fun. Because I wanted to forget that I was pregnant—' I broke off when my voice cracked. I tried to blink back my tears before Mum saw them.

'If you think I'm going to stand by and watch you destroy yourself, you don't know me at all.' Mum stood abruptly, causing the chair legs to scrape against the floor. The sound echoed around the room. Then she walked away without saying another word or bothering to look back.

I stared at the door long after it closed behind Mum. I felt sick with guilt, but also strangely triumphant for keeping Shay's name out of the frame. My emotions were so raw I thought I was going to choke on the lump stuck in my throat. I wasn't sure if I wanted to cry or smash something. The temptation to scream loud enough to rattle the windowpanes was overwhelming, but I somehow managed to keep my lips clamped together.

My eyes pricked with tears, so I turned away from the door. I had to blink hard to fight them back. I flopped back against the pillows, closed my eyes, and clenched my jaw. I was furious at myself for caring whether Mum came back or not. I was conflicted. I felt bad that I'd worried her, but I was angry that she was prying into my personal life and trying to rein me in.

My hands twisted the sheet. My chest ached with the burning rage I'd been carrying for years. Rage at Dad for dying. Rage at Mum for taking his place in the family business. Rage that it meant more to her than I did.

43

JOSIE

Cold air rushed at me the moment the sliding doors hissed open. The day had gone by in a blur. The sky was pitch black now, and the temperature had dropped. Majella was nowhere to be seen, but I was pretty sure the lad she'd been with was sitting alone on the low wall in front of me. It was difficult to say for certain, as whoever it was had a hoodie pulled up over their head.

My mind shifted from grief to calculation as I paced over to him with a fire in my belly. 'Hey, you,' I called as I got closer. The figure turned around. Sure enough, it was him. My eyes were wild when I stopped in front of him. 'You little bastard. Are you happy now?' I could feel my nostrils flaring as I waited for him to reply.

'How is she?'

'She's alive, no thanks to you. But she nearly died.' My voice cracked as I said the words out loud. He bowed his head in shame. His face was gaunt. His hands were trembling. But I had no sympathy for him. I wanted to put my hands around his throat and choke the life out of him for what he'd put my daughter through. Put me through. The two of us looked at each other, the silence stretching taut between us. Then the penny dropped, and a jolt ran through my chest. 'Christ, I thought you seemed familiar. I've just made the connection. You were at The Ink Pit when Mossy delivered the cocaine, weren't you?'

He appeared unfazed, as though I'd remarked on the weather. 'I don't know what you're talking about.'

Anger prickled under my skin. 'Don't play games with me. You're not a stray dog hanging around sniffing for scraps. You're a lookout. Did Lewis Slater send you?'

His expression didn't shift, but there was a faint gleam in his eye, like he was enjoying my suspicion. 'Nobody sent me. I'm here because of Orla.'

My jaw tightened and my hands were twitching. I wanted to grab him by the collar, but I reined my temper in. 'Is your boss worried he's sold a bad batch? The doctor didn't mention she'd taken cocaine as well.' I muttered, unintentionally saying my thoughts out loud.

'She didn't. She took ecstasy, not coke,' the young fella confirmed, which went some way to relieving my rising panic.

'You were the one who gave her pills, weed and alcohol, weren't you? Thanks to you, the baby's life is still in danger...' I let my sentence trail off when I felt tears prick my eyes.

The boy sprang up from the wall. 'She's pregnant?' His features changed as the realisation hit him like a hammer, which told me everything I needed to know.

'You're the father?' My words carried an undertone of disgust. I'd agonised over who it could be for months now. I'd tiptoed around the topic, trying to coax it out of Orla, but she'd refused to say. I'd thought the likelihood was he'd abandoned her. I hadn't considered the possibility that she hadn't told him. I'd expected him to be older. I'd expected him to be a decent human being. I hadn't expected him to be a teenage drug dealer. 'Why did you fill Orla with poison? Hadn't you done enough by getting her pregnant?'

He got up in my face in a fit of temper. 'Shut the fuck up, you stupid bitch. Why are you giving me grief? I brought her here, didn't I? If it wasn't for me—'

'Don't go acting all heroic on me. If you gave a shit about Orla, she wouldn't be here in the first place! What's your name?'

'Fuck off. Do you really think I'm going to tell you that so you can give it to the cops?' he sneered. When he straightened his posture, he towered over me.

My gaze flicked over him. He was just a lad trying to be a hard man. I wasn't going to let him intimidate me. 'I've seen what boys like you turn into. You'll burn yourself out before you're twenty, but you're not taking my daughter and grandchild along for the ride. Stay away from them!'

'It's no wonder she hates you. I don't blame her. You're an evil old cow, aren't you? You're trying to pin her overdose on me when you should be looking closer to home,' he fired back.

I felt myself freeze. His words were venomous, and they hit me hard, unsettling me. My breath hitched, and I began to shake from the cold, from the adrenaline, from the sheer rage that had been coiled inside me all night... But mainly from the agony his accusation left me with. I suddenly felt vulnerable. I had to get away from him. I didn't want him to see the guilt crawling up from within, which had quickly extinguished the fire inside me. I turned away from him. I couldn't let him see my tears as they started to fall. I rushed off towards the car park. The only sound around us was the echo of my heels striking the concrete, like drums.

I fumbled to unlock the car while blinded by grief. Niall had planted the seed of doubt and now I was plagued by thoughts that Orla might have been suicidal, and this hadn't been an unfortunate accident. It was no secret she was unhappy. Angry. Troubled. Had I missed the signs? Should I have done more to help her?

How I'd made it home from the hospital was a mystery. I must have driven on autopilot. I stepped inside the house. It was silent, except for the faint hum of the fridge. I followed the sound to the kitchen and sat down at the table. Putting my hand into my pocket, I pulled out my rosary and clutched on to the crystal beads. The clock ticked too loudly, needling me as I tried to pray.

When I closed my eyes, Orla's face was there in front of me. Tormenting me. Haunting me. Had I driven her to do this? Or was I being irrational? Only Orla knew the answer. The doctor told us he had no reason to believe she'd tried to take her own life. But the lad had tried to pin the blame on me. His accusation had wormed its way into my brain. Did he know something I didn't? Or was he shifting the focus away from himself? Both of those things were possible.

I put the rosary down on the table and dug my fingers into my temples, squeezing hard. Orla was wild. She was reckless. She was always pushing boundaries. Always pushing my buttons. But were things so bad that she'd want to take her own life? The life of her unborn child? If that was the case, I'd never seen it coming. Had everyone else known where this was going or was I being paranoid? Philomena had openly voiced her opinions on the way I was raising Orla. I'd thought she'd taken a swipe at me just to be a bitch. Being a single parent wasn't easy. Orla was going to find that out soon enough.

I was her mother. I liked to think I knew her better than anyone, but who was I trying to kid? That wasn't true. Not any more. I'd lost her. She'd been slipping through my fingers for the last few years, and I'd done nothing about it. I'd blamed her rebellion on the fact that she was being a difficult teenager. I'd tried to keep her from going off the rails, but all I'd done was push her away.

The lad had said Orla hated me. I'd tried to block his words out, but they'd bitten into me like something rabid. My eyes blurred with tears. I refused to allow them to fall. I didn't want to believe that was true. Hate was a strong word. Not one that should be used to describe a mother and daughter's relationship.

No matter how much I tried to ignore it, the facts were staring me in the face. I'd seen how comfortable Orla was with Philomena. Jealousy had swelled inside me as I'd watched them share a lingering hug. I would have given everything I owned to wrap my arms around my girl. But she'd never allow it. Not for a second. It sometimes took something huge to make a person see the light. I'd come so close to losing Orla, I wasn't going to waste my second chance. Life was fragile. I knew that better than anyone.

44

ORLA

The day was grey and damp. It was one of those London mornings where the clouds never lifted. I didn't think Mum was ever going to go back to work. She'd been watching me like a hawk since I'd been discharged, but she'd had to pop over to Mulligans to deal with some problems, although she'd vowed she wouldn't be long. I took the opportunity to slip to the corner shop. I was dying for a smoke and was out of cigarettes.

I pulled my hoodie up and jammed my hands into my pockets as I walked down the path. I still felt a bit shaky and the world around me seemed slightly muffled, like I was moving underwater. I pushed open the gate and stopped dead. Shay was sitting on the wall opposite our house. Neither of us said a word. We just stared at each other. Then he crossed the road. My heart pounded against my ribs as he grew closer. He stood in front of me wearing his familiar burgundy Fila tracksuit. But there was something different about him. He had a weight behind his eyes.

'How did you know where I lived?'

'Majella told me.' Shay started biting the nails on his left hand.

'So you're stalking me now, are you?' I laughed to hide my embarrassment. My hair was a mess, and I didn't have a scrap of make-up on. I hadn't expected to bump into anyone.

'I just wanted to make sure you were OK. How are you feeling?'

'I'm fine.'

'Your mum told me about the baby.' Shay swallowed hard.

'She what? Christ. She had no right...'

His words hung in the air as rain dripped off the guttering. I felt like I'd been hit by a train. Shay reached for me, but I took a step back.

'I'm glad she did. I need to ask you something. Is it mine?' Shay's icy-blue eyes fixed on me, and I felt my temper flare.

'What sort of a question is that? Do you think I'm a slag?' I was fuming. A rush of anger and shame tangled together. I had to get away from him, so I started pacing up the street. My breath misted in front of me as I hurried.

'Of course I don't. I'm sorry. I shouldn't have said that. Orla, wait!' Shay called after me. But I kept striding along. I hadn't gone far when he caught up with me. 'Don't storm off. We need to talk about the baby,' he panted. He had a look of desperation on his face. 'I want to be there for you. Both of you.'

'You'd better mean that. Because if you don't—'

'Of course I mean it,' Shay cut in. 'I'm not going anywhere. I'm going to be part of the baby's life, whether you like it or not. I don't want some other bloke raising my kid!'

'You say that now, but you'll get fed up when things get too heavy.' My bottom lip began to wobble, and I ran my hand over the bump concealed under my hoodie. I was carrying something inside me that neither of us was really ready for.

'No, I won't. My mum raised me on her own, so I know how hard it is to be a single parent.'

'I'm sorry, I didn't realise.'

'It's OK. It's no big deal.' Shay shrugged, like it didn't matter, but the way his voice wavered betrayed him. 'My dad wasn't on the scene much. When I was five, he died in a car crash. I don't really remember him.'

For the first time, I saw the person behind the bravado. He was scarred from the experience, but he'd never admit that.

'Why didn't you tell me you were pregnant?' Shay reached for my hand, and I felt tears well up in my eyes.

Leaving him in the dark was my way of pretending I still had control over the situation. Saying the words out loud made everything real. I'd been trying to buy myself some time. But the longer I kept the secret, the harder it was to come clean. I didn't want to drag him into the chaos. I thought he'd bolt if he knew the truth, so I figured I was better off dealing with things alone rather than watching him let me down.

'I'd better go. My mum will kill you if she sees you here,' I said to avoid answering his question.

'Let her try!' Shay laughed.

'Trust me, she'll have your head on a block if she catches us together!'

'She'll have to get used to me being around. I'm not going anywhere.'

'Is that a promise?'

'Yeah.' Shay pulled me towards him and wrapped his arms around me. I buried my face in his chest. 'I swear I won't run. Not from you, not from this. I'm going to stick by you. Whatever happens.'

I pulled out of his embrace and looked into his eyes. 'Mum will go mental if she finds out we're seeing each other.'

'Then we'll do it on the quiet if that's what you want.' Shay smiled before leaning in for a kiss.

We broke apart, breathless, when we heard a car approaching and stood in the drizzle, gazing into each other's eyes. The air around us was heavy with the words left unsaid. We knew we were on borrowed time.

'Go, before someone spots us.'

'I'll see you tomorrow. Same time.' A half-smile tugged at Shay's mouth.

He gave me one last look before he walked away. We'd been chatting for a while, so I didn't want to risk going to buy the cigarettes in case Mum returned in the meantime. I turned back towards home, already rehearsing the lie I'd tell her if she decided to question me about him.

45

DECLAN

The low-ceilinged storeroom in the disused lock-up near Limehouse Docks was the kind of place rats made a home. The smell of mould was heavy in the air, and thick, black cobweb curtains clung to the rafters. A couple of bare bulbs swung overhead, casting jagged shadows against the concrete floor.

Gavin Davis crouched by one of the crates stacked in piles while two of his guys hovered close by. My heart hammered as he cracked the box open with a crowbar. His hands delved into it, parting the packing straw before tossing it out, scattering it across the floor in every direction until the gleam of steel showed through. He pulled the rifle out like he was giving it life, beaming like a first-time father.

'You've done well, Declan. It's a beauty,' he said, pressing his lips to the barrel.

I breathed a sigh of relief. I'd been on edge since we'd left Dublin, but it looked like I'd been worried for nothing. 'I'm just going for a smoke,' I said, leaving Gavin to unload the rest of the order.

'Don't fucking play games with me, Declan.' Gavin's voice was as heavy as lead as he grabbed me by the back of the jacket a short while later. 'Did you seriously think you'd get away with this?'

I looked over at Cormac. He shrugged his shoulders, indicating he had no idea what Gavin was going on about, so I spun around to face him. He was glaring at me with his fist raised. By the state of his nose, I knew he was no stranger to a fight.

'I can see you're angry, but I can't fix the problem if I don't know what the issue is,' I said to try to pacify the situation. But my calm demeanour didn't have the desired effect, and I just seemed to rile him up more.

Gavin lunged at me and grabbed me by the lapels. 'Cut the crap, you arsehole. Don't insult my intelligence. Get inside now, the pair of you.'

My heart started pounding against my ribcage when Gavin dragged me into the warehouse. Cormac followed a beat behind. I glanced over in his direction. He was leaning against a stack of pallets with his arms folded, the picture of casualness.

'Did you clowns think I wouldn't know the difference between twenty-four and thirty? You think I'm some mug you can short-change?' Gavin's face was as hard as stone as he jabbed a finger at the open crate. The straw protecting the weapons had spilt out like guts.

My eyes flashed towards Cormac, who was looking as poised as before, but now he was wearing the slightest flicker of a smirk as if daring the tension to flare.

Gavin put his hand around my throat and got up in my face. 'Where the fuck are the rest of my rifles?'

Only Cormac knew, but I couldn't outright accuse him of skimming some weapons out of the drop, as I had no proof. But who else would have taken them? Nobody. Unless Gavin and his guys slipped them out of the crate while we were outside. I wasn't brave enough or foolish enough to suggest that.

'Answer me, you fucker,' Gavin roared as he crushed my windpipe.

I clawed at his hand until he loosened his grip. My lungs burned as I gulped down mouthfuls of air. 'I have no idea how this has happened, but I can assure you, I'll sort it out. The shipment was intact when it left Dublin, so I don't understand how something could have gone missing.' I regretted saying what was on my mind the minute the words left my mouth.

'What the fuck's that supposed to mean?' Gavin was fuming. His face was turning redder by the second.

'I think Declan's saying you've got a rat in your crew. Guns don't just walk away.' Cormac's voice cut the silence like a knife. I wish he'd kept his mouth shut. He'd just made things ten times worse.

Gavin's eyes narrowed. He wasn't buying it. When his hand dipped into his coat and he drew out a pistol, the tension jumped up another notch. 'You reckon? Well, you're wrong, shit for brains. Unlike you Paddies, my lads are trustworthy. They wouldn't dare try to shaft me!'

I needed to smooth things over quickly. I raised my hands in a show of submission to try to ease the pressure. 'Listen, there must have been a mix-up—'

Gavin shoved the order sheet at me before I had a chance to finish my sentence. 'I paid for thirty AK-47s. There are only twenty-four rifles in the crates. Where are the others?'

My jaw tightened. The air was heavy with suspicion. 'Are you sure your men didn't miscount?' The words hit like a spark in dry kindling, and Gavin erupted.

'There's a lot of money riding on this. My buyer is going to go mental when he finds out you've tried to rob him,' He bellowed into my ear and levelled the pistol straight at my chest.

'Don't point that at him, or you'll be the one with the bullet holes,' Cormac said. He'd stepped away from the pallets and had drawn his own revolver, which he'd aimed at Gavin. He had a faint smile on his face as though the situation amused him.

Gavin sneered, but he didn't lower the weapon. He glared at Cormac with his teeth bared like a rabid dog. My heartbeat thundered in my ears. Both of the men were ready to kill.

'Maybe your trusted circle isn't as tight as you thought it was.' Cormac's tone had sharpened. His words were edged with danger.

'I don't know why the shipment's short, but you'll get what you're owed,' I said a moment later to break the fingers of tension. 'That won't happen if you put me in a coffin. So what's it to be?'

Gavin's jaw clenched, and his finger twitched on the trigger. Cormac's eyes flickered. He looked reckless, as though he was daring Davis to fire. One wrong word. One wrong move. And the warehouse would be painted red. I felt the air shift, a split second before all hell broke loose and the warehouse exploded with sound.

The first shot cracked. The bullet tore past my shoulder, splintering holes into one of the pallets. My ears were ringing and my heart was pounding. Gavin had fired at Cormac. Instinct wrenched me sideways as Walsh's revolver responded. I was caught dead centre, balancing two storms, one English, one Irish, both of which were ready to tear each other apart. I hit the floor and rolled behind a stack of crates, as I dragged my pistol free.

Gavin retreated. His face twisted with fury as he swore at the top of his lungs. He fired wildly behind him, fuelled by rage as he ran to safety. Cormac broke cover and moved like a man possessed, ducking low, popping up and squeezing off shots with brutal precision. One of Gavin's men was hit in the thigh and went down like a sack of spuds, screaming blue murder as blood pumped out of the hole in his leg.

I could hear Gavin reloading. 'You're dead men walking, both of you!' he roared from the other side of the warehouse. His voice echoed off the rafters before he opened fire again.

'Cormac, stop!' I said, when he appeared next to me with his revolver raised. My voice was lost under the sound of deafening gunfire as he crouched next to me, firing into the distance.

He flicked his gaze towards me. His eyes were alight with something feral. 'No way. I'm not backing down,' he replied, and then spat on the floor.

Jesus Christ! We'd be lucky if any of us got out of here alive at this rate. I pressed myself against the crate and wiped the sweat from my brow. This had turned into a shit show. The deal was blown. Davis would never trust me again. Cormac had dragged us all into a war that couldn't be undone.

Another shot rang out. It was closer than the last one. Gavin must have broken cover. 'You should've known better, Declan. Crossing me was a suicidal move. There's only one way this is going to end,' he shouted, as he closed the distance between us.

I jumped up quickly and fired two sharp shots. One caught Gavin's other man high in the chest, jerking him backwards. He gasped as crimson bloomed across his T-shirt. The other hit Davis just below the shoulder. The gun dropped from his hand and skittered across the room. He stared at it in disbelief with eyes as cold as a winter's tide. Gavin's man fired bullets with no real aim as he moved towards the loading bay. Several of them sparked off the concrete, but none of them hit Cormac or me. I ducked for cover all the same.

Cormac sprang up and charged over to Gavin, thinking he was unarmed. But he must have been packing more than one weapon. He lined another pistol up and pulled the trigger. The thunder of the shot tearing through Cormac's flesh echoed around the room. He yelled and then tried to stagger behind a pile of crates while clutching the wound in his stomach. Gavin had him in his sights, so I raised my weapon at him. Before I had a chance to fire, his guy shot me in the arm. I dropped to my knees as the pain tore through me. Blood was dripping from my arm. A couple of seconds passed as I collected myself, then I fired back at him. One of the bullets hit him in the gut, the other blew a hole through the side of his face. The force hurled him against the shutter. His blood streaked down the corrugated steel as he slid to the ground with his eyes wide open.

The warehouse was a battlefield. Blood from both sides had been spilt. But I knew there was more to come before this was over. Gavin fired three more shots that splintered wood inches from my head. The bastard was still a good shot even with his right arm injured. I could hear his breath rattling as he reloaded. So I timed my move to catch him off guard. I flung a crate across the room, using the distraction to sprint low and fast. As Gavin leaned out of his hiding place, I dropped down beside him and pressed the gun into his temple. Rivers of sweat ran down my face as my pulse swooshed in my ears. I was tempted to blow his brains out there and then, but I paused. If I killed him, the deal would be off. I'd been through too much to let my hard work come to nothing.

The silence between us was broken by Gavin wheezing in sharp, ragged breaths. He writhed on the ground, clutching his shoulder, as blood seeped hot and sticky from the torn flesh. It had soaked through his shirt and pooled beneath him. Each gasp was a fight. His chest hitched as though the air itself was refusing to enter his lungs. He was in a bad way, but I stayed calm as the weight of the pistol rested steadily against his head. Cold steel bit into sweat-slicked skin. His expression was flat. Unreadable. There was no anger. No rush of vengeance. He faced me with the chilling certainty of a man who knew how this moment would end. He didn't put up a fight. He wasn't strong enough. He'd resigned himself to his fate. Gavin's gaze flickered towards me. I could see he was confused by my hesitation as his eyes begged for mercy.

'Are you wondering why I haven't finished you off? Put you out of your misery?' As I spoke, I pressed the gun into his temple, which turned the shallow gasps in his throat into choking sobs. 'Dead men make good martyrs. But the wounded? They spread fear better. I'll let you live, but you'll forever be indebted to me. Do I make myself clear?' My hand wasn't shaking. My face was set like stone.

'Y-yes.' Gavin's eyes were wild, but he managed to growl a reply back in a hoarse voice before he started coughing and spluttering.

Nothing would have given me greater pleasure than snuffing him out, but he was more valuable alive than dead. I hauled him up by his collar like he weighed nothing. His legs buckled under his weight. With a shove, I pushed him forward, and he fell in a heap on the ground, face-first. I crouched down beside him. He was half-conscious. He wasn't going to give me any trouble, but I disarmed him to be on the safe side.

Then I went over to where Cormac was lying sprawled out on the floor behind a pile of crates. He was alive – but barely. His lips moved when he spotted me, but no words came out, just a groan. I loomed above him while I assessed his injuries. Blood flowed between his fingers from the wound in his stomach. He tried to sit up, but his face contorted as the pain crushed him back down.

I knelt beside Cormac and met his glassy eyes. Holding the gun loosely in my hand, I tilted my head and studied the wreck of a man in front of me. My stare was unblinking. I wasn't raging. I displayed no fit of temper. I didn't need to. My calmness was worse than fury.

The thought was right there in my head. One squeeze of the trigger, and it would be game over for Cormac. He deserved to die. He'd almost derailed the arms deal. But without him, the chance to deliver the whole shipment would turn to dust. Gavin's buyer wouldn't accept a partial drop, and I couldn't afford to show weakness by running away from the mess he'd created.

Cormac's chest rose in shallow jerks. Each breath rattled like it could be his last. Time wasn't on my side, so I pressed the gun into the side of his face until the skin whitened beneath the steel. 'You sold me out, you bastard. Men have died for less.' My voice was flat.

Cormac whimpered something half-formed, but I cut him off with a savage kick to the ribs. He needed to suffer for what he'd done to me. He cried out in agony and then clutched his side, curling his legs up like a beaten dog. But I was just getting started.

'Get on your knees,' I snapped.

It took Cormac three attempts. His hands slipped in his own blood before he managed to prop himself up. His mouth was twisted in pain, but that didn't stop me from grabbing a fistful of his hair and yanking his head back, forcing him to look up into the muzzle hovering inches from his face.

Cormac's eyes were wide with terror. 'D-Declan, please. Please, don't do this. I'll put everything right. I swear. Just let me live.' His barely audible voice cracked with emotion.

I sneered as I watched him squirm, relishing the shift of power. I dug the barrel back into Cormac's skin. 'Look at the state of you. You're a fucking waste of space. You brought this on yourself. You shouldn't have tried to get one over on me.'

Cormac had been a pain in the hole since the first day I'd met him. He'd treated me with contempt and had made me jump through hoops to get to this stage, so it was satisfying to see how the mighty had fallen. He was grovelling at my feet. Broken. A shell of himself. But I wasn't going to let him be until I'd forced him to lose every last scrap of pride.

'I'm sorry. I'm begging you, Declan. Don't kill me. I've got the weapons you need. I can fix this.' Cormac's breath hitched, and blood bubbled at the corners of his mouth as he spoke.

I let his words hang in the air. He was pathetic. Spineless. He was attempting to cement our reputation after he'd been so dishonourable. I'd never be able to trust the bastard again. His power was gone. The raw fear in his face said it all. For a heartbeat, I considered pulling the trigger anyway, just to prove a point. But I resisted the temptation.

I pressed the barrel into Cormac's cheek. 'You're alive because I said so. You need to prove your loyalty. If you betray me again, I'll take my time and make you suffer to the point that you'll beg me to finish you off.'

'I'll do whatever you ask of me,' Cormac croaked. His breath shuddered, and he collapsed in a heap as he coughed up blood.

I wore a mask of cold calculation as I circled him like a wolf stalking its prey, while keeping the gun trained on his head. I intended to control Cormac completely. I wouldn't allow him to step out of line again. 'You get me those weapons, or I'll make sure your death is slow, cruel and remembered.'

Word would get out about what happened here. I hoped it travelled far and wide. I was operating close to Josie's patch. It would be good for her to know Declan Kelly was stronger than ever and ready to reclaim the power she'd taken from me. In case the little woman doubted my capability. Payback was a long time coming.

46

JOSIE

London, October 1985

Orla was in the front room, lying stretched on the sofa in her dressing gown. She looked pale and listless. She was still shaken from her hospital stay. A half-empty mug of tea rested on the nest of tables beside her. I eyed her from the doorway. The silence between us was thick with unspoken words.

Frantic banging on the front door made me jump out of my skin. I turned on my heel and raced down the hall to open it. When I flung it open, Niall stormed in without saying hello. He was flushed and breathless as he waved a crumpled letter at me; his hand was shaking with rage.

'They're a shower of bastards, Josie!' Niall shouted.

I'd been at home with Orla while she recuperated. Niall had been holding the fort at Mulligans.

'Fire safety, inadequate signage. Fire doors not to the required standard.' Niall looked up from the letter he was reading aloud when his voice broke with frustration. 'Food preparation areas not compliant. Evidence of damp. Vermin risk.' He stabbed a finger at the page, but kept going, spitting out the following lines as though they were burning the inside of his mouth. 'And to top it all, your application for a licence has been referred back to the magistrates' court following objections. The bloody council are giving us so much shit and the place hasn't even opened yet!' He flung the letter into the air in disgust.

'Objections! No prizes for guessing who lodged those.' I shook my head and blew out a long breath. Bennett had been meddling again.

'Never mind the objections. What about the rest of the issues? Reggie must have greased every palm in Westminster. Where's he getting the money from?'

Before I could answer him, the phone began to ring. I reached over and lifted the receiver to my ear. 'Hello.'

'Mrs O'Connor?' a no-nonsense voice enquired.

'Speaking.' My expression shifted. As I listened to what the caller had to say, my face tightened and my eyes flicked towards the front room 'OK. We'll come now.'

'Who was it?' A frown had settled on Niall's face.

A beat of silence passed. 'The school. They want me to bring Orla in,' I replied without looking at him. My mind was whirring as I paced down the hallway with Niall hot on my heels. 'Orla?' I called from the open doorway. I knew she'd heard the conversation.

'What?' Orla threw me a black look.

'Go and get dressed. The school want to speak to you right away.' My heart was pounding in my chest.

'For God's sake,' Orla groaned and pulled a cushion over her head.

'You can go in your dressing gown if you prefer.'

'Do as your mother asked,' Niall piped up. His intervention got through to her, as a moment later Orla threw the cushion on to the sofa and then stomped out of the room. 'Do you want me to go with you?'

'It's a kind offer, but you've got enough to deal with at Mulligans.'

I followed Niall out to the hall. As he slipped out of the door, I lifted my coat down from the hook and shrugged it on. I was waiting at the bottom of the stairs with my shoulders squared, ready for another fight when Orla walked towards me.

'What do they want?' she asked in a surly tone.

'I don't know. The sooner we get there, the sooner we'll find out.'

Orla let out a theatrical sigh and then muttered something inaudible under her breath.

* * *

When we stepped inside Mother Superior's office, she was sitting behind a large oak desk with a crucifix hung around her neck like a silent witness. I perched opposite her and clasped my hands tightly in my lap, hoping I looked more composed than I felt. Orla slouched in her chair wearing a scowl, but I could tell she was putting on a front. Her body language gave away her true feelings. She was restless. Fidgety. Chewing her bitten-down fingernails.

The silence in the room was suffocating. The deliberate pause was designed to intensify the stress, add weight to the situation and make us feel as uncomfortable as possible. Mother Superior had achieved her goal. A sense of relief washed over me when she eventually cleared her throat and began to speak.

'Mrs O'Connor, we've done what we can to support your daughter over the years. But in light of recent events, it's clear she can no longer remain in this school.'

Her words rocked me. 'I'm not sure I understand what you're saying.'

Mother Superior stared at me over her rimless glasses. 'Well then, let me spell it out for you. It's come to my attention that your daughter has been smoking, drinking and taking drugs. All of which are illegal. I cannot condone her behaviour or allow her to tarnish the name of my school. The Sacred Heart Catholic School for Girls has an excellent reputation, and I won't risk her leading others astray.' She tore her eyes away from mine to glare at Orla, who responded to the challenge by sitting bolt upright in her chair.

'Oh, Jesus, here we go. I'm the devil's handmaiden now, am I?' Orla mocked, and I felt my face flush with colour. I was mortified that she'd spoken to the headmistress in such a disrespectful way.

'Do not take the Lord's name in vain in this room, young lady!'

Orla smirked, delighted with the reaction she'd provoked. Mother Superior's eyes were blazing as they glared at each other for several moments before the nun turned her attention back to me.

'This is not the first time your daughter has displayed troubling behaviour. But her latest shenanigans are beyond forgiveness, Mrs O'Connor.'

'Beyond forgiveness? But, to forgive is divine, is it not? Where's your compassion? She's fifteen. She made a mistake. Surely Our Lord would want you to find it in your heart to give her a second chance. Ask and it will be given to you...'

'I have been a servant of God for thirty years, and I'm fully aware of his expectations. This institution cannot harbour pupils displaying reckless behaviour. Orla is beyond help and is a bad influence on others, so we have decided to expel her with immediate effect.'

'I'm sorry, Mother Superior. I hadn't realised having fun was a mortal sin!' Orla replied.

I sat in silence as rage simmered under the surface. What the hell was she doing? I could see my daughter out of the corner of my eye, leaning back with her arms crossed over her chest in a show of defiance. Although the twitch at the edge of her mouth gave away the fact that she was terrified.

'But what about her education? You can't send her out into the world with no qualifications. Please can you reconsider? She's sorry, aren't you, Orla?' Desperation had crept into my voice as I turned towards my girl.

'No, I'm not. I wouldn't stay here if you paid me,' Orla shouted, getting to her feet.

'Sit down,' I said through gritted teeth and shot her a look that could level bricks.

'I'm not running a social experiment, Mrs O'Connor. I'm running a school.' Mother Superior looked down her nose at me.

'For Christ's sake, I got drunk and took a few pills, big deal! It's not like I killed somebody.'

'This is precisely the kind of attitude I'm talking about. She mocks the authority of this school. She's disruptive. She's rude. She's defiant. You should be grateful I haven't informed the police. Possession of drugs is a criminal offence, Mrs O'Connor.'

My jaw tightened as I stood abruptly. 'You should be ashamed of yourself. You'd rather report a child to the police than show her mercy. May God forgive you!' I roared at the top of my lungs as my temper got the better of me. I was practically breathing fire. Orla's mouth fell open as she watched me in action.

Mother Superior's eyes grew wide. She stared at me with a look of disbelief on her face and pressed her lips into a thin line to restrain herself from responding. It was clear the conversation was over, so I grabbed Orla's arm and steered her towards the door, letting it slam shut behind us. Once we were in the corridor, I loosened my grip.

'You think you're so clever, don't you? But you've just ruined your whole life. Thrown your future away. And you're acting like you don't care? I thought you were smarter than this.' I was livid. Orla had shown both of us up, so the words came tumbling out like a leak I couldn't plug.

Orla stared at the ground, chewing her lip. She looked like she was fighting back tears. But my whole body was humming with rage. I'd done everything in my power to keep her on the straight and narrow, but she was impossible to control. God give me strength!

47

ORLA

'What are you smirking at? It's not funny, Orla,' Mum said in that sharp tone she used when she thought she knew best.

'Do you know what I nearly did?'

Mum shook her head.

'I came that close to whipping open my coat and flashing my baby bump at the old bag as my parting gesture.' I grinned, holding my thumb and forefinger an inch apart. 'Can you imagine the look on her face? I'd love to have seen her choke on it!'

'Do you seriously think making a show of yourself would prove a point? All it would prove is that you've got no respect – not for her, not for me, and not for yourself.' Mum spat the words out and then pursed her lips as she glared at me with a sour look on her face.

'Relax. Where's your sense of humour? I didn't do it, did I? I just thought about it. She's going to die when she finds out! They all will. I'd love to be a fly on the wall when the news reaches the sisters of no mercy. The evil bitches got a kick out of being cruel. I'm delighted I don't have to put up with their shit any longer!'

My smile stretched from ear to ear, but Mum's expression was sharp enough to cut glass.

'You're wearing your rebellious streak like it's a badge of honour. I don't know how to get through to you. You're utterly brazen. You're on a path to self-destruction.'

'Lighten up. I'm sorry I told you now.' I rolled my eyes.

'Are you deliberately trying to get under my skin?' Mum's eyes were blazing. 'You think this is funny? Dragging our name through the muck, carrying on like you're proud of it!'

The words landed like a knife in my chest. Mum was furious that my shame would stain the family, and that was hard to stomach as she was the one who'd encouraged me to have the baby. She was such a hypocrite! Whatever I did was wrong. I couldn't win! I'd been carrying the weight of the secret for months – swaddling myself in oversized coats and baggy jumpers to avoid people's questions. But I knew they were coming. It was only a matter of time until I'd have to face the gossip-mongers. My instinct was to go on the attack and dare others to judge me.

'What do you want me to do? I won't be able to hide it for much longer. The scandal's going to hit the street sooner or later.' I let out a bitter laugh as I paced up the path and slid my key into the lock. My heart was banging against my ribs like it was trying to escape. By the time I heard Mum step inside, I'd already reached the top of the stairs. I stomped into my room and slammed the door behind me.

48

DECLAN

London, November 1985

I drew on my cigarette and watched the ember flare. The smell of rot hung in the air as I stood in the half-dark waiting for Cormac to arrive. The fog drifted off the Thames and clung to the pylons, like a ghostly form. It curled around my shoulders like a snake, as a lone lamp overhead threw a circle of light across the wharf.

I heard the sound of Cormac's feet, pounding against the wet ground, before he came into view. As he walked towards me, I stepped out of the shadows with my collar turned up against the damp.

'What the hell kept you?' I asked through gritted teeth.

'I'm sorry I'm late, but these fuckers are heavy.' Cormac grunted, straining under the weight of the canvas-wrapped bundle. He gave me a half-smile to add to his apology, but I wasn't impressed by him or his timekeeping. I hadn't come here to make small talk.

Cormac's smile faded as he let the bundle drop at my feet. The thud echoed on the concrete. I glanced along the quay to check for signs of trouble. All was quiet, so I flicked my cigarette on to the floor and ground it out with the toe of my boot. Then I tugged at the canvas until it loosened, and I peered inside. Six rifles were lined up side by side in two neat rows.

'How did you think you'd get away with skimming these off the order?' I asked in a tone that would cut sharper than a blade.

Cormac shrugged. 'It was a big drop. I only took a few pieces, Declan.'

'I don't call six AK-47s a few pieces, not when I paid you seven hundred a pop for them!' I replied, putting an end to his crap.

'I was desperate for weapons. I wasn't expecting Gavin to check the order with a fine-tooth comb.' Cormac's arrogance was shining through.

'Why wouldn't he? He paid good money for these. You had no right to help yourself. They were spoken for by men you don't want to cross.'

'I didn't have a choice in the matter. I had to help a friend in need. Nothing's more important than the cause in my eyes. I told you that from the start.' Cormac laid his response down like a challenge.

Gavin was paying five grand each for the weapons, so I wasn't about to lose out on thirty grand to fund a war I didn't give a shit about. Cormac had already proved to me that he couldn't be trusted, so I crouched down and ran a thumb along one barrel, checking it for rust before I moved on to the next. Cormac shifted from foot to foot as I took my time inspecting the rifles, like a butcher checking a carcass.

'Jesus Christ, could you take any longer?'

I paid no attention to Cormac's impatience. He'd taken his own sweet time bringing the guns to me. A move I felt was deliberate. Once I was satisfied, I stood and got up in his face. 'You're a selfish fucker. We're lucky we're both still breathing after the stunt you pulled. Just so I make myself clear, if you ever try to double-cross me again, I'll pour concrete down your throat and throw you in the tide. I don't appreciate being dragged into your crap. In future, leave me out of the drama,' I warned. My voice was low and menacing.

Rather than appearing rattled, Cormac's expression was smug. 'It's too late for that, Kelly. Word will soon get around that the cell I was arming in London didn't get the weapons they were expecting, and then people will start asking questions. I'm not taking the heat for you.'

'That sounds like a threat.'

'It is. These men don't barter or forgive. I need to protect myself, so you can rest assured your name will be in the frame. Then you'll know what it feels like to have the IRA breathing down your neck. Once you're in their sights, there's nowhere to run. Do you still think Gavin deserved your loyalty? His buyer is no match for the beast you've unleashed. You should have killed him while you had the chance, and then you wouldn't be in this position.' Cormac grinned.

The dynamic had shifted. I was no longer the one pulling strings. Sweat prickled my back despite the chill, knowing I could be on borrowed time. The only sound filling the space was the slow slap of water against the pilings.

Cormac threw me a black look and then walked away, but I stayed on to collect my racing thoughts. His words hung over me like a curse. All was quiet, for the moment, but my instincts told me that things weren't going to stay that way. I knew how easily a man could be snatched off the streets. The IRA's reach was long. Did they already have eyes on me?

I didn't want to be out in the open. I felt exposed, so I hurried to where Gavin and I were meeting in a deserted car park in Camden. My hands were shaking as I made my way to the drop-off point. The tremors weren't just from the weight of the weapons; my nerves were in tatters. My senses were on high alert, and every sound made me flinch.

Gavin was already there. He was dressed as if he didn't want unnecessary attention, wearing a black leather jacket and cheap jeans, but his gold sovereign rings and heavy Rolex watch painted a different picture. He'd got money, and he liked people to know it. His knuckles were permanently scabbed or bruised. He was a man who liked to settle disputes with his fists.

'I'm glad to see you eventually came good on the deal. Now fuck off back to the bog,' Gavin said as he turned and slipped into the shadows.

I waited a beat, hoping to project a calm exterior while paranoia gnawed underneath the surface, and then I disappeared into the night. I'd delivered what I'd promised, but there was no walking away clean from a deal like this. It had left a bitter taste in its wake. The financial reward was far higher than smuggling barrels of whiskey. I'd made a small fortune, but in doing so, I'd stepped into a different war I hadn't signed up for.

The IRA weren't like the crews I was used to dealing with. They were harder, angrier, and they didn't forget faces. I was on the verge of being marked as a player in the political violence, whether I liked it or not. Being labelled a British sympathiser would stick to me like glue. Nothing could be further from the truth, but once the whispers started, they'd spread like wildfire, and my neutrality would disappear like a puff of smoke.

I'd started out as an opportunist, trying to stay out of politics. I hadn't banked on getting tangled up with the revolutionary networks, and I was out of my depth. I was walking away with the money, but the cost was clear. Once you had dealings with the IRA, you were in their shadow for good. If I ended up hunted and desperate, none of this would have been worth it. The cash would tide me over for a long time, which was a true blessing, but the money was useless if I couldn't spend it.

Josie hearing whispers of my return had to be put on hold. I needed to get out of London, but I couldn't go back to Dublin or anywhere I had connections until the dust settled. Although the future seemed uncertain, no good came from second-guessing. I hadn't survived this long by folding at the first sign of trouble.

49

JOSIE

Even before the awful business with Orla, I'd had no intention of sidestepping into drug smuggling. By opening Mulligans, I was trying to build a legacy and make the business appear more respectable, at least on the surface, while still keeping the whiskey smuggling Sean had fought so hard to establish when he was alive.

I wasn't trying to make a quick buck from peddling drugs. It was dirty money. I drew a line between my kind of business and the destructive path that cocaine led people down. Class A importation was in a totally different league from the whiskey runs. They were a family tradition, heritage work. The way I sourced the alcohol wasn't above board, but drinking it was perfectly legal, so the ends justified the means. I was happy to use the unexpected cash to finance the redevelopment project. It was the practical thing to do. Did I have double standards? So what if I did?

The storage facility we owned in Kilburn reeked of mildew. The air was heavy with damp. The high windows cut the afternoon light into hard strips as dust motes moved like spectators vying for the best spot. A forklift slept against the steel racking, which housed crates of the finest Irish whiskey.

Mossy knelt on the cold concrete with his hands shaking. They were bound tightly at the wrist with a length of cord that bit into his flesh. Niall's sleeves were rolled up, and his knuckles were taped. I paced back and forth, but my eyes never left Mossy, although he kept his trained on the floor.

'You should never have dragged me into this business. The authorities seized part of the shipment. Do you have any idea what would have happened if Eamonn hadn't got it released?' I asked when I stopped in front of him. The words tasted bitter, so I spat them out.

Mossy's head jerked up. His eyes were wide with terror. 'I never meant—'

'You never meant to get caught, did you? You thought you'd make a few bob behind my back and I'd never know the difference. You were happy enough to line your pockets and leave me to carry the shit if things went wrong.' I glared at him. My eyes were lit from the inside by pure rage.

'Please, Josie. I swear it wasn't like that.' Mossy's voice came out ragged.

'Do it.' I glanced over at Niall, who was leaning against the wall with his arms folded.

As he walked over to carry out my orders, his steps were slow and deliberate. His eyes were as dark as coal.

'I'm sorry I crossed you. I should never have done it—' Mossy tried to blurt out excuses, but the first punch cut him off.

The force snapped his head back, sending a spray of blood out of one nostril. Niall hit him again, and again, each blow echoing in the hollow room. The strikes were practised – not frenzied.

Mossy crumpled on the floor, holding his hands up in surrender. My brother-in-law's response was to boot him in the ribs. I didn't flinch. I watched. Mossy wheezed and coughed as he howled like a whipped dog. I lifted my hand and Niall instantly stopped as though I'd flicked a switch. He loomed over the turn-coat with his fists still clenched while Flaherty lay on his side, groaning, barely able to lift his head, trying to breathe through the pain.

I leaned down so that he could hear me. 'I'm showing you some mercy, Mossy. Next time, I won't ask Niall to stop. Are you still glad you tried to rip me off?' My voice was as sharp as glass.

Niall dragged Mossy back on to his knees. 'I m-made a mistake. A terrible one, but I've learned my lesson.'

I crouched until I was level with him and let his fear soak into me like a stain. Seeing the trembling of his mouth up close only heightened my desire to make him pay. Somebody deserved to die for what happened to Orla, so it might as well be him.

'You brought that filth into the country. My daughter almost died because of men like you.'

Mossy slowly lifted his head. Blood dribbled from a cut on his lip, so he spat it on to the concrete. 'I swear to God it wasn't me who gave her the drugs, Josie. I wouldn't do something like that. I'd never hurt—'

'Don't you dare say her name.' My voice cracked, but then I steeled myself. 'You don't get to betray me and walk away breathing.'

'Please, Josie. I've been loyal to the firm for years. You know that. I made one fuck-up, but I'll do anything to put things right between us. I can give you names. Information.' Desperation coated Mossy's words.

'I already know Lewis Slater's the boss, but what's his teenage sidekick called? The tall, wiry lad with the floppy hair?' My lip curled, such was my disdain for him.

'Shay Quigley,' Mossy replied without missing a beat.

'Shay Quigley,' I repeated, as if tasting the syllables. Hoping that if it was on the tip of my tongue as I searched my brain for some recognition, it might jog my memory, but I drew a blank. I knew a lot of Irish people in London. None of them had that surname. 'What do you know about him?'

'Not a lot. As far as I know, there's no dad on the scene. I think he lives in Camden with his mum, but he spends most of his time with Lewis,' he babbled. The words tumbled out of Mossy's mouth as he fell over himself to be helpful in a last-ditch attempt to redeem himself. It was too late for that.

His face was slick with sweat and blood. It was a swollen mess after Niall had worked him over. I could leave it at that, but I was still furious with him for involving me in the cocaine deal. If I let him walk, I'd look weak, and then I'd have every fucker in the city trying to take advantage of me.

Mossy was a pawn in the game – just another piece on the board. I'd promised myself that when the time came, I'd make sure he regretted crossing me. He'd outlived his usefulness, and I was riled up about what had happened to Orla. Drugs ruined lives. Even though he wasn't directly responsible for what happened to my girl, he was involved in supplying them, so it made perfect sense to me to punish him for that. How many other people had been destroyed by the gear him and Eamonn had delivered?

'Is there anything else you can tell me about Shay?'

Mossy shook his head.

I pulled Sean's revolver from my coat pocket and stared into his face as if weighing him up.

'Josie, please. Please, I'll do anything. Don't do this, for Christ's sake, don't do it. Take pity on me.' Mossy had resorted to bargaining for his next breath.

He'd turned grey with panic and seemed more pathetic than ever because he was pleading. That made me angry. Why couldn't he just accept his fate like a man? Mossy's eyes flicked to Niall and then back to me, hoping to find a crack in our armour.

'Pity was a coin you spent long ago.' There was no heat in my words. I'd already decided on the outcome, and no amount of grovelling was going to divert me.

Mossy started to cry, big theatrical sobs, which made my features harden. 'Please, Josie. Please.'

'You made a choice, Mossy. A bad choice.'

I walked behind him and placed the barrel against the base of his skull. I didn't look at him when I squeezed the trigger. I looked up at the rafters where the light sliced the dust. The sound was startling, sudden and absolute, but I didn't flinch. The echo hung in the air, making my ears ring. Mossy's body jerked forward, then slumped on to the floor. Blood, brain and bone fanned across the concrete in a dark spray before a puddle began to soak into the cracks.

For a moment, I stared down at the man who'd been in the inner circle. Now he was just a corpse cooling on the floor. Fury was still burning inside me, but the fire had nothing left to consume.

'Dismember him, then get him out of here. Make sure you leave no trace behind. Dump him in the canal. Let the rats feast on him.'

Niall nodded, and I headed for the door. The place reeked of death. The air was tainted with the decision I'd made. The score had been settled, private and final. News of that would travel through the streets far and wide.

50

JOSIE

London, December 1985

The advent wreath sat on the altar, with two purple candles burning. Votives shivered in red glass holders as I made my way to my usual pew. It felt icy inside the old church, so I pulled my coat tighter around me as I dropped to my knees. St Jude's was always cold. The chill seeped through the stone walls even on the hottest day.

'Bless me, Father, for I have sinned,' I whispered to myself as I looked at the rosary clutched in my hand, hoping it would anchor me in the storm I'd walked into. It was my trusted friend. My secret keeper. My closest confidant.

I bowed my head as I fought back tears. I was still wrestling with my guilt over what I'd done to Mossy. It wasn't the first time I'd taken a life, but the burden was hard to bear.

I mouthed the Hail Mary, as though I was trying to strike a bargain between my soul and the God I feared was growing tired of me. 'Forgive me, Lord. Forgive me for what I've done and for what I still have to do,' I whispered. A tear slipped down my cheek, so I wiped it away.

I glanced over at the darkened booth. I hadn't stepped inside it in years, not since Sean's death. I couldn't bring myself to share my wrongdoings with Father Riley. Confession was meant to be sacred. Confidential. And he was a decent man, but decent men feared the law more than God these days. If I told him the truth, I wasn't sure I could trust him not to turn me in to the police, which added weight to the worry. The thought of it made my stomach knot.

I kept telling myself that my prayers were enough to grant redemption. Truthfully, I was too ashamed to name my sins aloud. What I'd been involved in was too dangerous to confess. It was better to keep things to myself. I pressed the crucifix hard against my mouth, as though kissing it might absolve me. He already knew what I'd done. He'd already overheard my troubled conscience. He'd already seen the blood on my hands. Wasn't that enough?

I lowered my head again and let the rosary beads slide through my fingers like a life slipping away. Mossy's life. He'd been so scared. I'd seen the fear in his face. I'd heard his desperation when he'd begged for mercy, and yet I'd shown him none. I'd convinced myself I'd served justice. My chest tightened with guilt, so I prayed harder, hoping the force of my devotion would wash the sins away, even though I knew I was going to keep walking the path that had made me unclean in the first place. What I was doing was wrong, but what choice did I have?

As I sat alone in the empty church, the silence pressed down on me. My faith, my guilt and my fear of exposure were battling between themselves as the rosary slipped through my fingers. The edges of the crystal beads were worn smooth from years of use. I closed my eyes and clung to it as though it was the only one who would never betray me. For a moment, the quiet was absolute until a gust of wind pushed against the old wooden door, and it creaked open an inch. The candles flickered wildly, which made me flinch and my breath catch. I didn't turn around. I was scared of what I'd see. I stayed kneeling, closed my eyes and whispered a prayer no one could hear.

'You think I don't know it's you, Mossy? You visit me every night,' I said in a hushed tone, but my voice seemed to echo, bouncing off the cold walls.

The door creaked again, and the draft moved through the church. The flames trembled and danced. They nearly went out, but then they steadied. My hands tightened on the rosary until it dug into my palms. I glanced over my shoulder. Nobody there. I turned back to the altar and lowered my head, rocking slightly, to soothe myself. Outside, the wind howled. It sounded like laughter. It sounded like someone was mocking me.

'Dear God, take pity on me. I know I've done wrong. Terrible wrong. But I can't undo it. If there's a way back from this, show me the first step,' I muttered. Saying the words seemed to lift a weight from my chest.

I was praying for forgiveness, but it was also a desperate attempt to quieten my haunted mind. I closed my eyes and exhaled to slow my racing heartbeat. As the church bell tolled the hour, I almost jumped out of my skin. My nerves were shot to pieces. I slipped the rosary into my coat pocket and stood up, steadying myself on the wooden bench before I plucked up the courage to turn around. The church was darker now that the light had faded. The pews behind me stretched into shadow. They were empty, yet I couldn't shake the feeling that I was being watched.

'Who's there?' My voice trembled. Nobody answered. Mossy couldn't be here. He was gone. I had to force myself to breathe as

I walked towards the heavy oak door. I stepped into the cold, and my breath clouded in the air, so I turned the collar of my coat up against the chill. The street felt too still. Too quiet for early evening. My heels clicked against the pavement as I hurried away. The sound was sharp in the silence.

I sensed him before I saw him. My steps faltered, and my heart began beating like a drum as my eyes narrowed against the dark. Across the road, a figure half-hidden under the shadow of a shop awning was staring at me. I was almost certain it was Bennett. A cigar burned between the man's fingers. The ember glowed briefly as he drew on it. The smoke curled around his face. He didn't move. He just watched. I could feel the heat of his eyes on me.

'What are you doing here, Reggie?' I called, willing my voice not to waver.

He flicked the cigar to the ground and crushed it under his boot, but didn't approach me. A long moment passed before he turned and walked away. I stayed rooted to the spot. My hand drifted to the rosary in my coat pocket, and my fingers closed around it. His unexpected presence had rattled me. Had he been inside St Jude's while I was praying? Had he heard what I'd said about Mossy?

Panic started rising in my chest. I had to get away from here. I didn't feel safe out in the open. I felt more vulnerable than ever. More alone. Just when I thought I was learning to deal with Sean's loss, it would find the cracks in my armour and bring me to my knees. My grief still came in waves. But I couldn't allow myself to fall to pieces now. I'd have to suck it up and go into survival mode, which was an automatic response these days. Sean's words, as he lay dying, suddenly echoed in my head. 'You've got this, Josie. Don't let Reggie win.'

51

REGGIE

When Josie emerged from the church, her face was pale and drawn. She looked like she had the weight of the world resting on her bony shoulders. She seemed smaller than usual. Fragile. There was something brittle about her. I watched her walk down the steps. Her head was bowed, and her coat was wrapped around her tiny frame. I could tell from the way she was acting that something had rattled her. It didn't matter what had bothered her. What mattered was that I'd seen the cracks appearing. Josie wasn't as strong as she liked to make out.

'Finished praying for your sins, Josie O'Connor?' I muttered, and a muscle twitched in my jaw.

I wasn't sure if she'd heard what I'd said, but she suddenly noticed me. She stared at me wide-eyed. Dare I say she looked scared? Sean had tried to destroy me. And now Josie was picking up where he left off by building her shiny new pub on my turf. I had no intention of fading into the shadows. I'd seen the flicker of weakness, and it filled me with joy. A smirk tugged at my mouth as I disappeared into the night thinking about the best way to take revenge.

A short while later, I stood on the pavement outside the derelict building opposite what used to be The Velvet Ace. After I vandalised the place, Josie had boarded up the windows to stop anyone from seeing what was going on inside. But the covers had gone, no doubt in preparation for the grand launch in the not-too-distant future, which piqued my curiosity.

Newly unveiled brass letters above the emerald door read 'MULLIGANS'. The Celtic font was polished and proud as it caught the amber glow of the street lamps. The sight of it made my guts curdle, but I wanted to take a closer look so I crossed the road and peered through the gleaming glass. Bottles were lined up like soldiers on parade behind the mahogany bar. Polished lamps sat on wooden tables inside cosy snugs, while framed Gaelic prints and tricolour flags adorned the stone walls. Josie had chosen a green-and-gold interior. Typically predictable. She never missed an opportunity to flaunt her nationality. Fucking bitch. I hated the O'Connors and their fellow countrymen with a passion. She was really twisting the knife with this stunt.

My reflection stared back at me. I was a ruin of a man – a ghost of myself. I looked older than my years, with grey stubble, deep lines, hollow eyes and a face eaten away by bitterness. I pressed my palm to the glass. It was clear she'd spent a small fortune on the refurbishment, but she'd painted over history. Over me. Over everything I'd worked for.

Sean had crushed me when he'd burned The Velvet Ace to the ground. All the years of blood, sweat and tears I'd poured into my business, along with all my hard-earned cash, had gone up in smoke. I'd lost my livelihood, my home and my reputation in one fell swoop. But I didn't give up. I dragged myself back to standing. So if Josie thought I was going to let her turn my property into an Irish pub, she was wrong. I might be out of money, but I was never out of cunning.

I'd put constant obstacles in Josie's way, but she kept finding ways around them. The O'Connors had destroyed my legacy. It was time to settle the score before they turned the love of my life into a shrine to themselves. I tore my gaze away from the bar and crossed the road back to the derelict building where I was still living. I'd stashed a container full of fuel there, although the conditions weren't ideal. Drizzle had been falling for hours.

My chest was wheezing from the exertion by the time I slipped down the side alley. I unscrewed the jerry can and mirrored Sean's movements on that fateful night as I splashed petrol along the brickwork, over the bins, the doorframe and the steps while muttering curses. The smell was overpowering. The fumes punched the night air, so I put the empty can down at my feet as I coughed my lungs up. My hands were shaking, but not from fear. From fury. If I couldn't have the building, nobody would. I was still spluttering when I pulled the box of matches from the inside of my worn coat. Before I had a chance to strike one, a voice from behind cut through the dark, sharp as a knife.

'Reggie Bennett, don't you fucking dare!'

When I turned around, Josie O'Connor was standing at the mouth of the alley with her coat flapping like a bird trying to take flight. The breeze had caught her red hair and made it billow around her shoulders. Her expression was as hard as stone. Niall was beside her with his fists clenched and his jaw tight.

'Have you lost your mind?' Josie asked, stepping closer.

'You're the one who's lost their mind,' I sneered. 'This place was mine before you stole it. I won't let you turn it into a place for Paddies to congregate. The lot of you need deporting! Pretty soon you'll know how it feels to lose everything.' I laughed as I took a match out of the box and struck it to bring it to life.

The look of horror on Josie's face was priceless as she

watched the flame dance in my hand. I'd waited a long time to get even with the scrawny excuse for a woman, but finally the moment had come. I felt on top of the world, for the first time in years. I was going to love seeing the bastards suffer as they tore around in blind panic, trying to dampen the fire.

52

JOSIE

Reggie looked so smug when he struck the match. I charged towards him, lunged and knocked his arm away from the building. The lit match fell from his finger and hissed as it hit the wet ground, although it somehow managed to stay alight. Reggie shoved me back before I could stamp on it. He slammed me into the wall and pinned me there. His eyes were wild as rage churned within him; decades of resentment were bubbling under the surface. Niall tried to grab him, but Reggie reached down and swung the jerry can, which caught my brother-in-law across the jaw.

My knee came up fast and hit Reggie in the balls. He buckled, winded by the unexpected strike, giving Niall enough time to recover. The two men grappled in the petrol-slick alley, both of them were slipping, both of them were breathing hard. The fumes were thick and choking.

Bennett was surprisingly strong and was putting up a good fight against his much younger and larger competitor. The desperation seemed to have given him superhuman powers. I should never have spared his life. That decision might be about to cost me everything. I pulled Sean's gun from my coat pocket. Reggie smiled when he caught sight of the barrel aimed at him.

'You're no threat to me. You ain't got the nerve,' he goaded, spitting at my feet.

I didn't blink before I squeezed the trigger. The shot clapped like thunder in the narrow alley. Reggie staggered back as a bloom of red spread across his chest. He looked down at the wound and tried to speak. My second shot dropped him to his knees. His breath rattled as he toppled backwards. I watched Bennett twitch and then go still in the petrol puddle as his blood spread beneath him like a dark halo. This moment had been a long time coming. I'd never forgiven the bastard for murdering Sean. The match lay beside him with the tiny flame still flickering weakly. I crushed it under my shoe. I'd worked too hard on the restoration to let the fucker burn it to the ground.

'Jesus, Josie, that was a close call. I told you it was a mistake to give him a second chance. I knew it would come back to bite you on the arse,' Niall said in a judgmental tone.

But killing everyone who crossed me once wasn't my style. I glanced down at the body lying at our feet. The problem needed to disappear fast. 'Dump him where he won't be found.'

'You say that like it's nothing,' Niall snapped. 'How come I'm always the one getting my hands dirty while you give the orders?'

I studied Niall as he paced next to me. Hurt flickered beneath my anger. 'It's my job to lead.'

Niall stopped moving and threw me a black look. 'Lead? I'm not sure you can do that while you're hiding behind me.'

I stared at him as he towered over me. He'd never spoken to me like this before. What had got into him?

'The same blood as Sean's runs in my veins, not yours, Josie. You seem to have forgotten that. I should be the one running things – not you.'

My jaw tightened. 'When did you turn into Philomena?' I should have realised her influence would worm its way into his head and fracture his loyalty.

Niall's features darkened. 'Leave my wife out of this. I'm just saying what everyone's thinking. You're too soft where it counts.'

'Soft? You think I rule with weakness?' Ten years after taking control of Kilburn, I was running the business with precision and restraint to avoid the bloodbaths of the past. But my brother-in-law had the cheek to insinuate I wasn't doing a good job, even though the business was thriving.

'What you're doing is dangerous. For all of us. Sean would never have allowed Reggie an opportunity to come back like this,' Niall fired back.

'Sean's war with Reggie cost him his life!' I felt my eyes brim over with tears, and I tried to sniff them back.

Niall met my gaze, but he didn't answer. The silence between us was colder than before – something fundamental had shifted.

'I hope you know what you're doing. I told you right from the start that buying The Velvet Ace was a mistake. It's given you nothing but hassle since the day you got the keys, and I very much doubt that will change in the future. The place is bad luck, and rather than leaving it to rot, you've brought it back to life.'

'A word of warning, Niall. If you start questioning my authority in front of the men, we're going to have a different kind of problem.'

Niall laughed. 'Philomena's right. You're so caught up trying to play the big boss, you've lost sight of what matters. You should be at home with Orla – she's gone off the rails and everyone knows it.' Niall's words were bitter, and they landed like a punch.

'Don't you dare say that!' I jabbed my finger at him. I was seething. 'And tell your wife to mind her own business.' I was fed up to the back teeth with her poking her nose into my affairs.

'Why's that? The truth hurts, doesn't it?'

'She's an evil bitch, Niall, but you're too blind to see it!'

'Is that so? Well, I'm not too blind to see you're jealous of Philomena. It's been that way since the day you met her. You don't like her because she holds you accountable and is the only one brave enough to say things to your face.'

I swung my arm back and slapped him across the cheek. The action wasn't out of rage, but I wanted to break his momentum. I didn't want to hear any more of Philomena's words pouring out of his mouth.

'Enough talking. Get rid of the body.' I put my hands on my hips and glared up into his face as we locked eyes. Niall's betrayal cut deep. I could almost taste his resentment.

He turned on his heel, grabbed hold of Reggie's corpse and dragged it further down the alley, away from prying eyes. As I watched him go, it dawned on me that I was losing him. I never thought I'd have to question his loyalty. But behind closed doors, Philomena was clearly fanning the flames and driving a wedge between us. Hairline cracks in our relations were growing wider by the day, thanks to her interference. It broke my heart to think he'd allow her to fill his head with poison. Surely he knew me better than that?

53

JOSIE

No expense had been spared for opening night. I'd ordered ten-year-old casks straight from the distillery, and there was enough food to feed a small army. Every taste was catered for; bacon and cabbage, stew, and a mountain of oysters and soda bread were laid out on platters for my guests.

The place was heaving. A fiddler played over the chatter, stamping his foot, keeping the rhythm with a bodhrán and a tin whistle, while four young women in traditional costumes danced a reel as the floorboards trembled under their feet.

I stood near the bar in a forest green silk dress with my red hair pinned up, shaking hands and smiling in the centre of it all, playing my part as the hostess as glasses clinked around me. All the tables were taken by people who couldn't resist the lure of curiosity and free drinks. Whiskey bottles and pints of Guinness lined the surfaces. Laughter rose and spilt on to the street.

I glanced around the room. Green, white and gold bunting hung from the rafters. Fresh paint gleamed on the walls. The brass taps shone while new glasses behind the bar glinted under the lights. The smell of turf smoke and perfume clung to the air as a queue three-deep waited on the black-and-white checkerboard tiles to be served. Mulligans glowed like a hearth at the end of the night. The community had turned up in force to see what I'd done with the place, but there was one notable exception. Niall. He was nowhere to be seen. He'd always been a steady presence – for Sean, for me, for Orla. But not any more. His absence spoke volumes, which made a lump form in my throat.

My heart started racing when I saw the door open, but the sense of relief was quickly replaced by a feeling of dread when Philomena swept in as if she owned the place, wrapped in a black fur coat with her blonde hair set like a film star's. She'd arrived late. She was the kind of woman who liked to make an entrance. She paused in the doorway to allow everyone time to notice her. Her heavily made-up eyes swept the room like a hawk's as she took in the crowd. She looked out of place in her full-length red sequinned dress with matching stiletto heels and clutch bag, but that wouldn't stop her from making a slow circuit, pretending she belonged. I didn't think she'd have the nerve to turn up without Niall.

Voices hushed and a ripple passed through the crowd. It was the type of unease that always foreshadowed trouble. I could feel all the eyes in the room on me as they waited to see how I would respond. If Philomena had come to cause a scene, she'd be going home disappointed. I wasn't about to let her ruin something I'd worked so hard to achieve.

Philomena grabbed a crystal tumbler of single malt from a passing tray, and then she moved through the sea of faces, exchanging empty pleasantries. People flocked to her as though it was her event. The dress, the red lips, the confidence oozing out of her seemed to give her so much power. It hummed around her like static.

She was collecting fragments of gossip like a magpie. I knew what she was up to. She'd come here to spy. By the time she drew closer to me, I was ready for whatever she was going to hurl my way. My pulse was pounding at the side of my neck, but I wasn't going to back down. She was brazen, but she was the outsider. I'd survived worse than anything she could dish out.

'Is there room for one more?' Philomena laughed as she sidled up beside me, surrounded by a cloud of perfume, holding her drink like a sceptre to symbolise her authority. But the sound came out too loudly. Too forced. I knew she was putting on a front.

'I didn't expect to see you here. Figured this wasn't quite your scene, slumming it with the ordinary folk,' I replied.

'Oh, I wouldn't have missed it for the world, Josie. I wanted to stop by to wish you well on your big night.'

Stopped by? Who was she trying to kid? She was dressed up like a dog's dinner. She looked like she'd spent the entire day getting ready for the party, but for the sake of keeping the peace, I kept my thoughts to myself. 'That's very kind of you.' I somehow managed to smile even though my jaw was tight.

'You've done well raising this from the ashes. Quite the little empire you're building.' Philomena's hand wafted around the room like she was the Queen of England.

'Empire's a strong word. I wouldn't go that far. I'm just trying to keep a roof over our heads.'

'Of course you are.' Philomena's tone was sweet. Too sweet. I knew it wouldn't last. 'I do have to question your motives, though. I can't fathom why you wanted to pour pints in the place where Sean bled out. Morbid, don't you think?'

Her words landed hard, but I didn't allow myself to flinch. I wouldn't give her the satisfaction. A couple of nearby tables had fallen silent. They were pretending not to listen. I knew they were hanging on every word.

'No, I don't think it's morbid. Mulligans is a tribute to Sean,' I replied, owning my decision. Not that I needed to justify myself to anyone.

Philomena arched a perfectly sculpted brow, and her sly smile widened. It was laced with poison. 'A tribute?'

'Yes. He would have thought this was amazing.' Now it was my turn to sweep my arm across the crowded room, and it fell silent. Even the musicians and dancers stopped the entertainment as our heated words became the main focus.

'I get that, but why here? It seems like a strange sort of tribute to open a pub where he—'

'He built his name on what comes out of those bottles,' I cut in, gesturing to the bar. My eyes were drawn to the framed photo of Sean on the wall. He was grinning from ear to ear while holding a single malt in his hand. It seemed right to keep something of him here as a memorial. I didn't expect anyone to understand, but I felt close to Sean while I was here. I could sense him in the room.

'Niall says it's bad luck. And he's right. You can't just wash the blood away.'

I met her gaze and willed myself to stay composed. 'Bad luck? There's nothing bad about remembering someone. I wanted to try and make something good from something bad.' I wanted to carry Sean's legacy forward by honouring what he'd built and reclaiming the ground where he fell.

Philomena studied me for a moment. 'Each to their own, but this place gives me the creeps. Too many memories. Too many ghosts.' Her voice softened. Her venom had dulled a little.

'I live with them either way. This place isn't about what happened that night. It's about what came before, and what will come after.'

'Well, I suppose that's one way to make peace with it.' Philomena smiled.

I leaned in closer and lowered my voice so that only she would hear what I was about to say. 'I'm not trying to make peace. I'm trying to make sure he's remembered properly and that he lives on. Now mind your own business.'

Philomena's smirk faltered. 'You really know how to make a person feel welcome, don't you, Josie? I only came here to pay my respects.'

'Is that what you call it? Looks to me like you're taking notes so you've got plenty of news for your gossip circle.'

'Don't flatter yourself. I've got better things to do than tell tales on you.' Philomena laughed.

Her presence was ruining the atmosphere. I needed to send her packing before she ruined the whole night. 'Maybe it's time you went home.'

Philomena's smugness curdled. She drained her glass and set it down with a thud. 'Enjoy it while it lasts. This place is doomed. And don't come running to Niall when everything turns to shit. He's washed his hands of you!' She threw me a black look before she turned sharply and left without another word. Her heels clicked against the floor as she drifted off into the crowd. A moment later, the door swung shut behind her.

I felt tears stab my eyes, but I managed to hold them in. She'd always had a mouth on her and had behaved exactly as expected. I wasn't going to dwell on what she'd said. I had a party to enjoy, so I exhaled a long breath and then smiled over to the band and the dancers. 'What's happened to the music? I'm not paying you lot to stand around and chat.'

The fiddler got to work again, and a beat later the tin whistle and the bodhrán joined in. People cheered when the girls' feet came to life. The musicians were louder this time. It was almost as though they wanted to drown out the chill and tension Philomena had left behind.

'Who's having another?' I called out. A roar of approval answered me. 'Make sure everyone's got a drink,' I said to the bar staff. Once all the glasses were full, I lifted mine and watched the amber liquid swirl before I took a deep breath and straightened my shoulders. 'I'd like to make a toast. To Sean and everything he stood for.'

'To Sean,' the room echoed, and the cheer that followed was thunderous.

As I held my whiskey aloft, I felt a familiar warmth in my chest, like he was close by. Not haunting me, but standing with me. I could feel him there beside me. I let my fingers rest against the polished wood and traced the grain of the bar. For a moment, everything else fell away – the chatter, the band, the clinking of glasses. I glanced up at Sean's photo again. He had the bluest eyes and a spark that used to fill the room. I had my memories. But that didn't stop me from missing him more than ever.

This wasn't just a celebration; it was a test. Whether people uttered it or not, the question on everyone's lips was whether Josephine O'Connor could make this place a success without the support of her brother-in-law. Niall's absence was hard to accept. But it wasn't unexpected. He'd made his feelings clear, and that was his choice. We disagreed on the matter. He didn't get where I was coming from. Although I was convinced Sean would have approved of my decision, which made pride swell inside me.

54

ORLA

The cramps started as a dull ache, so they were easy to dismiss at first. It was nothing serious, I told myself. I was only thirty-four weeks. The baby wasn't due until the end of January. But the ache came again, sharper this time, and my breath caught in my throat.

'Are you all right?' Shay asked when I shifted. He was sprawled beside me on the sofa, glued to *The Bill* on the telly.

I pressed a hand to my bump. 'I've got a bit of a stomach ache.'

Shay sat up, and his icy blue eyes scanned over me. 'What sort of ache? Do you think the baby's coming?' Panic edged his voice.

'I don't know.' I had no idea what a contraction felt like, but when the cramp came again, I was seriously worried he might be right.

Mum had been gone the whole day. She'd been busy with last-minute preparations for the party, so for once, we hadn't had to watch the clock. I'd been looking forward to having the house to ourselves, but I'd been restless all evening. Something had felt off. By the time the pain tightened into waves, I couldn't ignore it any more. Deep down, I had a horrible feeling this wasn't a false alarm.

Shay swung his legs off the sofa and reached for his jacket. 'We're going to A & E. You need to see a doctor.'

'No.' I grabbed his arm.

'Orla, please. You need to go to the hospital.'

'No way.'

'You're in pain.' Shay stood up and put his jacket on.

'You can't come with me. What if they call the police? You'll be blamed for getting an underage girl pregnant—'

'I don't care. I'm not letting you go on your own,' Shay cut in.

'I'll call someone. I promise. Please, just go...' My words drifted off when the pain ripped through me. I dug my fingers into Shay's arm until the moment passed.

Oh God. I'd brought this on myself. The pills. The drink. The fags. The reckless way I'd acted was running through my head on a loop. When I'd had the overdose, the doctor had warned me about the risk of a premature birth. My stomach twisted, but not from a contraction, from guilt. If the baby didn't survive, that was down to my behaviour. I felt tears sting my eyes, so I sniffed them back. I had to stay strong. Not fall to pieces.

'I'm not leaving until I know somebody's coming. Do you want me to phone Majella?' Worry was etched into Shay's features.

'No,' I replied before another stab stole the rest of my sentence. When the pain passed, I walked over to the sideboard and picked up the phone. 'Something's wrong. I think the baby's coming.'

'Jesus, Orla, you're not due for weeks.' Philomena replied.

Mum wouldn't be happy that I'd reached out to her, but I didn't have a choice. She was tied up at Mulligans, and Soho was a long way from Kilburn, so it would take her ages to get to me, and I needed help fast.

'Where are you?'

'I'm at home.'

'I'll be with you in five minutes.'

'My auntie's on her way. She only lives around the corner. Please go before she gets here.'

Shay hesitated. He looked torn, like walking out was the last thing he wanted to do. 'Are you sure you don't want me to wait until she arrives?'

I shook my head. Shay kissed me on the cheek and then disappeared through the door. Moments later, Philomena swept in wearing a fur coat, party dress and heels like she'd been waiting for this moment all her life.

'Orla? Are you OK, love?' she asked as she burst through the open front door. I hadn't bothered to close it behind Shay.

'I keep getting terrible pains in my stomach. I think I might be in labour.' I sobbed as my emotions got the better of me. Then I doubled over and clutched my stomach.

'Right, darling, we'd better get you to the hospital. You need to see a doctor.' Philomena grabbed my arm and guided me down the path.

'This is all my fault. The baby's early because of that night.' Tears streamed down my face as the reality of the situation hit home. My whole body was shaking.

'Stop that now. It's not your fault. Don't fill your head with any of that guilt nonsense. Try to stay calm. You're going to be fine. Do you hear me?'

I nodded. I was happy to let Philomena take control. She was being commanding, but maternal, which was just what I needed. I stared out of the windscreen as she drove us to A & E. My nerves were twitching with pain and fear.

'My God, it hurts like hell!'

'I know, darling. Try to breathe through the pain.'

Streetlights streaked past me in smears of amber. The car ride went by in a blur. Philomena kept offering words of encouragement, but I barely registered what she was saying. All I could focus on was the pain, the panic and the guilt.

'We're nearly there,' she said as she pulled into a parking space. When she helped me out of the car, she wrapped her arm around me. 'OK, love? Deep breaths now.' Her voice was soothing. Comforting.

'I'm scared,' I whimpered and then swallowed a sob.

'You'll be OK. I won't leave you alone. I'll stay with you.'

The fluorescent lights were too bright. The air smelled too clinical. I felt like I was going to vomit as a wave of nausea washed over me. A nurse hurried over with a wheelchair, asking questions I couldn't find the voice to answer, so Philomena filled in the blanks.

'How far along is she? When did the pains start? Have there been any complications with her pregnancy?' the nurse rattled off.

Complications. The word made me flinch. A near-fatal drug overdose would tick that box, wouldn't it? They wheeled me into a small, curtained bay, and the sharp smell of disinfectant caught in my throat. When another contraction hit, I gripped the armrests and bit down hard on my bottom lip to stop myself from screaming.

Then a midwife appeared. 'You're doing brilliantly, Orla. I just need to check you over, OK?' Moments later she announced, 'You're in active labour and are already four centimetres dilated.'

My heart dropped.

'It's too soon. The baby's not due for another six weeks!'

Philomena clutched my hand. 'Try not to worry. Everything will be fine. Babies come early all the time.'

I wanted to believe her, but I had a bad feeling about this. The flurry of nurses and midwives moving around me was making me anxious. My thoughts turned to Shay. I wondered if he hated me for sending him away. What choice did I have? I didn't want to land him in trouble, but I wished he was here by my side.

55

JOSIE

Glasses clinked and laughter echoed from every corner of Mulligans. Opening night couldn't have gone any better. I glanced around the packed room with a smile on my face. The girl who'd left a tiny village in County Kerry with little more than the clothes on her back had done well for herself.

The streets of Kilburn hadn't changed that much in the last ten years. They still rumbled with trouble. I, on the other hand, was unrecognisable and had the price of every decision I'd made etched into the lines on my face. I was tougher, having been hardened by the events I'd lived through. I'd outlived some enemies, outlasted grief, and now I ruled my patch of London with a quiet ferocity. Although I was still struggling to balance leading a criminal empire with the demands of being a mother to a wayward teenager. It was a difficult skill to master.

The phone behind the bar began to ring, so I reached over and picked it up. 'Good evening, Mulligans. How can I help you?' The silence that followed stretched like a warning. At first, I'd thought the caller couldn't hear me over the racket, but my heart nearly stopped when they finally spoke.

'Josie, it's Orla,' Niall said, and my blood went cold.

'What about her?' I knew he wouldn't phone tonight, not unless something bad had happened.

'She's at the hospital.'

'Oh, dear God,' I replied, and my free hand flew up to my mouth. 'What's wrong?'

'She's gone into labour. Philomena's taken her to A & E.'

I froze. For a moment, the noise in the bar went hollow, like someone had sucked the air out of the room. Orla. Labour. I was struggling to fit the words together. Then the anger hit me like a punch to the gut.

'Why did Philomena take her? Why didn't you ring me?' I snapped.

'There wasn't time—'

I hung up before he could say any more. 'Christ almighty,' I hissed. Disaster seemed to follow me around. 'I have to go. Family emergency. Hold the fort for me,' I said to the bar staff before I slipped out the back door to avoid answering any questions.

My heels clicked hard on the pavement as I ran to the car. The cold air bit at my trembling hands while I fumbled for my keys. Why was I shaking? I'd faced men with guns, taken lives and kept my nerve through things that would have turned others to stone. But this was different. This wasn't business; this was about my girl. I knew she'd be scared. So was I. My nerves were shot to pieces.

I forced the worrying thoughts about the premature birth from my head and focused on Philomena instead. The idea of her stepping in and taking my place before I had a chance to burned a hole through my skull. Fury was tearing around inside me, like a living thing trying to escape the confines of my body. Would the bitch never tire of trying to get one over on me?

The drive felt endless. I'd tried to floor it through the city, but every light turned red as I approached it. It was as though Philomena was putting obstacles in my way and stopping me from being by my girl's side. My thoughts were jagged. Visions of Orla and my unborn grandchild flashed before me on the journey.

I slammed the car door and ran into the hospital. A & E was packed with drunks and people with a variety of injuries and illnesses. My heels clacked against the floor as I stormed through the doors with my coat half on. My heart hammered in my chest as I rushed up to the receptionist. 'I need to see my daughter, Orla O'Connor. She was brought in a while ago.' The tremor in my voice gave away my rising panic.

She faced me with a polite smile. 'Because of Orla's age and the fact that she isn't full-term, she's being treated as a vulnerable patient and has been transferred to the maternity unit. It's on the first floor. You can go and see her if you'd like.'

'Thank you,' I said as my feet carried me towards the staircase.

Philomena was sitting bolt upright on a plastic chair, wringing her hands, looking like she'd done something saintly, as I made my way along the corridor. I was on her before she had time to stand. 'What the hell did you think you were doing?'

Philomena blinked. She seemed startled by my presence. 'Being helpful! She was in pain, Josie. I had to do something—'

'You should have called me. You had no right to take matters into your own hands. I don't want an outsider interfering in family business,' I hissed.

A nurse passing by shot us a look, and Philomena's face flushed pink.

'Orla phoned me and said she needed help. What did you want me to do? Turn my back on her? It's not my fault she chose to reach out to me!' Philomena narrowed her eyes and glared at me.

A pang of jealousy stabbed me in the gut. Then my fury flared again. 'And you were only too happy to swoop in during the crisis and be the one to save the day! In future, don't you dare make decisions about my daughter without consulting me!' My voice was trembling with rage. I brushed past her before she could answer and pushed open the door to the delivery suite. Orla looked pale and frightened, which made my breath catch. My anger drained in an instant and was replaced by something raw and aching. 'Are you OK, love?' I whispered as I reached her side.

Orla's eyes fluttered open. 'Mum! What are you doing here? What about the party?'

'Never mind the party. You're far more important.'

Orla suddenly screamed as a contraction tore through her. My throat tightened in panic. I wanted to be calm. I wanted to be strong, but all I could do was stand by and watch as my daughter cried out in agony.

'That's it, sweetheart. Breathe through it,' one of the midwives said.

Once the pain passed, I sprang into action, brushing Orla's hair back from her face. 'You're a brave girl. You're doing really well. When the next contraction comes, squeeze my hand as hard as you like,' I said as I gripped on to hers.

The following hours blurred into one. The pains were getting stronger and coming more regularly. Orla was exhausted, but after a sudden flurry of activity, the baby's head began to crown.

'Push as hard as you can,' the midwife instructed.

Orla let out a low moan as she crushed my hand.

'It's a girl!' the midwife said.

My heart leapt for joy, but the moment was short-lived when

the baby didn't announce its way into the world with a cry. Silence pressed down on us as the medical team got to work. I squeezed my eyes shut and prayed to God that he would spare my grandchild's life. I jolted when I heard Orla sobbing. She blinked through her tears as she searched the faces in front of her. One of the midwives had wrapped the tiny body in a towel, while another pressed a button on the wall. A siren sounded, and more nurses and a doctor ran in.

'Why isn't she crying? What's wrong with her?' Orla's voice broke. No one answered. 'This is all my fault,' she wailed as she tried to sit up, but she was in too much pain. She reached out towards the bundle. 'Let me see her. Let me hold her. Please—'

A nurse gently touched her arm. 'We're doing everything we can,' she said, clearly having learned from experience not to promise anything.

My breath caught in my throat, but I managed to swallow down my fear as I did my best to comfort my daughter. She was inconsolable as the medical team battled to save her baby in front of her eyes. The little dot had been placed on a metal table under a harsh lamp. Multiple hands were working on her, rubbing her, pressing the smallest chest in the world, while suctioning her underdeveloped lungs. She was still. Lifeless. Orla's heart was breaking. My heart was breaking. Why was God so cruel?

Orla started shaking as shock and adrenaline raced through her body. She looked so vulnerable as she watched helplessly. She was too young to be dealing with this. I cradled her in my arms and rocked her, but nothing would soothe her. Nothing would take the pain away.

The noise of machines and the rhythm of desperation pulsed around us. Above the racket, I heard one of the nurses say, 'Come on, little one. You can do it.'

I had to stifle a sob. After the longest pause, there was the faintest sound – a whispered gasp. Then a wet, mewling cry pierced the air.

The midwife turned towards us, smiling. 'Congratulations. You have a beautiful baby girl.'

With that, the world came back into focus. The chaos had subsided, although the machines continued to hum and the monitors still blinked. But the panic had waned. The midwife walked towards us with the baby in her arms. She was like a little doll with a shock of red hair peeking out from a woollen bonnet.

'She's only four pounds and one ounce, so she'll need to go to the specialist unit for some medical support until she's stronger,' the midwife said.

'Can I hold her? Please?' Orla asked.

The midwife smiled, then placed the baby, swaddled in a pink blanket, in Orla's arms. 'Does the young lady have a name yet?'

Orla nodded. 'Kayleigh Josephine.'

A lump formed in my chest. 'Aww, that's lovely. She's beautiful.'

I had to fight to hold back my tears as I looked down at my daughter, holding my granddaughter. She was so impossibly small. Her fists were tiny, knuckles barely formed, and her skin was almost translucent. She was like a little bird, trembling with every breath. She'd had a tough start, but I could see she was a fighter. Of course she was. She was an O'Connor.

'Look at her, Mum. She's so tiny,' Orla whispered as she gazed at her sleeping daughter.

Her limbs were so thin I was afraid to breathe too hard near her. 'She's perfect,' I replied.

'I'll have to take her now, but she'll be in good hands. You'll be able to go and see her later. Try and get some rest, you've been up all night,' the midwife said.

Orla kissed the top of the baby's head, and then she turned to look at me. I bent and gently pressed my lips to my granddaughter's forehead. Then the midwife left with the tiny bundle, and the room suddenly felt too big and empty. I'd expected Orla to be an emotional wreck when they took the baby away, but her eyes were heavy with sleep. She was drained from the labour, so I held her hand and stroked her hair until she drifted off.

The news of Orla's pregnancy had come as a shock, but now that Kayleigh was here, I felt able to deal with the situation. Everything happened for a reason, so I was hopeful the baby would heal the rift between us. My girl would need financial and emotional support. I wanted to be there for her and shield her from the backlash being a teenage mother would bring. The name-calling, the bitter jibes, the snarky comments would be hard for her to cope with. And the whispering would start once people heard the news. The gossip-mongers were going to have a field day when word began to spread. But I wouldn't leave her to walk that road alone. If anyone had anything to say to Orla, they'd have to come through me first.

56

JOSIE

Philomena was still waiting outside the delivery suite. She stood up the moment she saw me. 'How's Orla?'

'She's had the baby. The little one almost didn't make it, but she's breathing now.' I managed a tight smile.

'Thank God.' Philomena's shoulders sagged in relief. 'She had a girl?'

'Kayleigh Josephine.' I beamed. I was delighted that Orla had chosen to pass my name on to her daughter. There was no greater honour.

Before I could say more, movement further down the corridor caught my eye. Shay was standing with his hands shoved into his jacket pockets. I froze when I saw Declan Kelly beside him. What the hell was he doing here?

Shay walked towards me. 'How are Orla and the baby doing? I heard you say I've got a daughter. Can I see them?'

I felt my features harden. I'd suspected that he was the father, although Orla had never confirmed it. 'You've got some nerve showing your face here. I don't think much of the company you keep.' My glare landed on Declan.

'The feeling's mutual, Josie.'

'You should go,' I replied with steel in my voice.

'We're not going anywhere,' Declan replied as he put his hand on Shay's shoulder. 'We have every right to be here. We're family, after all.'

My stomach dropped. 'Family?'

Declan's eyes gleamed with amusement. 'Didn't you know Shay's my nephew? He's Aidan's son.'

Philomena gasped as Declan's words echoed around me. For a second, the years fell away, and I was back in the tunnels with Sean's gun in my hand. I'd squeezed the trigger and hit Aidan in the throat. Blood had poured from his mouth and pumped through his fingers as he'd stared at me in disbelief until I'd shot him again to end his suffering. Now that I knew the connection, I couldn't deny Shay's resemblance to Aidan.

'You knew my dad?' he asked with a confused expression on his face.

I nodded.

'You're old enough to know the truth now, son. It's time I set the record straight. Your dad didn't die in a car crash. Josie killed him.' Declan pulled back his lips, grinning like a shark who'd spotted blood.

Shay's face went white. He shook his head and blinked repeatedly as he tried to process the information. 'What? No. That can't be true...'

'It was a case of kill or be killed,' I muttered by way of explanation.

Shay just stared at me wide-eyed with a look of horror on his face. His eyes were glossy with unshed tears as he searched my face, trying to find the answers to the questions I figured were racing around in his brain. But he was too shocked to string the words together to ask them.

'You took Aidan from me, from Shay, but thanks to your daughter, he'll live on with the Kelly and O'Connor bloodlines bonded together.' Declan's voice was almost mocking.

My eyes locked on his as I delivered the threat. 'You stay the hell away from my daughter and granddaughter.'

'The boy has rights, Josie. You can't just cut him out of their lives.' Declan's words were as cold as ice.

'Watch me. Have you forgotten you're only breathing because I allowed it? You'd do well to remember that. I spared you once – it won't happen a second time. Think long and hard before you try to cross me,' I snarled through gritted teeth.

Declan limped down the corridor without saying another word. Shay shook his head, and then he slipped away like a shadow. I stood frozen to the spot with one hand on the wall. The weight of what had just been unleashed made my legs want to buckle.

'Dear God, Josie. What are you going to do?' Philomena asked.

I couldn't bear to speak to her now. I had too much on my mind, so I walked back into the delivery suite, safe in the knowledge that she couldn't follow me as only family members were allowed. I needed space to process what had just happened. Orla looked so peaceful as I sat down next to her. She should enjoy the quiet while it lasted.

Shay wouldn't walk away from this, and neither would Declan. Niall was right. I should've killed him while I'd had the chance. He'd come back to taunt me. Haunt me. Now that the truth had come out, there'd be no hiding from it. Instead of bringing us closer together, Kayleigh's birth might be about to tear our fragile relationship apart.

I suddenly had an overwhelming desire to be near my granddaughter. As I walked towards the neonatal unit, I could see her through the nursery window in her tiny incubator. She was the only girl among all the babies, so she was easily spotted. Wires like spider legs curled around her, as her chest rose and fell. I pressed my hand to the glass and willed her to live. It was heart-breaking watching the struggle of a baby born too early having to fight for every breath.

I craved the closeness Orla and I used to share. I'd had high hopes that Kayleigh would bring us back together, but now that I knew she had Kelly blood running through her veins, I wasn't sure that would happen. I loved the baby unconditionally and none of this was her fault. The weight of her heritage was huge. Orla didn't know about Shay yet. I'd have to find the words soon before the truth came out. Ugliness always had a way of crawling its way into the light.

Kayleigh stirred, and I felt something tighten in my chest. I could already sense the storm clouds gathering. This next chapter could be the most challenging one I'd faced yet, but I wouldn't shy away from it. I'd do what I'd always done. I'd protect my family until I took my last breath. The same way Sean had. The pull of legacy was heavy and inescapable. It was threaded through me.

Thank God Sean wasn't alive to witness this. The Kellys and the O'Connors bound together by blood. The innocent baby beyond the glass had defied the odds stacked against her to make it into this world, and now she was at the centre of all this drama. Life was cruel sometimes.

I was unsure of what the future held. Trouble had a habit of finding a way back, no matter how far you thought you'd run from it. I crossed myself and prayed for guidance. Could I dare to believe this child would break the cycle of hatred? Only time would tell. All was quiet for now. But how long would that last?

* * *

MORE FROM STEPHANIE HARTE

Another book from Stephanie Harte is available to order now here:

https://mybook.to/OConnorsBook3

ACKNOWLEDGEMENTS

Thank you, Emily Ruston, for all your help and suggestions. It has been a pleasure working with you again.

Thanks to everyone involved in the production of this book, especially Jenna Houston, Wendy Neale, Debra Newhouse, Helen Woodhouse, Colin Thomas, Ben Wilson, Caroline Lennon and Gerard Logan.

A big shout-out to my amazing cousins, Ray, Don, Mark, Claire, Greg, Darren, and Alan. I'm counting on you to keep Auntie Carmel's Facebook cheerleading alive. No excuses!

Last but not least, special thanks to the readers, reviewers and bloggers. Without you, none of this would be possible. I hope you enjoy the book!

ABOUT THE AUTHOR

Stephanie Harte is the bestselling gang-lit author of crime novels set in London's East End. Stephanie taught beauty workshops at a specialist residential clinic for children with severe eating disorders for ten years. She also previously worked as a Pharmaceutical Buyer for the NHS and an international medical export company. She lives in North West London.

Download your exclusive bonus content from Stephanie Harte here:

Visit Stephanie's website: www.stephanieharte.com

Follow Stephanie on social media here:

facebook.com/stephanieharteauthor

x.com/@StephanieHarte3

instagram.com/stephanieharteauthor

ALSO BY STEPHANIE HARTE

The Kennedy Twins

Double Trouble

Double Dealings

Double Cross

The O'Connors

Dublin Rogue

Dublin Widow

Printed in Dunstable, United Kingdom

80759387R00179